The Entean Saga
Episode 4: Vision Dreaming

C.B. Williams

COPYRIGHT

Published by: Bryn Williams LLC
655 Orville Rd. E., Eatonville, WA 98328
cb@cbwilliams.us
www.cbwilliams.us

Vision Dreaming
Ebook ISBN: 978-0 -9909461-4-4
Print ISBN: 978-0 -9909461-3-7

Cover design by Al Williams

Edited by: Faith Freewoman, Demon for Details
www.demonfordetails.com

Formatted by: Maria Connor, My Author Concierge
www.myauthorconcierge.com

Bryn Williams, LLC Edition: First, December, 2018

DEDICATION

For Michal, with love and gratitude.

Our brainstorming sessions helped more than can you know.

OTHER TITLES By C. B. Williams

Under the name C. B. Williams:

The Entean Saga
Champion of Entean (2015)
Brightness Calling (2015)
Chaos Tamed (2016)
Vision Dreaming (2018)

Sky Dancers (2014)

The PeaceKeeper Corps (2014)

The Walkers Trilogy
Walkers (2012)
The Place Between Worlds (2012)
The Shield (2013)

Under the name Cynthia Campbell Williams:
This Fools Journey, Tarot Tales for Modern Minds (2011)

Prologue

Across light-years, the Planetary Consciousness of Longwei reaches out.

Entean!

(A pause.)

Longwei, my Planetary Sister.

Did you feel it?

(A pause.)

Yes. Our Planetary Sister in the Vela Kentaurus galaxy has ceased to exist. She is gone from us.

How many more, Entean? How many more?

(A pause.)

Our Champion. He must save the remaining. He must leave now.

Yes. It is time.

(A pause.)

It is past time.

Yes.

(A pause.)

I fear.

CHAPTER 1 – LETTING GO

Aboard the colonizer interstellar ship, the **Valiant**

Grale stormed into the science labs, nearly colliding with Spider, who was unpacking a container of test tubes and putting them away.

"Hey!" Spider scolded as he dodged out of the way. "I nearly dropped these. These tubes are glass. Very fragile and hard to come by. And expensive. You should know."

Grale ignored him and charged over to where Genji sat, bent over his info-console. He whipped Genji's chair around, gripped both armrests, and leaned over the startled science officer. "Where is it?" he growled.

Genji's nostrils flared and he shoved at one of Grale's arms. "Where is what? Calm down, Grale." Genji narrowed his eyes, looking somewhat predatory.

Grale repositioned his hand on the armrest and leaned in closer. "Aiko and I just spent three days dirtside," he said between gritted teeth. "Three effing days haggling over your precious state-of-the-art instruments that you couldn't travel without and needed *yesterday*. And what do you do in those three days?" he yelled, his face red.

Genji frowned when flecks of spittle landed on his cheek.

"I'd be careful, there, Grale," Spider warned. "You don't want

Genji going all Nuri on you."

Grale locked eyes with Genji. "I don't care if he turns into a bloody sniffer," he growled. "This module stuff stops," he stated, poking Genji's chest.

Genji hissed and half rose from his seat. "And if it doesn't?"

"What's going on, boys?" Wren asked mildly, leaning against the doorframe. Little Sister, her sniffer, hovered at Wren's side, the huge carnivore's smooth black head at waist level.

Aiko stood behind the pair scowling, hands on her hips.

The two men looked up.

Wren crossed her good leg over her animated limb and cocked a brow. "Care to share?"

"I told you to wait," Aiko said, glaring at Grale. "Why couldn't you wait just ten minutes, so I could get Wren down here before you went all macho?"

Grale glared back. "Well, Kitten," he drawled, "I guess I just wasn't in the mood to wait, now was I?"

"So what's up?" Wren asked again. "And Grale, I think it'd be wise if you give Genji a little space."

"Fine," Grale said, pushed himself away from the chair to whirl and slam his fist against a cabinet door.

Something inside tinkled .

"Test tubes!" Spider snapped. "Hard to get and costly, remember?"

Grale ran his hand through his already untidy hair and stared at Spider. "Oh, fuck it," he said, shaking his head as he shoved past the lab tech. "I can't deal with this right now."

He began to push past Wren.

4

The giant sniffer rumbled a warning from deep in her chest. "Hush, Little Sister," Wren said and rested her hand on Grale's arm. "I know you're tired, Grale," she said softly, "and I have an idea what might have set you off. Aiko mentioned—"

"We couldn't find the bloody Navigation Bridge," Grale roared, "We're gone for three days, and they go move it on us. No warning. No courtesy call. Nothing. We had to wander the whole circumference of this rust bucket—"

"We could have asked someone," Aiko interrupted. "There are com links all over the place."

"We shouldn't have had to ask someone, Kitten," he growled. "That's the point. It's the Navigation Bridge! It's *our* domain. They should have asked *us* if they could move it. It's not right."

Aiko threw up her hands, "Hey, don't get all shouty at me, Cowboy," she said, her voice rising, "I'm on your side over this."

"And you're not on the Committee," Genji called from his chair. "We don't need to ask you."

Wren squeezed Grale's arm. "That's enough!" she commanded, her voice slicing through the cacophony of raised voices. "Grale, unclench your fist. Genji, stop with the lizard eyes. And you, Spider, for the love of God, close that cabinet and quit inspecting the test tubes. It's not helping."

She released her hold on Grale's arm and waited for two beats. "Thank you," she said. "Now then, here's what we're going to do. I will personally take Aiko and Grale to the Navigation Bridge. Then they will freshen up, and we will all meet in two hours at the usual place." She glanced at Grale and Aiko, "No, the galley module wasn't moved this time. It's still near our sleeping modules."

"Be still my heart," Grale scoffed.

Wren ignored him. "We will all sit down and have a civilized conversation. In the meantime, Genji, will you round up the rest of the crew and tell them to come to the meeting?"

5

Genji nodded, his pupils having returned to normal. "Eloch too?"

Wren hesitated. "I'll touch base with Eloch." She shrugged. "He'll either be there or he won't. But either way, we're going to resolve this situation."

"Thank the stars," Grale said. "I am so sick of this bloody Module Migration."

"Hey!" Spider said, "We just want it right."

Wren held up her hands. "Boys," she warned, "we'll all talk this through in two hours." She looked up at Grale, then glanced over at Aiko. "Let's go."

The corridor snaking around the perimeter of the *Valiant*, their interstellar ship, was wide enough for all three to walk abreast as Little Sister trotted ahead, her paws clicking in rhythm with her trot. "I really need to file those claws again," Wren said, making small talk. "She is starting to skid around corners during my morning runs."

Aiko nodded. "Can't get enough of a grip."

"So, when you're doing your running thing, how come *you* don't get lost with all these migrations going on?" Grale asked.

Wren laughed. "But I do. As soon as I get it all sorted out, something gets moved. I suppose I could look at the new schematics Spider always posts, but where's the fun in that? It reminds me of my days in SubCity when I learned all the tunnels in my KinLands."

"I'm telling you," Grale said, "they really need to stop."

"Yeah," Aiko agreed. "This Navigation Bridge thing has finished it for me."

"I couldn't agree with you two more," Wren said. "Speaking of which, here we are." She came to a halt beside Little Sister, who stood waiting, "Your Navigation Bridge."

Grale glanced at the sniffer. "How did she know where it was?" he asked.

"Smell," Wren said. "Little Sister informs me it smells like the two of you."

Grale lift a brow and shrugged.

"I wish Spur had gifted me with a keener sense of smell," Aiko said, "like She gifted you with the ability to communicate." She glanced over at Grale, "But then again…" she drawled.

Grale scowled at her. "I smell just fine."

"I beg to differ," Aiko said.

"Don't you two want to go in now you're here?" Wren asked.

Grale swept his hand over the door panel, which slid open. "After you, ladies."

Aiko raised a brow before she strode into the module. Little Sister followed Wren in and began to nose around.

"What is it?" Wren asked just as Aiko gasped.

Grale came up alongside the two women, took one look inside, and wheeled around. "That does it," he said. "I'm not waiting no two hours. I'm dealing with this now."

"Stop!" Wren barked.

Grale stopped.

"You are going to wait, Grale," she said quietly. "You're going to go to your room module and clean up, and then we'll all meet as planned."

"I don't need to clean up," Grale scowled.

"Yes, you do," Wren said. "You smell like dirtside."

"*Dirtside?* What does that mean?"

"It means," Aiko said, "that you smell like cheap alcohol and women. And nobody needs to be gifted with a keener sense of smell to notice it."

Grale lifted his eyes heavenward, "What did I ever do to deserve this?" he moaned. "Just because I know how to have a little fun while I can," he muttered. "Fine. I will see you in two hours, smelling blossom sweet," he said, making his way to the exit.

He paused and glanced over his shoulder at Wren, "Uhhh, which way?"

"To the right."

"The right. Okay."

Wren waited until the sound of Grale's footsteps had faded. "Grale seems more out of sorts than usual," she said to Aiko.

Aiko nodded. "It was a rough three days. Lots of price gouging going on." She turned to Wren. "Just make sure Genji and Spider thank Grale because he worked hard getting that equipment for them. I gotta hand it to him."

She swept her hand around the room. "Then all this, and especially that." She pointed at the pilot chair. "I'm pretty livid myself, truth be told."

Wren linked arms with her, "Come on, then. Let's get you smelling like a blossom, too, and then resolve our problems."

~~~

They sat on separate sides of the table. On one side Kalea sat beside Genji, her hand on his arm. Mink was wedged between Spider and Wade. On the other side of the table sat Aiko and Grale.

Grale leaned over to Aiko, his thick hair still damp from his shower. "Do I smell blossomy enough for you, Princess?"

"Ugh." She pushed him away.

"Eloch won't be joining us," Wren said as she took her place at the table's head, a mug of tea in her hand. "So let's begin." She glanced around the table and grinned. "You know, you might be a little more comfortable if you all spread out a bit."

"But we're the Committee," Genji said solemnly.

"And I need to be by Genji to help him calm his Nuri," Kalea explained.

Wren's grin widened. "It's okay for the Committee to be split up. We know who you are." She sobered, "Look, this isn't an 'us versus them' thing. Mink, you and Wade move over to the other side. Get comfy."

"We've showered," Grale said, waving them over "We smell all blossomy over here. Hey, Wade, can you bring me whatever you're having?" he added as Wade moved to the beverage unit with an empty glass in his hand.

"It's just H2O," Wade said.

"Sounds perfect, thanks," Grale said. "I'm buying."

Wade snorted and shook his straight dark hair out of his eyes. "Be right back," he said.

Wren caught Grale's eye and nodded.

He winked.

As Spider, Genji, and Kalea rearranged themselves, Mink took a seat by Aiko. She leaned over and sniffed. "Blossoms!" she said, her green eyes dancing.

"I think we need to get a new fragrance of washing liquid," Aiko laughed.

"Dirtside might be nice," Grale offered.

Wren chuckled.

Wade returned, handed Grale a glass of water, and sat.

"Everyone comfy?" asked Wren.

"Very comfy, thank you," Spider said dryly.

"Okay, then," Wren said. "Grale, I believe you have an issue?"

"We both do," Aiko said before Grale could respond. "Where is the second pilot's chair?" she demanded, fixing her gaze on Genji.

Genji cocked his head at her. "We didn't think it necessary since you two will be taking shifts."

Aiko went very still. She fisted her hands. "Put the chair back, Genji," she said slowly.

Genji blinked. "But why? There was only one on the *Stardust*."

"The *Valiant* is a modular ship," Grale said hotly. "You can't compare it to the *Stardust*. And that's not the issue here. The *issues* are," he counted on his fingers, "first you moved the Navigation Bridge without consulting us, and second, you took out the other pilot's chair—again, *without consulting us*. And third, why are you constantly moving modules? Leave them alone. The ship is fine the way it is."

"It was lopsided."

"Lopsided?" Grale slammed his palms on the table. "*Lopsided?* You're moving it all around because it didn't look pretty enough for you? We're in space! Who cares whether it's lopsided! It's going to fly right just fine."

"Eloch wasn't happy with it," Wade said quietly.

Wren straightened. "Eloch? What? When was this?"

10

"Three days ago," Wade said, "Eloch came to us and asked us to make the ship more symmetrical. He wanted it ovoid."

Wren sighed and ran a hand down her coilmats. "And is it ovoid now?"

Spider nodded. "It is."

"And can we stop moving modules around?" she asked quietly.

Spider shot a glance at Genji. "There's one more move."

Grale groaned.

"And what would that be?" Wren asked.

"The galley," said Genji. "It's too close to the med and science labs. As we travel, we will be capturing and studying various organisms. We don't want our food supply to accidentally come in contact with a foreign contaminant."

Aiko glanced at Grale. "He makes a point."

Grale nodded, "But if the Galley is moved, then all our sleeping modules will need to be relocated too. Mine will, anyway. I'd die of starvation before I could find the galley again. This ship is a monster, even without the modules we sold off."

Genji looked over at Wade. "We hadn't considered that."

"What, Grale dying of starvation?" Aiko quipped.

Genji frowned.

Mink giggled.

Aiko leaned over to Grale. "I'd still make them put back the other pilot chair, Cowboy, even if you did die of starvation," she told him.

"That's a relief. You're a real peach, Kitten," Grale said.

"What hadn't you considered, Genj?" Wren asked.

"It is much more convenient to have the sleeping modules close to the galley."

"Let's take a vote," Wren said after taking a sip from her mug. "Who agrees that it's a wise decision to separate the galley from the labs?"

All hands raised.

"And who wants their sleeping modules near the galley?"

Again, all hands raised.

"Okay then. Committee, make this final Module Migration and be done with it. No more after that," Wren said.

"But—" Genji began.

Wren raised her hand. "Not another module move after you move the galley and rearrange the sleepers, Genji. That's final."

"And put the pilot chair back," Grale said, glancing at Aiko.

"Definitely," she said. "And never, ever do anything to the Navigation Bridge without first consulting us." She sat back and crossed her arms. "Ever."

"And you might want to thank Grale, Genj and Spider, for the equipment he worked so hard to acquire for you," Wren said.

"Of course," Spider said. "Thank you, Grale."

"Yes," Genji said. "Thank you."

"I want to thank you too," Kalea chimed in. "I'm going to be learning how to use it."

"I'll toss in my gratitude," said Wade. "I'll be using it."

"As will I," Mink said. "You worked hard, Grale, and it's

appreciated.

Wren smiled when she saw Grale's deep flush of pleasure. "Meeting's adjourned then. Put that pilot chair back first thing you do, Genji." She stood. "I'll be with Eloch in the Solar Farm."

~~~

Wren passed a hand across the door panel, which slid open to reveal the midsection of the *Valiant*—the Solar Farm, a vast array of greenhouses named for their ability to capture and store the energy of any passing star to provide light and energy to grow enough food to service some 15,000 souls.

Since there were only nine people going on their mission, Mink suggested they off-load some of the greenhouses and use a smaller module for the ship's middle area. But Eloch insisted they leave that inner space alone.

Little Sister, never far from Wren's side, slipped past her in search of Eloch. Wren followed, allowing the panel door to quietly slide shut behind her as she paused to get her bearings before following Little Sister.

At first glance, Eloch's domain was a warren of plant life. But closer scrutiny revealed a convenient web of pathways much like a spider's web. The paths crisscrossed from a central hub to all points of the ship, allowing everyone to take shortcuts through Eloch's domain.

Eloch and his Solar Farm. It was here where he unleashed the creative force gifted to him by the planets he championed, and the Solar Farm had become his private domain, where he spent most of his free time.

Ahead, Little Sister let out an excited *woof*.

Seconds later Eloch joined her, matching his long strides to her shorter ones.

"Hey there," she said.

He shot her a grin. "I was inspecting the growing things and felt you nearby."

Wren nodded, relieved to find him focused and alert. Alert enough to sense she'd just been thinking about him and decide to join her. When he was present, they were that attuned with each other. She laced her fingers with his.

"You missed all the drama with the crew," she said.

"I knew you could handle it easily." He squeezed her hand, then turned to face her. "I have some drama of my own to share."

She scanned his face. "That bad?"

He nodded. "One of the Sisters in Vela Kentaurus has died."

Wren gasped. "We need to get out there, Eloch!"

"We will, but we need to wait a few more days. The Lady Talamh visited me," he explained. "She has a gift for us, a Seer who will accompany us."

"A Seer? What's a Seer?"

"One who dreams the future. One who gazes beyond normal reality."

Wren quirked an eyebrow. "You sound like you're quoting someone."

Enoch smiled, taking her hand. "I was. The Lady."

"So you really don't know what this Seer is, either."

He shook his head. "I have no idea. But she will be coming with us, so we should make a room for her."

Wren stopped with a groan. "Which means the *Valiant* is going to undergo another change," she cried in mock dismay.

14

Eloch chuckled and pulled her to him to rumple the top of her head, sending her coilmats swinging. "I'm afraid so. But as soon as our Seer arrives, we depart."

She gave his waist a quick squeeze and stood back to look up at him. "Walk back with me?" She whistled for Little Sister.

Eloch nodded and took her hand, lacing their fingers.

"So it's happening. We're actually leaving," Wren said.

"Should be very soon now," Eloch agreed. "Time to tell the crew."

"Yeah. I'm going to meet Mouse in about an hour down dirtside. I'll let her know." She grew thoughtful. "Now I know we're leaving, I'm feeling greedy for her company."

"You know you could remain here," Eloch said tentatively.

She pulled her hand from his grasp and turned to look up at him. "Why would you even suggest that?" She punched his arm. Hard. "As if I would ever think of leaving you, Eloch."

He smiled and pulled her to him. "That's good because I would miss you." He paused and rested his chin on her head, then buried his nose in her hair and breathed deeply. "I need you to keep me here, keep me present."

She nodded and nuzzled his chest. "I know, Eloch," she said softly.

"And I need you because I love you and don't want to be apart from you."

"I love you too, Eloch. Always. Now, time to let me go. If I don't hurry, I'll be late to meet Mouse."

He kissed the top of her head before he released her.

~~~

Wren walked beside Mouse along the wide, chalky path leading to

Hern, the village closest to the walled City of Talamh. It had been a year since the old government toppled and Max took over leadership of the city dwellers, those who had settled from Spur.

Negotiations between the indigenous people—Talamh's people—and the settlers from Spur were going well under Max's skillful guidance. The Lady, the Spirit of the planet, approved of Max and instructed Her people to trust his goodwill.

At first, distrust was prevalent, but curiosity on both sides began to erode the skepticism and Max was encouraged.

"There's no longer a guard at the city's wall," Wren commented when they paused and looked back at where they started. "And the city is looking much prettier now you've taken over its design." She glanced at her friend. "Who knew you had all this talent? You're amazing."

Mouse smiled, transforming her face from ordinary to extraordinary. "It's what happens when you're not fixated on keeping yourself and others alive."

"Still have nightmares?" Wren asked when she saw a shadow skim across Mouse's expression.

Mouse nodded. "I think I always will."

"Yeah," Wren agreed. "I know I will too."

They shared a glance, one filled with a sorrowful wisdom.

"We did what we needed to do," Wren said.

"And we'd do it again."

"Yes."

The shadows of two winged creatures swept over them, and Mouse looked up. "That just isn't natural," she commented as she watched Genji and Kalea, in their Nuri forms, spiraling above them on a wind current. "I just can't get used to them being able to transform from people into those creatures."

"Yet they do," said Wren, her eyes twinkling. She followed the pair's flight. "Beautiful," she murmured.

"They do it a lot, too," Mouse said and shivered.

Wren sighed. "They know we're leaving soon. I don't envy them being cooped up in a ship for who knows how long. Sure, they'll be able to shift and fly in the Solar Farm. Eloch made sure of that. But it certainly won't be the same as this." She swept her hand in a gesture, which included the sky and the vast meadow stretching to the horizon.

"All this natural space, it is beautiful, isn't it?" Mouse said. "Talamh was wise to keep the Spur colonizers behind a wall. We would have ruined it."

Wren nudged her friend. "But no more. With you and Max in charge, we ignorant Spurians will learn how to play well with others."

They began to walk across the meadow toward a leafy grove surrounded by chalk hills.

"Spurians?"

"My nickname for us cuz we came from Spur."

Mouse snorted. "SubCitians would be more like it."

Wren grinned and called to Little Sister, who was straying away, captivated by the strange scents. The enormous sniffer came bounding closer, her sleek, dark fur catching the sunlight.

Mouse smiled. "Never thought there'd come a day when I would actually love sniffers." She reached out her hand, and Little Sister bumped it with her huge head, nudging Mouse until she stroked behind a silky ear. "Remember Little Brother?"

"Your sniffer back on Spur, right? The one who has stolen Ingot's heart?"

"That's the one," Mouse said with a grin as she watched Little Sister go trotting off to explore again. "I'm having him shipped here. I can't wait."

"Mouse?"

Mouse glanced at Wren. "What's wrong?"

Wren shook her head. "Nothing's wrong. I have a favor to ask, is all."

"Okay, what's the favor?"

"Could you keep Little Sister here with you on Talamh?" The words came out in a rush.

Mouse slowed to a stop so she could study her friend. "You sure?"

Wren watched the sniffer playfully batting at a flying insect. "No. I love that beastie. I'd love to take her along, but it's just not fair to her." She turned to Mouse. "Who knows how long we'll be gone or whether we'll ever set foot on a planet again? It's just too much to ask of Little Sister. Genji and Kalea know what they're getting into. But Little Sister? She'd follow Eloch and me anywhere, but she would be so unhappy, Mouse. I can't do it to her."

"But you're her pack. She loves you two."

"You're part of her pack, Mouse. She knows you and Max. And Little Brother will be arriving soon."

Mouse's face lit up with a smile. "Little Brother would sure love a playmate. But two sniffers..." her voice trailed off.

"Two very well-behaved sniffers."

"Two very well-behaved and extremely large sniffers living with Max and me in our getting-smaller-by-the-minute dwelling." Mouse flashed her beautiful smile. "Sure, why not?"

"Don't you think you should ask Max?"

"No need. Max will say yes."

"You've got him that twisted around your little finger?"

Mouse snorted. "Not at all. But I know him, and he'll say yes because you asked, Wren. We'd both do anything for you."

Wren reached out and touched Mouse's hand before she started walking again. "Thank you."

They walked together in silence.

"So, tell me about this building we're going to see," Wren said.

"In a sec. Wren, is everything okay?" They had stopped again, and Mouse faced Wren. "Seriously, what's wrong?"

Wren looked skyward, her mouth trembling, then dropped her gaze to her friend. "The enormity of it all, I suppose," she replied. "I'm leaving you and Flick, my two best friends in the universe, and traveling light-years—*light-years!*—away. So far, in fact, we're talking about taking turns in the Cryo beds so we don't get too old. Do you know what that means? None of us are immortal, here." She put her hands over her heart in a protective gesture. "It hurts, Mouse. Hurts."

Mouse sighed and cleared her throat. "I know what it means. These last few days may be the last time we'll see each other. So yeah," she agreed. "It hurts. Especially—" she broke off.

"Especially what, Mouse?"

Mouse hesitated. "Can this be in The Narrows?" she asked, referring to their long-ago code word for secrecy.

"Of course."

"I haven't told Max yet, but in a few months I'm going to be making him a daddy."

19

Wren stilled. "A little Mouse or a little Max," she murmured, then laughed and grabbed Mouse in a hug so tight the other woman squeaked. "I love this! This is the best news! And with vids, I'll be able to watch Little MaxMouse grow up and all the little MaxMouses after that." With another laugh, a little more shaky, she released her friend and steadied her. "Why haven't you told Max?"

Mouse shrugged, her expression softening. "I just wanted to keep it to myself for a span. Get used to the idea. I'm planning to tell him soon, though. I've gone to a med lab, and the baby and I, we're both healthy."

"Mommy Mouse. I'm so happy for you," Wren said softly.

"But what? You didn't have to say it, I heard it in your voice."

"Just makes the hurt worse."

Mouse sighed. "I know. Feeling it too." She paused, "However, on the bright side, I've got Max and my architecture. And don't forget, Flick can keep us in touch through his connection with Spur. And you've got Eloch and the others. We're going to be fine. Just fine," she added for emphasis.

She punched her friend. "And when did I become the one who does the cheering up? There's something more, isn't there, Wren?"

Wren glanced around. "Are we still in The Narrows?" she asked quietly.

"Of course we are."

"'Kay, then. I've never mentioned this, and I wouldn't have mentioned it to you, but you've, per usual, called my bluff." She ran a hand down her auburn coilmats. "I'm worried about Eloch, Mouse."

"Eloch! *Why?* He's amazing. And he's invulnerable. I mean, he saved us from an exploding building...just appeared when you needed him. And he loves you so much, Wren."

20

"I know. I know all that. But those damn planets broke him down and put him back together again, gave him all that knack..." She paused. "He's doubting his own humanity, Mouse. And he goes away someplace. In his head. His eyes get all distant, and he's just...gone. A couple of times I noticed him start to fade a bit, like you've seen Spur do. Like I've seen all of them do. Scares the crap out of me. It's like he has to be so focused to stay who he is. And he's not ready to talk about it yet. That's what he tells me when I ask him. The most he'll say is he needs me to keep him present."

Wren shook her head. "And then he'll ask things of the crew without consulting me. This last time, I first heard of it in this morning's meeting. He had Genji and rest of them moving modules around because the ship was 'lopsided' and he wanted it 'ovoid.' That's not like Eloch...or the Eloch I knew, anyway. It's costly to move modules, Mouse. You have to schedule the service cranes, and then make sure everything is sealed up so we don't die when they disconnect and reconnect the parts. That's...I just don't know what to do. I—"

"Stop, Wren. Stop right there." Mouse shook her head and glared at her friend. "Forget about Eloch for a moment. Where did *you* go? Where did KinLord Wren go? This"—she waved her hand at Wren like she was trying to erase her—"Wren person in front of me is *not* the Wren I know. Not at all. This is *your* and Eloch's mission. These planets may have sent Eloch, rearranged Eloch, but Spur sent you. *Your* planet sent *you*, Wren, because She knows what you're capable of. She knows you've got this."

"But Aiko, Grale—" Wren began.

Mouse clapped her hands once, a sharp sound, echoing across the meadow.

Little Sister's head darted up from her digging.

"Spur did *not* send Aiko!" Mouse stated, her voice rising. "Nor the others. *She sent you, Wren.* You're the KinLord on this journey. They are not, and it's time you recognized that fact."

"Eloch—"

"Eloch is not the KinLord either. Not while he's Champion. He can't be both. It's you, Wren. Own it. Fight for it if you have to." She snorted. "It'll be so much easier than what you did in SubCity." She paused, breathing heavily.

Wren's eyes widened. "Easy, Mama Sniffer. Calm down. I'm hearing you. I'm listening. You always have been one to tell me truth whether or not I want to hear it."

Mouse took a deep breath and smiled shakily. "Sorry. Hormones."

"No, I'm sorry, and thank you, Mouse. Thank you from my very soul. It's exactly what I needed to hear."

Wren took a deep, calming breath and let it out with a nod. "I'm good now." She hugged her friend. "Thanks to you. You are absolutely right. Spur did send me. I do have this. I am KinLord of that ship. I see it now. I know what to do. Thanks," she said again.

"Just don't ever forget again, promise?" Mouse said.

"Promise."

"Okay, then."

"Yeah." Wren flashed a grin. "What a powerful Mama Sniffer you are." She laughed and brushed the tears off her cheeks as she linked arms with her friend. "And what a lucky baby. Now tell me about this building you've created."

Mouse's face lit up, and she began to describe her latest building, designed to honor The Lady Talamh, inspired by a dream Mouse had. It would be where the two different peoples could gather in peace and harmony, where the new government seat would be, and it was to be built beyond the wall that Lady Talamh had created to keep the colonizers apart from Her people.

As Mouse described the details, they crossed the meadow, following the route through the trees and down a rise. Small thatched homes began dotting the landscape. Seeing the homes, Wren called Little Sister to them. The sniffer ambled docilely between the two friends.

"It was my inspiration, Wren. Max had been wondering what gesture of goodwill we could offer. They were so wary of us at first, and wise to be wary, because you know what we"—she elbowed Wren and grinned—"Spurians are like."

Wren elbowed her back. "That I do. Give us an inch, we'll take a mile and turn it all into rubble." She held up a hand. "But no more. That's in the past."

Mouse smiled. "Yup. In the past, although it's still taking some convincing. Spurians are stubborn too, and slow to change."

"Willful, yes."

"Anyway, it's nearly done, and as soon as we go around this corner, right here, you will see it," she said just as the building came into view.

Wren sucked in a breath and halted, her eyes widening.

The walls were the same chalky stone as the path they were on, quarried from nearby hillsides, cut into blocks, and polished so they were smooth. Low steps, graced by delicately arched pillars, led to the entrance, two large bronze doors which stood open, revealing an inner courtyard where Wren could make out the statue of a woman. Large, arched windows spread in even rows on both sides of the door, flanking both the first and second story. These were embellished with intricately carved stone garlands. The third story windows were small arches forming a scalloped pattern.

"It's beautiful, Mouse," Wren whispered. "It's feminine. How a building can be called feminine, I don't know, but this one is. So lovely. But strong, too, you know?" She looked at Mouse. "It's not going to go anyplace."

Mouse let out a breath she'd been holding. "You like it, then? I've been so close to the project, I just don't know anymore."

Wren glanced over at Mouse, her fingers stroking Little Sister's fur.

"It amazes me, Mouse. You amaze me. What did Max say?"

Mouse chuckled. "He called it *exquisite*, but you know Max."

"No, he's right. That's exactly what it is. It's exquisite, Mouse. I'm sure The Lady is honored."

"I wouldn't know. I haven't had the guts to ask Talamh's High Priest. That's what they call their Champion here," Mouse explained. "There are priests and priestesses, and then there's a High Priest and a Seer. The Seer dreams the future and consults with the High Priest."

"Interesting. Just this morning Eloch mentioned a Seer who will be coming with us, but I really haven't paid attention to how that part works on this planet. I leave that up to Eloch and...well, I've been working on other stuff."

"Like getting the *Valiant* ready for intergalactic travel?"

"Yeah, like that. Getting her ready for Vela Kentaurus. But since we're not leaving until the Seer is ready, will you walk me through your exquisite creation?"

Mouse reached for Wren's hand and tugged her forward. "But of course. This way."

CHAPTER 2 - PERIN

The dream shifted and she began to Dream True. Everything became crystalline clear. Every detail, every nuance, every word spoken would embed itself in her memory. She used to enjoy the shift, to look forward to the True Dream, knowing its message would benefit her people.

But that was before.

Now, she only dreamt one True Dream. Countless times, over and over and over again until she was sure she was going mad. And what was in the dream made no sense to her whatsoever. And yet she continued to dream it. Madness was the only explanation.

She had begun to fear sleep. Would only sleep when utter exhaustion drove her to it, or when she convinced one of her handmaidens to give her a potion that made dreaming impossible. Her maidens were worried. She could hear their concern whenever they spoke, could feel it when as they helped her dress.

So it was no surprise when Rayne, The Lady's Champion, came to see her. In fact, she wondered why he hadn't come sooner, although she knew he was usually busy with The Lady's wishes. The people of Talamh were finally in negotiations with the Others, those who came from Spur, those The Lady Talamh had walled off.

Rayne took her hands and led her to a comfortable sitting bench. His hands were warm and dry, a bit papery, but then Rayne was not a young man.

"How are you, Perin?" Rayne asked in his deep, rumbly voice, a voice that belied his years.

"I am well, Champion," she replied. "Tea?"

"Yes, that would be nice, Perin. Thank you."

She signaled the handmaiden who always stood at the room's entrance. Her handmaidens were never far away. "And how are the negotiations with the Others?" she asked politely while they waited.

"I am quite pleased with the progress," Rayne replied, a smile in his voice. "Their new leader is very reasonable, although he has highly defined boundaries he refuses to cross."

"What sort of boundaries?"

"He insists they keep the city's structure, and The Lady is not pleased, but She will agree to it reluctantly. When he learned of The Lady's displeasure, he was willing to compromise by redesigning the larger buildings so they will be more pleasing to the eye. His bondmate has some ideas and is building one now to honor The Lady. If it pleases The Lady, then so much the better."

"The Lady has not seen it? That is unlike her."

Rayne chuckled. "The new leader made Her promise not to look until it is ready."

"That is surprising, that She would make such a promise."

"Yes."

"There is frustration in your voice. What troubles you?"

"The timing. These Others want to bring the two peoples together sooner rather than later."

Perin sighed. "We are slow to make decisions, Rayne, it is true, but I've heard the distrust is lessening and people are becoming curious about one another. This is good."

Rayne touched her hand. "They need their Seer, Perin. The Lady's High Priest and the Seer's True Dreams, as it has always been."

A discreet cough came from the door, announcing the tea's arrival. The pause for Rayne to pour tea gave Perin time to regain her serenity.

Rayne handed her a cup.

She took a sip, allowing the warmth to soothe her. It was time to confess. It was best for the people of Talamh for her to face reality. Besides, she was tired of the burden of hiding what was. "I am aware our People need their Seer, Rayne," she began, hearing how despairing the words were sounding, "but I only dream one dream, that of people I do not know and of places I could never imagine. Over and over and over again." She gripped the handle of her cup. "I have begun to dread sleep."

"Oh, child! I was not aware."

"It is my fault. I have told no one, hoping a True Dream would come soon." She took a deep breath. "Yet no True Dreams come." She turned to face in his direction. "I fear I have lost the Gift, Rayne." She hadn't meant to sound so pitiful, even if it was how she felt.

The clink of a teacup, the rustle of fabric, and Rayne's arms were wrapped around her. "You have not lost the Gift, Perin. Otherwise, your normal sight would be returned to you."

Hope fluttered beneath her collarbone. "My sight would be returned if I no longer Dreamed True? I didn't know this."

"Few do, it happens so seldom." He released her, and she heard the rustle of his robes when he sat again. "So you are still Dreaming True. Of what, we do not know, but it will come to pass, be sure of that."

A chill ran through her, but Perin remained silent. "What of the People?" she asked into the silence. "My dream cannot possibly help them."

Rayne sighed. "Then The Lady will bring us another Seer." He patted her hand. "But for now, describe to me this True Dream of yours. I will discuss these events with The Lady and will return in the morning with solutions."

"Very well." Perin set down her cup, took a deep breath, and told him of the dream. She had dreamed it so often, the details she described seemed more real than the reality in which she sat.

"I am filled with terror, nearly paralyzed by it. I enter a room unlike any I have ever been in before. It has seats facing a large window that looks out onto nothingness. There are people there, dressed in strange clothing, and there are other people there who are traveling through the room.

"You would think the traveling people would be seen, but no one pays attention to them. And then one of the travelers aims a weapon at the tall man standing in the room."

She swallowed. "The tall man is shot clean through and falls. I am filled with deep sorrow and feel as though I have failed these people. I have failed them all, and the world will never be made right because of me."

When she finished, she was greeted with silence. Perin ducked her head, allowing the fall of her long hair to mask her emotions. "I know it makes no sense," she said. "It makes no sense to me either. I am not even sure I am describing it accurately because it is so strange. All I know is, it is a True Dream."

She waited, but The Lady's Champion remained quiet. "I am sorry, Rayne, that I waited so long to tell you."

"The timing is perfect, Perin. You know it always is so. But you are right, this dream is strange and perplexing. What you describe has nothing to do with The People and everything to do with those beyond the wall." He patted her hand, then returned her cup. "Finish your tea, dear one. I will return tomorrow."

She nodded, disappointed he did not comment further. But he was the High Priest, had been The Lady's Champion for so many years that perhaps he went to others to share its contents. Perhaps even to those beyond the wall.

Rayne patted her hand again, "Drink. I am not leaving until you drink."

She took a swallow of the tea and enjoyed the spreading warmth.

"The tea will soothe you." The sweep of fabric against her arm told her he had risen. "Until tomorrow, my dear."

She listened to him leave, the rustle of his clothes and the soft cadence of his voice as he greeted her handmaidens and asked about her well-being.

That night, she decided, she would sleep and would accept whatever happened. Perhaps her confession to Rayne would stop the repetition of that one True Dream which had been haunting her for so long.

~~~

"The Lady has need of you, Perin. A great need which calls for a great sacrifice," Rayne told her when they were once more sitting side by side the next day.

Her heart quickened. "I am relieved," she told him, "I thought..." She trailed off. She could not express how inadequate and useless she had been feeling.

R's hand covered her own, which she only now recognized had fisted. "I understand, my dear," he said quietly.

His kindness was nearly her undoing. She forced her fist to unclench, and she shifted to face him where they sat together on the bench in her little courtyard. "What is the need?"

"Your True Dream, Seer," he began. "It is not for the people of Talamh, however. It is much larger than that. There is a quest, you see."

"A quest?"

"Yes, my dear. Something is happening out in the stars, far beyond this world. But it is approaching. The Lady and Her Sisters have been following its path. In its wake are misery and death."

Perin leaned toward him. "Death?"

"The Sisters whom this *something* has passed by have become sick. They lose their reason. They are easily confused. Slowly, They lose their ability to function, lose Their will to function. Their inhabitants..." Rayne paused.

"What of Their inhabitants?" Perin prompted.

"Their inhabitants perish," Rayne finished quietly.

Perin gasped, her hand covered her mouth. "And it is coming here?"

"It is. Not for a great many years, but it is coming. And so," he continued, "the Sisters in this region of stars have banded together. They have found a Champion who will intercept this unknown carrier of misery and defeat it."

"The tall man from my True Dream," Perin breathed when understanding flooded her.

"The man from your True Dream, yes. He is here on Talamh, making preparations to depart in a great ship. They will be gone a long, long time, possibly to never return." Rayne covered one of Perin's hands with a gentle squeeze. "The Lady asks that you go with them. She believes you will begin to Dream True again. For them. She believes you are the Seer for this Champion."

Perin felt her whole body tense as Rayne's words sank in. "If I do what The Lady asks of me, I will never step foot on Talamh again," she said.

"You are likely correct, my dear."

"The great sacrifice," she whispered.

"Yes. That is why The Lady is asking and not demanding. You

30

have a choice."

She took a breath and steadied herself. "This Champion. May I meet him before I make my decision?"

"Of course."

"I want to know in my heart that he is the one from my True Dream."

"The Lady believes he is."

"If I am to offer myself as his Seer, I want to know for myself."

"I understand."

Rayne made rustling noises like he was about to rise, but Perin touched his arm. "There is something you're not telling me. I can hear it in your voice."

Rayne resettled himself with a sigh. "I forget how sensitive you truly are, Seer."

"What is it?"

"I am not at liberty to say, other than I do not believe The Lady was surprised when I told Her of your dream."

"Ah," Perin said. "If She wasn't surprised, then She already knows and perhaps has already offered my support?" she guessed.

"Perhaps, but you still have a choice."

That night Perin dreamt a True Dream, a different Dream from the one haunting her sleep. This one showed her a group of people not from Talamh. They were sitting together in a sterile room sharing a meal and laughing, joking with one another as comrades often do. She felt included.

When she awoke, she understood she never really had a choice.

~~~

He was huge. She nearly took a step back to regain her balance when his power slammed into her. And he was so bright, nearly as bright as The Lady Herself. Yet Perin was unafraid.

"I am Eloch," he said. "And you are Perin?"

She nodded and smiled. His voice was deep and rolling. "You are so bright," she told him. "Your light."

"You can see?" He sounded surprised.

"The Lady did not tell you about Seers," she guessed. For some reason, this put her more at ease. She felt more of an equal to this powerful being, this individual who was a man, yet more than a man. Much more.

"No," he confirmed. "Perhaps you would?"

They were outside in her small courtyard. She sat on the same bench she had shared with Rayne the day before. Like all parts of her home, she knew exactly where everything was and how many paces from the entrance to her favorite spot for contemplation, beneath a flowering tree. She loved to smell the blossoms in springtime. It was summer, now, and the tree's leaves rustled in the breeze, which also eddied the blossoms' fragrance around her.

She patted the place beside her. "Come," she said. "Sit with me." She waited for him to sit, felt his warmth and his energy as he lowered himself beside her. She turned toward him, waited for her Inner Sight to adjust to his brightness. "It is true I cannot see the world as you may see it. I used to, before I began to Dream True. Then my vision changed. Perhaps to accommodate the dreams? I do not know. It is what we are told."

"How did your vision change?" he asked.

By the way he brightened, she knew his curiosity was piqued. "I see the energy patterns of the living, so I am not entirely blind," she explained. "And colors. Every individual has a distinct color.

Sometimes it is very subtle, especially with families. But you, you are a bright white. Nearly blinding, until I have time to adjust. Much like The Lady, but not like Her at all. Her light flows around Her, like shimmery smoke, which touches and caresses everything around Her. Your light is bright, and if I squint, I can see vines of light moving within you. You are like a world all your own, contained in your flesh."

"Interesting," he said.

"Are you new to your powers?" she asked. "You sounded unsure."

"I am," he said. "I have been made and remade. I'm still trying to define what I have become so I can feel comfortable about it."

Perin felt moved to reach out and touch his hand. "Do not be afraid of what you are becoming," she told him. "You are perfect in your design."

"How can you be so sure?" he asked warily.

She couldn't hide her smile, in fact she didn't want to. "I am a Seer. I just...know. And," she paused. "it appears I am your Seer."

"How so?"

She laughed. "You are very curious. You enjoy knowing things."

"I do," he agreed. She heard the smile in his voice.

"Then I will answer you," she said with a little nod. "I am your Seer because this *knowing* does not come to me for all people, only those I See for."

"I don't quite understand."

"A Seer dreams dreams. We call them True Dreams. They are foretellings. But a Seer also has knowings. As the Seer for the people of Talamh, I would share my True Dreams and my knowings with the High Priest Rayne." She paused. "I believe you would call Rayne The Lady's Champion. Together, our combined wisdoms care for The Lady's people.

"But I stopped having True Dreams for the people. When I had a True Dream, it was the same one over and over again. I don't understand it because it doesn't take place on Talamh. I have no idea where it takes place. It is all very foreign to me, so foreign I don't even have the words to describe what I'm seeing. But you are in it.

"And now that we have met face-to-face, I know things about you. Helpful, supportive things. I am definitely your Seer." The laugh bubbled out of her. "I cannot tell you how happy this makes me. I truly thought I was going mad. Dreaming one dream over and over, a dream that served no one, that was terrifying."

"What is the dream about?"

She waved her hand dismissively. "I tried to describe it to Rayne, and it made no sense to either of us. I just don't have the words for the things I saw. But you were in it, and it will serve us as a warning to pay attention."

"A warning?"

She nodded. "In the dream, you were injured."

"How?"

"You were...struck down." She paused. "I am sorry. I can't explain, because I don't know what it was I was Seeing." She paused again. "I can understand your frustration, and I am sorry for it, Eloch. When I understand, I will tell you, I promise. It is how a Seer serves."

"You are coming with us."

It was not a question. "Yes. I must."

"You are willing to leave all you know, to fly off-planet without the promise of ever returning?"

Sitting in the warm sun beneath her tree, which smelled so good in springtime, Perin shivered. "In truth, I am terrified and filled with great sadness. But, yes, I am willing, Eloch."

She felt his warm hand cover her own, engulfing it.

"Thank you. I admire your courage and do not take your sacrifice lightly. We are good people, Perin, and we have all made the same choice you are making today, so we understand. Wren, my beloved, is kind. She will make sure you feel welcome and will do all she can to help you get comfortable and adjust to what I am sure will seem very strange. We all will."

Perin bowed her head. "Thank you." She felt more at ease, yet still could not hide the tremble in her voice. "I sense your urgency and will make myself ready within the week."

CHAPTER 3 – LEAVE-TAKING

Five days later, Eloch and Wren were in the galley having their morning coffee, as was their habit. He handed Wren a cup and took a sip from his own. Knowing she had something on her mind, he remained silent as he followed her to a seat in the galley.

She savored the aroma before she took a taste, then looked up at him. "Eloch, I think it's time to take Little Sister to Mouse, don't you?" Wren asked.

He felt her sorrow. He felt his own.

Eloch nodded, setting his cup on the table and turning around and around. "Yes. It's time," he said finally. "Prolonging the inevitable is only making it harder for all three of us. Little Sister will be happier on Talamh. We're making the right decision."

"Knowing she will be happier is the only reason I can let her go."

"Do we have a departure date?" Aiko asked Eloch when she saw them sitting together. She had been asking so often it had become a joke among the crew, a way of greeting each other.

Eloch smiled and shook his head. "Soon. Just a couple more days, in fact. The Lady has a gift for us, and we'll leave shortly after we receive it."

Aiko nodded with a sigh.

"Waiting is always hard," Wren said. "Why don't you take a shuttle to the surface? Buy Manabu that drink you keep promising your mentor. I'm heading down in about an hour to see Mouse. Why don't you come with me?"

"I don't want to leave the ship," Aiko said. "Thanks anyway."

"The ship will be fine," Grale chimed in from behind her. "I'll be here."

"That's supposed to make me feel better?" Aiko asked, turning to face him.

Grale barked out a laugh.

"Come with me, Aiko," Wren said. "I'm leaving Little Sister with Mouse today, and I could use the company on the way back."

Aiko shot Wren a glance. That was the closest she'd ever heard Wren come to asking for help. "Sure, Wren," she said, watching Eloch drape a comforting arm around his mate. He gave her a nod of thanks. "Let me call Manabu and get my ident."

Wren smiled. She leaned into Eloch, surprising Aiko with how small and fragile she appeared next to Eloch. "Thank you, Aiko. Little Sister and I will meet you at the gangway."

Grale nudged Aiko as she moved past him. "I saw the look Eloch gave you. You really wanted to stay on board. How come you never challenge the Big Guy over there?"

She scowled up at him. "Because that Big Guy is so full of knack, I don't want to bust him open. Besides, this is Eloch's quest. He and Wren are the bosses. I'm just the pilot." Her scowl deepened. "So are you, for that matter. Best not forget that."

He grinned. "With you reminding me every chance you get? Not likely. And Kitten," he added, as she turned to leave, "if you keep looking at me that way, I may start to think you're developing a hankering for me."

"Dream on, Cowboy," she huffed.

"Oh, I plan to," he said, grin firmly in place. "This trip's just getting started."

Aiko snorted as she left, ignoring the little thrill that raced through her. Instead she decided she was glad she was going dirtside.

It was a good day to hook up with Manabu one final time. She had something she wanted to give him, and today felt like the right moment. She walked to her cabin, snatched up a jacket, shoved her ident in her back pocket, and pinged Manabu, who was more than happy to meet her.

"Better yet," he said, "Why don't I pick you and Wren up? You caught me just wrapping up a short flight with Max. I can be there in twenty."

"Make it in sixty and you've got a deal," Aiko said. She disconnected and pinged Wren. "Manabu will pick us up in an hour," she told her when Wren answered her ping.

"That saves me the trouble finding someone willing to carry a sniffer. Thanks, Aiko."

"You bet. See you shortly."

"Sounds good. Gives Eloch and me time for one final romp with our Little Sister."

Feeling restless, Aiko exited her cabin and headed back to the galley, the crew's usual meeting place. Grale had left, as had Eloch and Wren, but Spider was there, and she visited with him until it was time to go.

She found Wren and Little Sister waiting for her at the *Valiant's* gangway. Wren looked sad as she stroked the soft hair behind the sniffer's ears. Aiko reached out and fondled Little Sister's other ear. The huge beast closed her eyes and rumbled her pleasure.

"I'm going to miss this beastie," Aiko said.

Wren sighed. "It's going to be bad for a while, but I just couldn't bear to keep her cooped up on a spacecraft for who knows how many light-years. It's just not fair. I want her to live out her days on the ground."

Aiko nodded and smiled softly. "You've done the right thing, Wren."

Wren ran a hand over her coilmats. "Yeah," she sighed. "I know. And Mouse says Little Brother is arriving any day now, too." She glanced at Aiko and flashed a smile, "Mouse told me Ingot was rather upset. Asked Max if he could get his replacement sniffer pronto," She giggled. "Pronto. That was the word he used."

Aiko laughed, envisioning Ingot, Max's perfectionist aide. She'd met him once or twice back on Spur, and he didn't seem the type to develop an attachment to a huge, drooling sniffer. "You don't say?"

"I do say," Wren responded. "Who knew Ingot would become so devoted to a huge beasty like a sniffer?" She tapped on the animated that had replaced her organic leg. "Who thought *I* would, after what Little Sister did to me?"

Aiko grinned. "Love's a funny thing."

The intercom pinged. "Ladies," Grale announced, "your shuttle awaits."

"Yeah," Wren agreed while she thoughtfully studied Aiko as she exited the ship. "Love's a funny thing."

~~~

"That's good," Manabu said, smacking his lips. "Thanks, Aiko." He hoisted his glass to her.

"Hey, don't thank me yet. You're buying the next round," she said as she clinked her stein against his.

"Wouldn't have it any other way." He took another swig. "So, still no departure date?"

Aiko shook her head. "No, all I get is some variation of 'any day now.' It's killing me. We're waiting on some gift from The Lady. That's all I know."

40

"So different from being a captain on a colonizer ship, isn't it?"

"There was still a wait," Aiko reminded him. "Big difference is, when you got your assignment, you'd be taking off within two or three days. Not like us with our two to three months of planning, purchasing, and organizing. Delays, delays, delays."

"You may be frustrated, Aiko, but I welcome the delay. Because of my age, I doubt I'll ever see you again."

Aiko tilted her head back as the rush of feelings swamped her. "That sobered me up quick."

"It's the truth, Aiko."

She sighed and looked at him, feeling tears threatening to spill over if she blinked. "And who's to say we're going to ever make it back here? Gods, Manabu, *a whole other galaxy*." She took a long pull from her glass.

"You okay with the crew?"

Her thoughts flashed to Grale. "Most of them. Not many of us to be not-okay with."

"That upstart rock pounder still giving you fits? Seems like he loves to push your buttons."

She smiled, "He does. But that's the good thing about this ship. It's so huge, there's lots of room and plenty of privacy. I don't have to interact with him that much."

"Is he as good a pilot as the rumors say?"

She made a face. "Unfortunately, the rumors are true."

"Unfortunately?"

"Means I have to respect his skills. He's near as good as I am. Better, when it comes to handling the *Valiant*. I haven't logged in as much flight time with the modulars."

"You'll catch on quick enough."

Aiko grinned wickedly. "I plan to."

Manabu set down his glass. "One smooth beer. Ready for the next round?"

Aiko nodded. "And some food to go with it. I'll buy the food."

Manabu signaled the waiter, and they placed their orders. "How are you planning the cross to Vela Kentaurus?" he asked while they waited.

"We haven't discussed it yet. If I'm asked, I'll recommend we hit the Cryo beds with a rotation plan. Going to be a long journey."

"I wonder how long it's going to take."

"No idea. Uncharted quadrant." She leaned forward eagerly. "My knack's going to be tested to its limits, for sure."

"And you're excited about that."

Aiko felt the grin tug at her mouth. "More than excited. You know how I love a good challenge. This one is the chance of a lifetime."

"Yeah. In a way, I wish I was going with you. But then I think of all that vastness..." Manabu's voice trailed off.

"And the space sickness grabs your gut," Aiko finished for him.

"And the sickness grabs my gut," Manabu agreed. "And I grab an intoxicant, so I doubt this here liver would last the journey. Not for me anymore. I'm just happy I can fly Max around and about this planet." He glanced heavenward. "And the occasional hop up to the space stations so I can feel a little weightlessness. I'm good."

Aiko returned his smile. "I'm glad. You ever going back to Spur?"

Manabu shrugged. "Depends on the boss man, but I doubt it. His mate has the space sickness worse than me. Besides, Ingot's managing my property. Making a nice sum off it, too." He paused. "Sold the shuttle I had stored and now have two places to rent out."

"You *sold* the shuttle?"

"I did. That sweet ride of mine is now someone else's."

Aiko shook her head. "Never thought you'd sell her. She was a beauty."

"Not to worry. I'll get a new one someday. And," he winked, "you know how sweet the ride is that I get to use whenever Max wants me to take him anyplace. Saves me all that maintenance expense."

"A win-win."

Manabu snagged the beer stein from the waiter just as he was setting it down. He raised his glass to Aiko. "A win-win," he said and took a deep swig.

Aiko waited for her food and glass to be served, then saluted Manabu with her glass. "To win-wins and long goodbyes."

Manabu's eyes misted. "And to good friends we'll never forget."

They drank.

Aiko set down her stein and picked up her fork. "That ship in your future?" she stated.

"Mmm?"

"I'm giving you the *Stardust*," she said and took a bite of her meal.

Manabu gawked at her and slowly set down his stein. "No, Aiko," he said with a shake of his head. "She's your baby. I can't."

Aiko swallowed and picked up her glass, gesturing with it. "It's a done deal. I signed off on it a while back. Been waiting for the right moment to tell you." She smiled. "This feels like the right moment." She took a gulp. "Feels like I'm going to be having another one of these, too."

"But Aiko—"

"You're the closest thing to family I've got, Manabu. There's nobody I'd rather give her to." She took another long drink. "Please, just be gracious and let's celebrate."

Manabu reached across the table and clasped her hand. "Gracious, I don't know if I even know what that means," he sniffed. "But drink with a comrade who's like family? That I can do." He released her hand and lifted his stein. "Thank you, my dear friend."

The rest of the lunch was spent laughing over shared experiences, accompanied by maybe too many glasses of lager, but Aiko didn't mind. She knew it was the last memory she would ever create with her dear friend and mentor.

She made sure it was a great one.

After their meal, Manabu walked her to the shuttle station.

Wren greeted them with hugs when they reeled over to join her.

"I could have taken you two ladies back up," Manabu said.

Wren waved a hand. "Too much trouble. You've already parked your shuttle, would have had to get back in line, all that stuff. We can bus it one time." She gave Manabu a hug. "Thanks anyway. Stay safe. Take care of Max and Mouse for me."

"I certainly will," Manabu said. He turned to Aiko. "Well, this is it, kiddo. Fly right."

Aiko hugged him hard. "You, too, Manabu. Fly right. And thank you for everything."

"Ready to line up?" Wren said, watching the queue forming for their scheduled shuttle back up to the space station where the *Valiant* was berthed.

Aiko nodded to Wren. "Why don't you save me a seat? I'll be right behind you." She waited for Wren to say another last goodbye to Manabu, then smiled at her old friend. "You be good to the *Stardust*, and she'll be good to you."

Manabu gave her a thumbs-up. "I will. May have to rename her the *Aiko*, though. You know, after the best pilot this old teacher ever met."

The tears welled too fast for Aiko to hold them back. Speechless, she nodded, and sent him one final wave before she hurried to catch up with Wren.

The pair remained silent the first part of their journey. With its scheduled route, the shuttle would take longer than the ride down since it stopped at two other stations orbiting Talamh before reaching theirs.

After the first stop, Wren turned to Aiko with a sigh. "That was hard, huh?"

Aiko nodded. "Pretty bad in a good sort of way." She smiled. "Made a new memory to take with me."

"I like that," Wren said.

Aiko considered Wren. "And you? How are you feeling?"

Wren shrugged. "A little empty, but I'll get over it."

"I know that feeling. Had one too many lagers over lunch trying to get over the empty."

Wren snorted. "I'm going to be hitting the gym when I get back. Throw some knives or something to get rid of it." She shot a glance at Aiko. "You feel like sparring with me, or are the lagers still too many?"

Aiko pursed her lips. "No," she said. "I think I'll be able to go a couple of rounds with you. Should help me sweat some of the poison out. Spare the liver." She chuckled.

"Good. We'll spare our livers together." Wren blew out a breath. "This leave-taking is the hardest. I almost want to be gone already."

Aiko nodded. "I hear you," she sighed.

"Thanks, Aiko," Wren said after a few moments.

"For what?"

"For making this trip with us. It's a big sacrifice. I'm sure you're giving up some dreams."

Aiko nodded. "No need for thanks. It's my choice, and I chose. And we all are giving up something, aren't we?" she added.

"True, that." Wren paused, thinking. "What are you giving up, Aiko? Unless you don't want to talk about it?"

"It's fine. It's something I gave up a long time ago. I'm over it."

"Over what?" Wren asked gently, not convinced Aiko was.

Aiko sighed and looked at her hands. "I always wanted a family. Worked my ass off to get out of SubCity, to better myself so I could have something. Finally had my own ship, and family was the next part of the plan." She looked over at Wren. "But when I was ready for all that, I learned that love isn't that easy to come by. The men I met weren't the..." she hesitated. "Let's just say they weren't father material. So I put that dream to bed."

Wren touched Aiko's arm. "I'm sorry."

"No pity, Wren."

"No pity given. Just sad is all."

"How about you? You want any children? Baby Elochs?"

Wren smiled. "I don't know. Maybe? Want to stop this *something* that's coming before I even consider that possibility."

46

"But haven't you and Eloch ever talked about it?"

"There really hasn't been the time. Eloch has been on one mission after another since we became partnered. 'Sides, I'm not even sure if I'd be a good mother. Didn't have the best role model."

Aiko snorted. "You're a KinLord. You have an amazing understanding of people. KinLording and child-rearing? Same thing in my book."

Wren wrinkled her nose, "Hopefully not. KinLording wasn't something I did for fun. I did it because I wanted to make SubCity a little easier for people, and because I was good at it."

"You'd be good at mothering, too, Wren."

Wren smiled. "Well, I'm not going to be dreaming about it. Just glad that Mouse and Max will have their chance. They're so happy."

"I didn't know they were having a baby. How wonderful."

"Yup! I was sworn to secrecy until Mouse found an opportunity to tell Max, and since she has, so can I."

"That's great," Aiko said. "I'm happy for them."

"What about Grale?" Wren asked out of the blue.

"What about him?"

"Ever considered him as partnering material?"

Aiko burst out laughing. "You're kidding me! Grale?" she hooted. "You're crazy, Wren. I take back all I said just now about you understanding people. He's one the most un-father-like people I've ever known."

Wren shrugged. "People change. You never know. We're embarking on a very long journey."

Aiko kept on laughing.

And for weeks—maybe even months—afterwards, whenever she caught a glimpse of Grale, she'd chuckle all over again.

~~~

Two days later, Perin arrived.

CHAPTER 4 – HEADING INTO CRYO

Rayne went with Perin up to the ship, and she was very grateful. The sensations were new and disconcerting. As they shot above the planet's atmosphere, she clutched at Rayne's hand, wondering if she was making a terrible mistake. To calm herself, she repeated to herself, *The Lady asks this of me*, again and again. It helped some.

Accompanying her and Rayne were Max and Mouse. It was the first time she had met either of them, which increased her discomfort. Yet when she heard the sorrow in Mouse's voice as she explained her relationship with the various crewmembers Perin was about to meet, Perin saw how correct Eloch was when he mentioned others who had to make sacrifices as well.

"You will miss them," Perin said, softening toward the couple.

"Very much so," Mouse agreed, her voice quavering with emotion. "Wren is like a sister to me. She will always be my KinLord."

"And a daughter to me," Max said.

Perin nodded. "I believe the love you share with each other will always keep you close, despite the distance."

"And technology will help substantially," Max added. "We'll have a few years when communication will be fairly easy."

"I don't know if that's a blessing or a curse," Mouse muttered.

"I think you will find it a blessing, My Mouse," Max said.

Perin liked the way they glowed at that moment.

~~~

Wren was throwing knives at a battered target when Eloch alerted her through their connection of Perin's arrival. *Be there in a few,* she replied silently. Snatching up the towel she had slung over a barre in the exercise room, Wren wiped the sweat off her neck as she strode to the target. Retrieving her knives at the various kill spots, she slid them back into their sheaths and concealed them within her clothing, smiling as she remembered her reply to Aiko when the pilot wondered why Wren still wore concealed weapons. "I feel naked without them," she told her.

And she did. Her knives and her skills were a part of her, just like the scars crisscrossing her back and the black animated replacing one leg.

Deciding she hadn't worked up enough of a sweat to smell, Wren finished toweling off and hurried to the gangway where she would have opportunity to say one final goodbye to Mouse and Max, and greet Perin.

She was curious to meet Perin, and was surprised by how young the woman was. And lovely. Tall and willowy, with long golden hair, a heart-shaped face, a small straight nose, and a full mouth. The eyes below the dark gold brows, which winged at the tips, were such a cloudy blue they were almost white. She was dressed simply in a loose white tunic and trousers tucked into cloth booties. A red sash belted her middle.

Wren heard Eloch introduce Perin to the rest of the crew, giving Wren a chance to hug Mouse and Max one final time.

It hurt to watch them go.

To keep her mind off the pain, she offered to take Perin to her new quarters, deciding it was a good way to get to know The Lady's Seer, Her gift to them.

"I hope you like your new space," Wren said as she led the woman

50

down the corridor to the sleeping wing of the ship. "It's going to be your home for a long time."

"I'm sure I will," Perin said politely, her hand resting lightly on Wren's forearm. "Everyone seems very nice," she added in a pleasant tone, but Wren noticed her tighten her grip on the duffel bag she insisted on carrying herself.

"We are a nice group of folks," Wren assured her. "We've all got our quirks, but underneath it we're kind. And," she added, "we know we're going to be together for a good many years, so we allow each other plenty of privacy."

"That will be a new experience for me," the Seer said.

Wren frowned. "You didn't have much privacy back on Talamh?"

Perin shook her head, "Not since I began having True Dreams and became blind. For nearly twenty years privacy has been hard to come by."

Wren's step faltered. "I don't mean to pry, but did you say twenty years? Exactly how old were you when you became a Seer?"

"I was eleven when I experienced my first True Dream."

"That must have been frightening when you were so young."

"The Dream didn't frighten me. But waking up without sight terrified me."

"I can imagine," Wren said as she slowed their pace. "I'm sorry, Perin."

"I've had a few years to adjust," Perin said wryly.

Wren chuckled and decided she liked the girl. As they walked, Wren explained the setup of the *Valiant* and how its modules surrounded the large Solar Farm area in the middle.

"I don't think you can get lost if you stick to the outside corridors,"

Wren said, "but until you get used to the ship, I wouldn't advise trying to take a shortcut through the Solar Farm without someone to lead you."

She paused, "The *Valiant* is enormous, so walking the perimeter can take a long time. We have little automated carts we can drive, but most of us just go through the Solar Farm. Based on the way you insisted on carrying your own baggage, I assume you want to be as independent as possible, but give it a few weeks, won't you? Let us help you learn your new home. Along the walls are com links, and there's one in your room, too. You can ping any of us at any time, and we'll lead you wherever you want to go."

Perin nodded. "I would like to tour the ship. Walking, not riding. Walking is how I will find my way around."

"Okay, then I have an idea. I run around the perimeter nearly every day for exercise," Wren told her. "I can take you with me during my cooldown."

Perin brightened. "I run, too," she said. "I love to run. I just need an arm and someone to match pace with." She hesitated. "Unless you prefer your privacy."

"No worries, Perin. I do like to run to clear my head or solve problems, but I like company now and again as well. Let's begin tomorrow morning, shall we? But for now? Now, we're here," Wren said, halting in front of Perin's room.

"There's a door panel right in front of you. On the right of the door panel is an activation panel. It's the same with every single door on the ship, which should make it pretty easy for you. The activation panel is heat sensitive, so you need to be close enough. Either waving your hand or touching the panel activates it, and your door will slide open. Want to try?"

She glanced over at Perin and noticed her frown. "What's wrong? Did I confuse you?"

Perin shook her head. "No, not at all. I simply forgot to count the steps while we were walking. It's how I know where I am."

"You'll have plenty of time to count," Wren told her. "Don't worry about that. And take it easy. This ship is enormous, and if you take your time you won't get so overwhelmed by all the things you're going to have to get used to. A little bit at a time is the best, you know. Here, try the panel. Let me help." She guided Perin's hand to the panel. "Slap your palm on it, and the door opens like magic."

Perin touched the activation panel and grinned as she heard the door whisk open. Delighted, she touched it again and it closed. She looked where Wren's colors were and grinned. "Easy," she said and opened the door for them.

"The activation panel is always on the right-hand side," Wren said. "Come, let's explore the room together. It's very spacious. And we'll remember to count. I'll count the paces with you."

Together they wandered about the suite, counting the paces to the bed, where Perin deposited her duffel. Then they counted over to the built-in closets and dressers, where Perin played with opening and closing the receptacles.

Next they wandered into the bathroom, where Wren showed her how to use the various appliances. Still counting, they strolled over to the long couch, which stood across from two easy chairs. "Careful with the side tables by the chairs and the coffee table in front of the couch," Wren warned.

"Not sure I'll be using this much," Perin said dryly when Wren led her to the desk with its info console.

Wren snorted. "But you will want to know where all the com links are. Besides the ones by the door and near your bed and in your bathroom, there's one here by the desk."

"I would love for you to describe the colors for me," Perin said when Wren brought her back to where her duffel lay on the bed.

"Well, all the furnishings are a light golden-colored material that looks like wood but isn't. The walls are deep green. Very restful. The carpeting is an orangey-gold, and it matches the bathroom walls, only the bathroom walls are lighter than the carpet.

"The couch is a floral pattern that has the same dark green as the walls, and the two chairs are pale orangey-gold like the bathroom walls and blend with the carpet. It's pretty nice. Comfortable, too."

Wren looked around and then thought of one more thing. "This ship was built to be a colonizing vessel and was created to transport the upper classes from Spur, my home planet, to wherever they were going to colonize. The UpperUppers loved luxury and fine things, and I'm not going to complain about it. I think we'll want...and probably need...as much comfort as we can get during this voyage."

"Is this the ship the people used to travel to Talamh?"

"No, this one came from Longwei, but the people living in the walled city would have used a similar ship."

"Many years ago."

"Yes. Many years ago, and now we're finally making friends with your people. I'm glad. It was wrong for my people to colonize, but it's been so long that Talamh is their home, too."

"Just so they don't try to overpower us," Perin said. "It would be a bad thing for them if they did. The Lady Talamh will never allow that to happen."

"The people of Spur don't want it to happen either, Perin. Max is a good leader. He wants a peaceful union of our two people."

"We do, too, but it may take us time to trust you." Perin smiled. "Do you have time to sit and describe the people I just met?"

"Of course, although I don't want to wear out your poor brain."

Perin chuckled. "I think there's still a little bit more room in there. Let me see if I can lead the way to the couch."

Wren watched Perin move forward hesitantly, arms outstretched. She took slow, careful steps, found one of the chairs, and maneuvered her way around it to the couch, where she settled herself with a sigh. "You're right. It is quite luxurious," she said, smoothing her hand over the rich fabric.

"And comfortable," Wren agreed, sinking into the chair closest to her. "So," she began, "I'm going to assume that Eloch has already been described to you since you met him before."

She waited for Perin's nod.

"Good, now I'll tell you about the crew you just met." Wren gathered her thoughts. "Aiko and Grale are our pilots. Aiko comes from Spur, from SubCity, so she is small like me. Her skin is the color of honey, dark longish hair and dark eyes. Her hair used to be short when she worked for the colonizers. She also used to have her own ship—a scouting vessel. She and Genji were the first ones to meet Eloch. Brought him back with them from Entean, his home planet." Wren paused and sighed. "She and Genj have seen Entean, and I really envy them that. Have Eloch describe it to you one of these days."

Perin nodded. "It must be very hard for him to be away from his planet."

"It is, but Eloch has adjusted. Moving on, now. Grale was what we call a rock pounder. He used to mine ore from various asteroid belts. I have no idea where he originated, but I suspect from the City of Talamh. He knows a lot of people here, which helped us get some good deals selling the modules we didn't need so we could buy the supplies we do need.

"Like Aiko, he had his own ship, a modular mining ship, put together very much like this one, so he's had more experience flying this kind of ship. I like Grale, but he can be pretty sarcastic, and he take a lot of pleasure in antagonizing Aiko."

Perin nodded. "I noticed all sorts of colors swirling around them when we were introduced earlier. Is it possible they share feelings?"

Wren hesitated, "I'm not sure. If they do, they're unaware of it. I mentioned something similar to Aiko and she burst out laughing."

"In time we will know," Perin said, nodding.

Wren chuckled. "True, that. Now, where was I?"

"You were describing Grale."

"Right. He's a big man, but graceful for all that. Dark hair and eyes, always looks a little scruffy. Seems rough, but I suspect he's hiding a sensitive soul. His people were extremely loyal to him, and that says a lot. Longwei, the spirit of the planet, insisted he come with us. I know there's a story there, but Grale won't talk about it. However, Longwei put her handprint on his forearm like a tattoo, and I know it has something to do with why he's here. How am I doing?"

Perin blinked, then laughed. "That was a question, wasn't it? I was so absorbed, I didn't realize you asked me something. You are doing very well, thank you."

"Going too fast?"

"No, no, it's perfect, and just enough background so I can connect who they are with the colors I saw when I met them."

Wren settled more deeply into her chair. "Good. I figure you'll be forming your own opinions and developing your own relationships with them, so I'm spending more time on what they look like."

Perin nodded. "Please continue. It is helping."

"Okay," Wren said, tucking her legs underneath her. "Who haven't I talked about?" Wren snapped her fingers. "Spider. Of the crew, I have known Spider the longest. He was one of my most trusted advisors when I was KinLord in SubCity on Spur." She paused. "A KinLord is the a leader of a group of people for whom he or she provides guidance and protection," Wren explained. "SubCity was a rough place. The weaker ones needed looking after."

"I see," Perin said, sounding like she understood more than Wren had let on. "So is Spider from SubCity like Aiko?"

"No. He was an UpperUpper. Got himself in trouble and came to my KinLands for help. We worked out an agreement. I'd protect him, and he'd tell me as much as he knew about living in the UpperUpper." Wren paused. "Although he could pass for someone from Sub on account of he's so wiry and he's not too tall. He's got wild bushy hair he wears kind of long, thick slanty brows, and eyelashes that don't belong on a man they're so thick and lush. His eyes are dark, too. Spider is smart. Wicked smart, but he's quiet, so you may not notice at first just how much he knows. He and Genji are in charge of sciencing out anything we may come across.

"Now Genji. Gengi used to work under Aiko. She calls Genji a walking question mark." Wren snickered. "He is that. Genji is the most curious person I've ever met. He looked after Eloch when he was new to Spur, and I would say Genji was Eloch's first true friend. Genji and Aiko. They really looked after him."

Perin nodded, hearing the warmth in Wren's voice. "And Genji's mate? Kalea? They seem very bonded. Their colors tangle."

"Very. It's a love story and not mine to tell, but I'm sure they'll tell you. They love telling their story. All I'll say is they would die for each other. Nearly did, too. Genji and Kalea look very similar, although Genji is taller. When Kalea dances...well, it's one of the most beautiful things I've ever seen. She's tall like you, but is dark, with thick black hair that flows down her back. She and Genji have mirror tattoos."

Wren paused. "They're Nuri, but I'll let them explain that, too, because I'm sure you're going to start getting confused if I give you too many details. And I still need to tell you about Mink and Wade. Let me just finish with Kalea and Genji by saying Kalea asks nearly as many questions as Genji. They'll never get bored."

Perin giggled. "You're very entertaining, Wren."

"Thank you. I think," She snorted. "Lastly, we've got Mink and Wade. They came with the ship. Met them on Longwei. They know this vessel inside and out." She chuckled. "Although with all the remodeling that goes on here, I'm not so sure anymore."

"Remodeling?"

Wren slid her hand over her coilmats and sighed. "Yeah, yeah. We have a module committee who got a little too carried away. Nobody could agree about where to put what module when. Too many people and too many reasons why, is what I say.

"I stayed out of it. But it sure was annoying. You'd just get used to where one section was and it would be swapped out with another, which changed all the perimeter corridors because not all modules are the same size. It was like an ever-changing maze for a while. We all kept getting lost.

"It came to a head a few days ago when the committee moved the ship's Navigation Bridge without consulting our two pilots. I did get involved then. We finally took a vote and put a stop to it.

"Anyway," Wren continued, "Mink and Wade. They're both techs, so if you need to know how anything works on the *Valiant*, they're the ones to ask, although Genji, Spider, and Kalea are catching on fast. And Aiko and Grale rule the Navigation Bridge." Wren uncurled her legs. "And there you have it. Our crew."

"Wait. Mink and Wade. What do they look like?"

"Oh, sorry. Uh, let's see. Mink is shorter than you but taller than me, and has a fuller figure. She's light-skinned, has green eyes that change colors depending on what she's wearing. Wears her blond hair short, which suits her personality, I think. It's curly. She's got a twinkle in her eye. Wade is more serious. Tall, slender. Even features. Dark hair and eyes. Quiet. Even quieter than Spider."

"What about you?" Perin asked.

"Me?"

"What do you look like?"

Wren laughed. "I don't know. Nobody's ever asked me to describe myself. I'm small like Aiko. Pale skin. Dark red-brown hair, more red than brown, that I've got in coilmats cuz it's so easy to take care of that way. And I've got gray eyes."

She stood and stretched. "Listen, Perin, I need to shower, so I'm going to leave you to get settled. We'll be eating in a couple of hours, and either Eloch or I will fetch you and take you to the galley. You won't want to miss the meeting after dinner to plan our trip." She leaned over and touched Perin's hand. "Think you can make it over to the bed where your duffel is?"

Perin nodded and smiled. "We counted steps, so I should be fine. Thank you for taking the time, Wren. And for making me feel welcome."

"You *are* welcome," Wren said as she moved to the door and touched the panel. It slid open. "See you soon," she said before the door slid shut.

~~~

Later, enjoying the solitude of her stateroom, Perin reflected on their conversation, linking Wren's descriptions to the colors her Inner Vision provided when she was introduced to the crew.

Having met Wren, felt her warmth, and basked in the lovely orangey-pink of her aura, Perin understood a little better why Mouse and Max came to care for the woman who was Eloch's mate. Wren took her responsibility for the people under her care very seriously. Even after the little time she had spent with the woman, Perin knew who was the true leader of this mission.

She had assumed it would be Eloch, but it was Wren. Eloch and his mission might be the why of the group, but Wren was the how. She was the one who created the cohesiveness that made it all work. And she did it with love and respect for each of the individuals, innately understanding their strengths and weaknesses. Perin smiled. In her way, Wren was very much like The Lady.

And she liked to run! An added blessing. Perin looked forward to getting to know her more while they explored the ship the next morning.

~~~

"Good news!" Wren said when everyone was seated at the galley table. "Now that Perin is here—and welcome again, Perin—it's time to leave. Aiko just informed me we have a spot and are slated to cast off tomorrow morning."

"At last!" Mink said. She raised her glass. "This deserves a toast." She lifted her glass higher. "To smooth sailing and positive outcomes," she said, quoting the traditional colonizers' pre-sailing toast.

"Smooth sailing. Positive outcomes," they all replied in unison.

"I've got some notes here that I want to go over after we eat," Wren said. "So let's dig in," she said, setting down her glass and raising her fork.

Spirits high, the group enjoyed a spirited and good-natured conversation along with their meal. Topics mainly revolved around Perin, as they shared experiences with her and listened to her own. Then, their meal over, the group waited in comfortable companionship while Spider and Mink cleared the table and Grale refilled people's glasses with their beverages of choice.

Drinks refilled, Wren cleared her throat and held up a piece of paper scribbled with notes. "Genji and Spider have located the wormhole jump that will begin our trip to Vela Kentaurus. It's pretty far, nearly twelve years out."

Grale whistled and paused refilling Kalea's glass. "The first one? There will be more than one?"

"Oh, yeah. We really don't know how many. It's uncharted territory, but Genji here thinks at least three or four."

Grale shook his head, "We'll be too old to move even before we get there. Either that or we'll be shriveled up with boredom," he said as he topped off Kalea's beverage.

Spider snorted, taking a seat beside Genji, making room for Mink.

Wren grinned at Grale, "Yeah. So, we're going to go Cryo. Take shifts. Eloch and I were figuring we could do two three-year shifts, with an overlap year in between." She looked at Mink and Wade. "How's that sound?"

Wade glanced at Mink. "Good decision. I'd recommend we rethink the length of time after we go through the first wormhole and locate the next."

"Can we stop and investigate if we come to a solar system with intelligent life?" Genji asked.

"I'll second that request," said Spider.

Wren glanced at Eloch, who gave her a brief shake of his head. "How about we note them and visit on the way back? We can't lose sight of why we're doing this. One Sister has already died over in Vela."

She paused and lifted a brow at Genji, who nodded.

"Great. Moving on, then. Eloch and I went over all our strengths and weaknesses and came up with two separate groups, but I want to get everyone else's insights before we proceed. Some of us may need extra training so we have all situations and responsibilities covered. Don't want to have to wake anyone before their time."

She waited for Grale to reseat himself between Aiko and Perin. "Spider, we'll start with you. You'll sleep while Genji and Kalea are awake and vice versa. Grale sleeps while Aiko is awake. Mink and Wade, you two can sleep, since you're partnered, but you're going to have to train someone to work the Cryo beds."

Mink glanced at Wade and raised her hand. "I think you've got the wrong idea about us," she said after Wren nodded for her to continue. "We're Cryo partners, but not really partnered." She looked at Wade.

"She's right," he confirmed. "We were sort of the leftovers back on Longwei and wound up with each other."

"Not that it hasn't been great," Mink said.

"No, I'm not saying it wasn't," said Wade with a grin. "But what we're trying to say is we're open to being split up."

"And," Mink added, "I think everyone on board needs to know how to operate a Cryo bed. I think it should be mandatory. You just never know."

"Good thinking," Wren said with a grin. "*Caution First* is the way I like it. Mink, you're a woman after my own heart. We all will be trained on the beds then."

She wrote something on her paper, then looked at Perin. "Even you, Perin. Since Wade and Mink don't mind, I'll split you up. Each shift needs an expert working with the Cryo equipment."

"I'd like to be awake when Eloch is awake," Perin said. "I feel my Seeing is tied to him, is meant to serve him."

"I will be awake the full time," Eloch said.

Wren nodded. "It's true."

"Then I will remain awake as well," Perin said quietly.

"But you'll age, Perin," Wren said. "The whole reason for us traveling this way is so we will still be in our prime and able to cope with whatever we find out there in that next galaxy."

"I understand," said Perin, "But I have promised The Lady I will use my skills for this endeavor. And my age won't change my ability to Dream True. Plus," she smiled briefly, "we people of Talamh are known to live nearly two hundred years."

"Shall we compromise?" Wren asked after a brief pause. "Shall we revisit this idea twelve years from now, after the first wormhole jump?"

"Of course," said Perin. "Although I doubt my mind can be changed."

"How are we going to decide who takes the first shift?" Aiko asked.

"Let's wrestle for it," Grale said as he leaned closer to her. "I'll go easy on you, Kitten." He winked.

Aiko glared at him.

"Play nice, you two," Wren said before Aiko could respond. "We're going to flip a coin."

She glanced down at her scribbled notes. "To recap, here are the two groups, although it's gotten a little uneven." Wren glanced at her notes and made a couple of notations. "Aiko, Genji, Kalea, Wade, and I make up one group. Then Mink, Grale, and Spider are the other group. Eloch and Perin will remain awake. Everybody happy with this?"

She waited a few moments. "We can switch things around if you'd like. I just need to keep the pilots and the science officers separate." She glanced at Spider and Genji. "That's you two, with Kalea helping Genji. Genj, think Spider's up to the task?"

Genji smiled at Spider. "He's more than ready."

Spider beamed.

~~~

Aiko eyed Grale and wondered what it would be like to be without him for three years.

When he caught her watching him, he grinned wickedly. "Gonna miss me?" he asked in a voice only she could hear. "We can still wrestle if you want, Kitten. Just say the word."

She rolled her eyes. "No thanks, Grale. I'm good." She leaned away, trying to ignore his teasing chuckle. *Maybe it will be nice to have a break from that gargantuan ego,* she thought and then turned back to the group's conversation.

"I think we should remain in Cryo state longer," Mink was saying.

Wren glanced at Eloch and sighed. "Can we revisit that after the first jump gate as well?" she asked. "It's all new for me and"—her cheeks flushed—"I frankly don't want to be separated from Eloch for so long."

Mink nodded. "Understood. But it doesn't feel long once you get used to it."

"It will for me," Eloch commented.

Aiko blinked at the vulnerability in his voice.

Wren reached out and touched Eloch's hand before glancing around the table. "This okay with all of you?"

She paused and when no one spoke, she continued. "Okay, then." Wren pulled out a coin from her pocket. "Perin, since you're not affected by this, why don't you call it?"

"Call what? I don't understand," Perin said, reminding Aiko of the first time she met Eloch on his home planet. Perin had the same combination of innocence, power, and wisdom. It made her curious to see what Perin would be like in a few years, after having adjusted to a more technological existence.

~~~

Wren laughed, "Oh, sorry, Perin. I'm flipping one of the new Talamh coins. Have you heard of them?"

Perin nodded. "Yes, I've held one. On one side is an image of The Lady and on the other is the planet."

"That's it," Wren said, "Our Mouse designed them. Okay, to continue, I will toss the coin in the air and catch it, covering the coin with my hand. You say which side you think will be exposed when I take my hand off it. If it's The Lady, Aiko's group sleeps first. If it's the planet, Grale's group goes first. Does that make sense?"

"It's like a game," Perin said.

"It can be a game, but it's also a good way to make a decision to keep things fair or if the leader doesn't want to make the decision."

"You don't want to make the decision?"

Wren chuckled. "Not really, for personal reasons." She glanced at Eloch. "Eloch and I had quite the discussion," she said, then swallowed and took a deep breath. "Unlike you, my argument for remaining awake wasn't good enough. Eloch told me he could still contact me while I'm in a Cryo state if he wants to discuss anything or just connect. Not sure if I believe it, but time will tell, I suppose."

Time did tell, sooner than Wren wanted. When she flipped her coin, Perin chose the Lady (no surprise there, Wren thoughtyly), and Aiko's group, herself included, would be heading into Cryo first.

"Okay," Wren said. "I guess that's that. Let's wait a couple of weeks to make sure the *Valiant* is behaving herself while we get used to our new habitat. I want Perin to feel comfortable with the ship and crew before two-thirds of us fall asleep on her for three years." She pushed herself away from the table. "And now I'm heading off to bed. Early day tomorrow. Perin and I are taking a run around the ship first thing, and I don't want to miss our departure." She looked at Eloch. "You ready for sleep?"

He smiled at her and rose, placing her hand in the crook of his arm. "Lead on," he said.

"You okay, Eloch?" Genji asked. "You've been pretty quiet tonight."

Eloch frowned and shook his head slightly. "I'm fine, Genj. In a thoughtful mood, I suppose, because I've been reflecting on the tremendous responsibility we've taken on to make sure this journey has a positive outcome."

Genji nodded. "And the heaviest responsibility falls on your shoulders."

Eloch nodded. "It does indeed."

"We will do all we can to help you, Eloch."

"I know that, Genji, and I appreciate it." He studied the group, "Frankly, I couldn't have gotten even this far without all of you. Thank you for your loyalty and sacrifices." He looked at Wren, who was smiling up at him. "Ready?"

She nodded. "Good night, all," she said as they moved toward the galley's exit.

Kalea turned to Perin, "Genji and I are just next door to your stateroom module, Perin," she said. "May we accompany you?"

"Yes, please," Perin said. "I'm looking forward to getting more acquainted with you. Your colors are beautiful," she added.

Genji took Perin's elbow to guide her out of the room. "Our colors?" he asked.

She nodded, following his lead and sensing Kalea on her other side. "Yes, you are both so warm, almost like a fire burning within you. And your colors are all different shades of orange, red, and yellow. They swirl around together when you are near each other. You are very bonded to each other."

"I like that," said Kalea. "It sounds like a sunset."

"It's very lovely," said Perin with a smile.

"So you see colors?" Genji asked. "I was under the impression that you're blind."

"I cannot see as you do. But I do see the colors and shapes of living things with my Inner Vision," Perin answered.

"Does that make it easier or more difficult to maneuver?" Genji asked.

Kalea laughed. "You must forgive Genji if he gets too personal, Perin. He is always full of questions."

Perin smiled and shook her head. "I don't mind at all. It's easy for me to avoid running into people, but until I memorize my surroundings, I will run into things since I can't see anything that isn't alive," she told Genji.

"Will you need help in your stateroom?" the two asked in unison.

Perin smiled, feeling better and better about her decision. "You are both very kind. Wren has taken me around my room and shown me where things are. Since then, I practiced and learned while I unpacked this afternoon. I am a fast learner and feel quite capable of putting myself to bed and getting ready in the morning." She hesitated. "I may need help with my hair, however, without my handmaidens to assist."

"Oh, blessings!" Kalea exclaimed. "I would love to help you fix your hair. My sister and I used to spend hours decorating each other's hair. And yours is so beautiful, like golden sands. It would be my pleasure, if I may?"

Perin laughed delightedly at Kalea's enthusiasm. "Thank you, Kalea, very much." They came to a halt. "We're here already?" she asked.

"Yes," Genji confirmed.

"Oh, dear," she said. "I was enjoying our conversation so much, I again forgot to count the steps," she laughed. "I forgot to count them when Wren took me to my room, and forgot again when Eloch came to bring me to dinner, and now I have forgotten again."

"Never fear," Kalea said. "We will all count them tomorrow morning. Wren said you were both going on a run."

"Yes, early."

"Tap on my door when you're back, and I'll come by to fix your hair, and then the three of us can breakfast together before we take off."

"That will be perfect."

"Good," Kalea said. "Good night, Perin. Rest well."

The pair waited until Perin had skillfully opened her door panel and entered her room.

Chapter 5 – Nuri in Cryo

Since they were the most experienced, Wade and Aiko went into the sleep first.

"Who's next?" Mink asked while she turned on the Cryo bed next to Aiko. She had begun the sequencing checks when she noticed the silence filling the room and raised an eyebrow.

Wren considered Genji and Kalea, who seemed focused on each other. "I think that's my bed," she said and released Eloch's hand. She moved alongside the bed and stood beside Mink, gently tapping the side of the unit. "This is new," she told her. "I'm not too good with not having control of a situation."

Mink nodded. "You saw how easily it worked with Wade and Aiko," she said. "Granted, they've done this before, and I do remember my first time, wondering if I'd ever wake up."

"Exactly," Wren said.

"You will wake up, Wren. Guaranteed," Eloch said softly.

She glanced at him. "Okay," she said and swallowed. "Let's do this."

She took off her robe. Underneath was the dark blue Cryo suit, the hood resting at the nape of her neck. She fastened her coilmats into a tail and climbed into the cylindrical bed, using the footrest as she had seen Aiko and Wade do. With Mink's help, she settled on to the soft bed, and Mink began attaching the hoses to the fittings on the suit. "Time to pull up the hood, Wren, and say nighty-night."

Wren swallowed and looked up at Eloch, who had come to her other side.

He picked up her hand and cradled it between his own. *My love, we will still be able to connect,* he said into her mind.

Even in this sleep state?

Even then.

Slipping her hand from his warm grasp, she nodded and drew the hood over her head, leaving only the top half of her face exposed.

Mink adjusted the formula flow. "Okay, Wren. I'm going to slide the hood shut, and you'll soon be asleep. See you in three years, fit and fine," she added with a smile.

The hood slid shut. Wren watched their faces fog and warp through the thick plastic dome. Then the cold hit, and she knew why both Wade and Aiko gasped. She had never felt as cold as she felt in that moment, even during that terrible time on Spur when she lay naked, beaten, her back one massive wound and exposed to the elements, by the fountain with The Lady. She welcomed the numbing that spread through her body as she relaxed into a sleep so deep and unnatural, she doubted Eloch could reach her. But by then it was too late to say a word.

With Wren asleep, Mink readied the next Cryo bed. She glanced at Eloch, who still stood by Wren's side, his expression unreadable. "She's fine, Eloch."

"I know," he said, not looking at Mink. "I'm just not sure if I will be," he added to himself.

Mink turned toward the remaining pair. "Which one of you is it going to be?" she asked, gesturing to the bed beside Wren.

Genji smiled. "I'll go next. This isn't the first time for me, either." He looked at Kalea, "You can watch me and see how easy it is."

"I have been watching, Genji, and I know it is easy. But..." she

70

paused. "I am uncertain."

"Everybody is the first time," Mink said.

Genji laughed. "So true," he said as he expertly slid into the bed. Kalea stood at his side, looking down at him while Mink attached the hoses. "That's exactly what I want to see when I open my eyes in three years. I love you, Kalea," he said, pulling his hood in place.

"I love you, too, kind Genji," she whispered as the lid slid shut.

A few moments later, Genji was sleeping peacefully. Kalea stood watching him, her hands resting on the lid. His initial gasp had frightened her, and when his eyes flew open, it frightened her even more. They sought her out, and she watched his eyes close again, his face and body relax as the Cryo sleep state enveloped him.

"Okay, Kalea," Mink said. "It's your turn."

Feeling empty, she nodded and crossed to the bed Mink had prepared. But something felt wrong. She hissed and whipped around toward Genji's bed just as a warning signal sounded, its shrill tone accompanying her hiss. "What's that?" she asked and raced over to Genji's bed, peering in through the hood.

"Stand aside, Kalea," Mink ordered while she rushed to the readout pad by the machine. "It says he's awake. Unstable." She looked inside the hood. "But he looks fine. There must be a malfunction with this particular bed. We're going to have to wake him up and put him in a different one. Good thing we've got plenty."

"No," Kalea said. "It's the Nuri," she said, noticing the lizard-like slits when Genji's eyes flashed open. "The Nuri is not asleep." She gasped. "He's going to change!"

She looked at Mink. "Stand back," she commanded. "He is very dangerous. The Nuri is frightened. A frightened Nuri attacks. Maybe—"

There was no time. Instead of explaining what she intended, she simply shifted into her Nuri form. The room was suddenly too

71

cramped, so she kept her wings folded closely to her side. In her Nuri form, she reached out to Genji's Nuri. It was very frightened, unable as it was to connect with Genji. She tried to soothe it with small hisses, but it refused to calm itself.

It felt trapped. Caged. It wanted out. *It's breaking out.*

Plastic shattered and metal groaned as Genji's Nuri exploded out of the Cryo bed, wings unfurling, neck snaking as the bed's hoses whipped around it and spewed fluid, which instantly froze whatever and wherever it landed.

Mink cried out as she was thrown against the adjacent bed, her arm shielding her face from the fluid.

Kalea hissed at the Nuri, and it whipped its head toward the sound. The Nuri did not recognize her, seeing only a potential threat. It snaked its head, the thick throat muscles undulating as it prepared to breathe its fire.

Terror hammered through her. Even in her Nuri form, she would be badly injured. *And the others! Helpless in their Cryo beds!* Hoping to draw the Nuri away, Kalea moved swiftly toward the exit, steeling herself for the pain from the blast.

"Hold!" a deep voice commanded.

Kalea froze in mid-step. She could do nothing else.

The room went silent, as if time stood still. For several moments, nothing happened. All Kalea could hear was the bellows-like breathing of the Nuri, which was behind her exposed back.

Cautiously, Kalea turned her head and hissed in surprise.

Genji's Nuri stood quietly with its head bowed, frill flattened, and wings folded, gently breathing into Eloch's palms.

She hissed again and returned to her human form. Slowly, she crept to Eloch and stood behind his broad back.

"It's okay now," he told her in a calm, low tone.

"How?"

He shot her a sidelong glance. "I've had experience with dragons. On Entean."

"But how? I tried to reach him, and I couldn't do it."

"You were trying to reach Genji-as-Nuri, Kalea. This is not Genji. This is a beast. A dragon. It needed to be soothed as one would soothe a beast."

"I-I tried that. It wouldn't listen to me."

Eloch shook his head. "I'm not sure, Kalea, if you can separate the two things. All you know is Nuri. You are Nuri and you see a oneness, but with Genji asleep..." His voice trailed off as he concentrated again on the beast.

Kalea was quiet, feeling Eloch's power. "I think," she said slowly, "there is more to this than you knowing how to soothe beasts."

"Perhaps. Come, let's take this dragon someplace more comfortable. Give it something to do."

"Genji?"

"I believe Genji is safely asleep. When he wakens, he will be able to shift. Mink can—"

They both looked over to where Mink lay huddled under the Cryo bed where she had been thrown, her eyes squeezed shut.

"Go," Kalea said. "I will stay here with Mink."

Eloch looked at the Nuri. Some kind of silent exchange happened between them, and then he turned. The Nuri dutifully followed Eloch out of the Cryo lab, nearly wedging itself in the doorframe.

Kalea slipped on a lab coat to cover her nakedness and knelt down by Mink, afraid to touch her.

Mink was breathing softly, which made Kalea relax. Until Mink moaned.

Kalea touched her shoulder. "Mink?"

Mink's eyes fluttered open and slowly focused. "Kalea?" she groaned. "What happened?"

"Genji went to sleep, but his Nuri didn't. Genji shifted into the Nuri form, but there was no Genji to control it and it went mad with fear. I was helpless to calm it, but Eloch could. Can you sit up? Are you hurt?"

"Where *don't* I hurt?" Mink replied with a grunt. "But I think I can sit up." She started to push herself up and immediately cried out and collapsed. "Maybe I need some help," she gasped.

"Your arm."

"Yes, yes, I see. Don't worry. Help me up."

With Kalea's help, Mink managed to slip onto one of the chairs placed haphazardly around the Cryo lab.

"Your arm," Kalea said again.

"It's been frozen, Kalea. But accidents happen, and all Cryo labs are equipped with med kits that can heal this." She nodded to a black med kit attached to a wall. "If you'll fetch one of those, I can take care of it right now."

Kalea nodded and rose to get the kit. When she returned, she noticed the beads of sweat on Mink's forehead. "Why don't you sit back and tell me what to do." She drew up another chair next to Mink and opened the kit.

While Mink described to Kalea what steps to take, Kalea soon had Mink's arm wrapped in a casing, which was programed to slowly bring the frozen limb back to body temperature.

"It mainly takes time," Mink explained. "And when this casing comes off, my arm will look dreadful—all black and blue—but that's just the blood circulating and cleaning out the dead cells. Good thing I won't be going into Cryo for another three years or so. My arm couldn't take it. An injury like this takes a full eighteen months to heal completely." She grimaced. "Hurts like a sonofabitch. Can you hand me one of those pain relief injects? Should have done that first."

As the pain relief meds took effect, Mink and Kalea considered the damage and debris, which was all that was left of the exploded Cryo bed.

"Should have been worse," Mink commented.

Kalea nodded. "Plastic and metal were flying everywhere but"— she nodded over at the beds where their three companions slept— "look how it all stops and lands in a line right before it can touch any of the others. How?" She paused, thinking. "Oh— Of course. Eloch."

"Eloch," Mink agreed. She took a breath. "I'm sure they're fine, but I want to double-check to make sure they are. Come with me, will you? Still too light-headed." She looked at Kalea. "You need to learn all this stuff anyway. I was serious when I said everyone should know how to work the beds."

"Not a problem for me," Kalea said. "I love learning new things." She sobered. "Genji?"

"If he was a normal human, I would say Genji will wake up on his own when all the Cryo fluids flush out of his system," she said as Kalea helped her over to Wade's bed, "about a year or so from now. And he would need immediate medical attention."

She pointed to the bed's control panel. "Wade checks out. See how all the readouts are somewhere in the middle range?" She waited for Kalea's nod of understanding. "That's what we want. If they are too extreme on either side of that range, we have a problem. Let's check Aiko and then Wren."

As Kalea helped her toward Aiko's bed, Mink nodded at her arm. "Genji will be like my arm if he's not properly taken care of, which means we need to get him into a Cryo bed, dose him with pain meds, and run the wake-up cycle." Leaning heavily on the hood of Aiko's bed, she glanced at Kalea. "But he's not a normal human being, is he? So I'm not exactly sure when or how Genji will wake up."

Kalea shook her head while watching Mink read the panel displaying Aiko's vital signs.

"Nuri are very hardy," Kalea said after a moment. "We heal very quickly."

"That's good to know, Kalea. Then we will think positively. Aiko's fine, too. Help me over to Wren. Even though I suspect she'll be fine as well, I need to be sure. I'm going to let you check the vitals and tell me what you notice."

Kalea nodded and helped Mink cross over to Wren's bed, noticing that Mink seemed stronger. Perhaps the pain meds were helping.

"Listen, Kalea," Mink said. "I'm so sorry. This is all my fault, and I'm not sure I'm ever going to forgive myself if…" She paused and looked at Kalea.

"Nuri are very hardy," Kalea repeated. "I am sure Genji will be fine."

Mink nodded, not feeling reassured in the least. "Well, I am so very sorry this happened. Please forgive me. I should have taken into account the Nuri physiology. I honestly have no idea how to put you people into a cryogenesis sleep stasis."

Kalea was silent for several moments. "Perhaps Genji and Spider can science it out. When Genji wakes up, he will understand more of the Nuri's experience."

"And perhaps it's only possible for humans."

"I believe I can put the Nuri to sleep," Eloch said from the doorway.

The two women looked over at him.

"When Genji wakes up and contains his Nuri, I will try it with the two of you, Kalea," he said, frowning at the stuck door panel, which was damaged when the Nuri wedged its body through the tight doorjamb.

"Where did you take him?" Kalea asked.

Eloch smiled. "He is in the Solar Farm, the forest there," he answered as he straightened the door panel and popped it back in place. "He's hunting a wily boar, which should keep him occupied for some time. I put a field around the area so his fire won't harm the ship. I've also told Perin, Spider, and Grale to stay away from that area."

Kalea blew out a breath and nodded. "I was worried. I am still worried for Genji."

"Don't be. I will be able to sense when Genji wakens," Eloch said.

Kalea glanced at Mink. Eloch rarely spoke of what he could or could not do, but this was so reminiscent of something Longwei would say, she wondered just how extensive his powers truly were. She forced a smile, wishing Wren was awake so they could talk. "Thank you, Eloch."

"We've been checking on the other sleepers," Mink said. "All is well with them."

"Good," Eloch said. "And you, Mink? Are you injured?"

She lifted her arm. "I got frozen, but it will heal. Kalea helped patch me up."

"I'm sorry you were injured," Eloch said.

She shrugged. "I'm just happy it's not worse. Like I said, I will heal, and in the meantime, I've got pain meds." She made a face. "Could use some help cleaning up this mess, however."

Eloch hesitated. "The damaged Cryo bed," he began. "If you like, I can repair it."

Mink glanced at the bed where Genji, in Nuri form, had erupted. The hood was shattered, and the bed was bent at an awkward angle on its pedestal. The readout panel dangled beside it. Hoses still dripped fluids. Pieces of plastic and metal were strewn about the room. She laughed. "Even if you did, I wouldn't trust it. These beds are precision instruments."

"Nonetheless, I believe I can repair it. I would appreciate the challenge."

"Then by all means, be my guest."

At Mink's direction, Eloch and Kalea carefully cleaned up the fluids and put the bed's bits and pieces in a semi-organized pile.

Eloch looked at Kalea and smiled. "The Nuri just caught the pig. He is enjoying his meal. Shall we go wake Genji?"

Kalea nodded. "Mink said he could be in serious trouble. Frozen like her arm."

Eloch glanced at Mink. "Good to know," he said with a nod. "I think it will be all right, Kalea. I believe I know what to do."

Kalea turned to him. "You do? How?"

He shrugged. "I think I can do a lot more than I expected." He laughed. "I was searching for something to occupy the Nuri and I just created an actual pig. A pig! From the aminos we've got in the protein labs, I created a pig. Let's go, Kalea, Genji is waking," he said.

CHAPTER 6 – THREE YEARS INTO THE MISSION

Three Years Later...

Perin seated herself on the bench with a contented sigh and leaned her back against the young tree so reminiscent of the one shading her favorite garden seat on Talamh. Here on the *Valiant,* there was no breeze to rustle the leaves, but there was the lovely scent of blossoms and growing things.

She sighed again, soaking up the peace, and stretched her legs out, making sure she didn't accidentally kick the tapping stick Spider had crafted and then showed her how to use.

She loved her tapping stick. Owning it had given her freedom, freedom to walk the ship without needing to count steps or wait for a person to lead her someplace. Over the past three years she had reveled in her ability to explore in solitude and discover the places she most enjoyed visiting. She was even able to keep up her daily runs.

She liked visiting the science labs, where Spider and Mink gathered data, measured distances, analyzed radiation, and studied the ever-increasing variety of flora and fauna Eloch was creating. She'd sit in an out-of-the-way corner and listen quietly while the pair discussed findings and hypothesized what it all meant.

Sometimes she even participated. The task and traditions of being a Seer had defined her existence and never allowed her to even imagine other ways of learning and gathering information. She'd been surprised to discover that learning fascinated her.

And instead of being impatient or resentful about her questions, Spider and Mink seemed to welcome them, and welcome the discussions, and she appreciated the developing friendship. Their friendly banter was refreshing after years of being treated as a Seer.

Grale was harder for her to connect with. He mostly kept to himself. She sensed that, like her, he was taking longer to adjust to this new life. Since she was enjoying her solitude and freedom, she decided it must be the same for Grale, so she only engaged with him if she chanced to meet him at mealtimes.

Another place she had discovered was a room full of musical instruments. It wasn't far from the staterooms, and, surprisingly, rarely frequented. There she spent many hours reacquainting herself with the lute, picking out songs from her childhood and making up new ones.

But Perin's favorite spot was this bench under the tree Eloch planted for her two years ago.

As his first year without Wren wound down, Perin noticed Eloch had become more and more withdrawn. It concerned her, and she began to pay regular visits to the Solar Farm to check up on him. Based on something she overheard Wren say to Eloch about how he might disappear, she decided Wren would have wanted her to be there to draw him out of himself.

She sensed the concern in the tone of Wren's voice then. And since Perin was Eloch's Seer, she took it upon herself to watch over him for Wren. After that first year, she began to make daily excursions to Eloch's domain.

Every morning, after she had eaten, Perin would make her way to the Solar Farm, sit on her bench, and wait. After a while, Eloch, sensing her presence, would join her. As time went on, he would often arrive before she did, his light shining so brightly it was a beacon.

At first they said very little to each other. Or if they conversed, Perin did most of the talking. Then, with Perin's gentle prodding, Eloch gradually began to talk about what he was learning about his power.

Within a few months, the two of them had slipped into an easy friendship, and as the friendship deepened, her Knowings and True Dreams began to be more supportive. The dreams, especially, had guided Eloch into controlling the all-consuming need he had to create. She was delighted when he had told her he no longer feared he would be devoured by that need.

Now that Wren would be waking soon, Perin was curious about how the new dynamics would play out. She understood Eloch's devotion to Wren, but would Wren understand his friendship with Perin? Or would Wren be jealous of her?

"Good morning, Perin," Eloch said, his deep voice interrupting her thoughts.

Perin started.

"I'm sorry, I didn't mean to startle you," he said, taking his customary place beside her.

She smiled and shook her head. "I'm fine. I didn't notice you were there. Deep in thought," she explained as she felt the bench shift slightly with his weight. "How are you?"

"Happy. Wren wakes up tomorrow."

Perin smiled. "It's been difficult, hasn't it?"

"More long than difficult." He looked at her. She could tell by the way his glow increased that he was studying her. "I've enjoyed getting to know you."

"I've enjoyed it as well. And it has helped me be a better Seer for you."

"For which I am grateful," he said. "Your True Dreams gave me the courage to press forward, and I've enjoyed experimenting with what I can do." He paused. "I think I know how to keep Wren from aging so she can remain awake." He paused again. "You, too. Why should you age if you don't need to?"

"Why should anybody?"

"Exactly. Then the others can remain awake as well."

"But what about the boredom? Spider told me long flights can cause boredom and then discord among the crew."

"Have you been bored, Perin?"

"Me? No. Everything is so new to me. I've been too busy learning and adjusting to ever be bored. But I've noticed how Grale seems more positive this morning. And dinner last night held the air of anticipation. I think we are ready to have our crew together again. If there were no Cryo sleeps, then people could get used to one another, squabble, get annoyed at people's peculiarities, like a family who spends too much time together."

"Hmmm," Eloch said. "That's something I've not considered. Possibly because, like you, I feel there is so much to learn about myself, how could I ever be bored? A very keen observation, Perin."

She laughed. "Only because I've experienced it with my handmaidens. As a blind Seer, I was constantly with people. They were always underfoot, seeing to my every need. I had no challenges, and if there were no True Dreams for a spell, I would get bored and irritable with my maidens. I relished my solitude when I was able to find it, which wasn't often at all." She touched her stick. "When Spider taught me how to *see* with this stick, I felt truly free for the first time since I became blind."

"You know I could make you see again, Perin."

She was touched by his offer and smiled. "Thank you, but no," she said gently. "What if my blindness affected my ability to be your Seer? I don't want to take that chance."

She touched his hand. "Let's change the subject," she said, clasping her hands in her lap. "What are you creating today, Eloch?"

"Butterflies. There is a need. My flowers need pollinating."

"So you chose butterflies. What about bees? We can have honey."

"I will consider bees, but butterflies seem easier. It's challenging to keep my world, here, in balance," he said. "Butterflies seemed easier to control. I already have a bird species in mind that eats caterpillars."

Perin smiled. Listening to Eloch ramble, she realized just how contented she was now.

~~~

The cold was intense. Wren's entire body shook uncontrollably. Her eyes shot open, but for a moment she couldn't remember where she was.

"Welcome back," Eloch said, easing her up to a sitting position.

"Mummph," Wren replied, burrowing her face into his warmth. "D-does this g-get any e-easier?" she asked through chattering teeth.

Mink laughed as she checked Wren's pulse. "Sorry, it never does," she said. "Lie back now so we can disconnect you, Wren. Sooner you're disconnected, sooner you can get warm."

"Then disconnect me, please," Wren said, allowing Eloch to help her lie down again. She smiled up at him. "You're a sight for sore eyes," she told him as she reached up and pulled her hood back, then noticed her coilmats were much longer. "I loved it when you were able to visit me, but this is so much better. My poor frozen brain jumbled it all together." She touched her hair. "Apparently, my hair kept growing, even in Cryo."

"What?" Mink exclaimed. "That's not possible."

Wren narrowed her eyes up at Eloch. "Did you have something to do with this?"

Eloch grinned. "I missed you."

"He moped a lot while you were asleep," Mink said.

Eloch nodded. "I did."

Wren squinted at him. "Didn't you ever hang out with the others?" She looked over at Mink, who shook her head.

"He preferred his solitude."

Wren nodded and reached for Eloch's hand. "I was afraid of that," she said.

"I needed the solitude, Wren. And Perin made sure I wasn't always alone."

"Perin?"

Eloch nodded. "She would find me and make me talk to her." He smiled. "I'm glad The Lady Talamh sent her to us. Her True Dreams have helped me gain better control of my power."

Wren smiled and squeezed his hand. "That's wonderful, Eloch. You must be relieved."

"I am. Very."

"I must thank Perin when I see her next."

"You're checked out here, Wren," Mink stated, reading the data from her scanning wand. "Go get warm while I wake the others. Eloch insisted that you be first."

Mink squeezed Wren's arm and rolled her eyes, "It was like he missed you or something. Welcome back." She glanced at Eloch. "I'm going to wake Aiko and then Wade. Wade can help me with the Nuri, but I'd appreciate it if you can be here, too, when we wake them."

"Of course," Eloch said.

"Why?" Wren asked as Eloch helped her sit up. "Did something happen to Genji and Kalea?"

Mink chuckled. "You might say so. I'll let Eloch tell you the details later, but briefly, Genji's Nuri didn't like the idea of Cry, and it broke out when Genji was asleep. Eloch got the Nuri stabilized. Did the same for Kalea, and we had no problems after that. However, Eloch needs to wake the Nuri after I've awoken Genji and Kalea." Mink shook her head. "I still don't understand how all that works, but it does."

Wren looked at Eloch. "Sounds like it was pretty dramatic."

Enoch's deep green eyes sparkled. "You could say that."

"I want to hear about it, but tell me while I'm getting warm. I am *so* cold. Ohhhhhh…" She paused and sighed when she felt the warm energy flooding her body. "Thank you."

"All you need to do is ask," he replied as he hoisted her out of the Cryo bed and carried her all the way to their shared stateroom. "I've missed holding you, Wren," he said as he set her down.

She hugged him tight. "That's the one good thing about Cryo. You don't notice the passage of time. Otherwise, I would be the one who was moping. And," she looked down at her toned body, "Grale was right. Cryo keeps you in great shape. I don't think I've ever felt this fit."

~~~

After Wren had warmed up and eaten a meal, Eloch led her to the Solar Farm. "I still feel most at home here," he told her as they walked hand in hand. "For me, this is the true heart of the ship."

She stood at the entrance and breathed in the rich, moist scent of growing things. "I won't argue with you. It's magical in here." She looked up at Eloch. "Want to show me what's new?"

"You know I do," he answered with a laugh. He tugged her forward. "Come see what I've done with the place," he joked.

Wren laughed and followed his lead.

They sat together on a knoll overlooking the crops. Eloch put an arm around Wren, drew her close, and fiddled affectionately with one of the coilmats that now reached to her waist. The tightness in his chest eased.

With a sigh, Wren leaned against him. "I don't remember this hill being here before." She straightened suddenly. "In fact, I don't remember a lot of this landscape being here before. You've been busy."

"It began with Genji's Nuri," he told her. "The ship's corridors were too small for it, which added to its panic." He glanced at her, "I had to act fast."

She nodded. "A panicked Nuri spits fire," Wren commented. "A panicked Nuri spitting fire in a spaceship is not a good combination."

"Not a good combination."

"But since we're all still here, your fast action solved the issue of the panicked Nuri."

His mouth quirked at the corners. "Indeed."

"Do tell." She shifted so she could see his face.

"I simply expanded the corridors leading to the Solar Farm so it was the only route the Nuri could take."

"Wait. Did you say you *expanded* the corridors?"

"That's what I said. And then I narrowed them again after the Nuri passed through so the only place it could go was here."

"You herded the Nuri."

"I herded the Nuri. And then, once it got here, I created a pig for it to hunt. The Nuri's hunter instincts distracted it from its panic. After that, the Nuri calmed down and relaxed until Genji awoke, regained control, and shifted back into his Nuri."

Wren absently smoothed her hand over her coilmats as she studied him. "So you can create."

He grinned. "From the most basic materials. The pig came from the amino acids used in the protein farm."

"And manipulate your environment."

He nodded again, his grin widened.

"Like Entean, Spur, Longwei, and Talamh."

"Like all the Sisters."

"Can you make a planet?"

"I-I'm not sure, Wren. All I know is I have this constant urge to create."

She nodded. "I knew that."

"And when you're not here, when you're asleep, I feel it even more strongly."

She looked around and studied the landscape. Really studied it, noticing the patchwork quality of natural growing things, which blended with the technology of the solar greenhouses of the Farm. She recognized the vegetation as plants she had seen on Spur, on Longwei, on Talamh, and, she suspected, there were plants from Entean as well. "So you started experimenting," she guessed.

A butterfly landed on her hand.

"The butterfly is new, as of yesterday. Experimenting passed the time while I waited for you," he said drily.

She snorted and looked at him. "But that's not why you did it."

"No. It is a need. One I can control to a certain extent, thanks to Perin's True Dreams, but the urge is always there."

She nodded and leaned back on her arms to gaze some more at his experiments.

"There's more, Wren." He took her hand.

"What's that?"

"I can feel the ship as it moves through space, as if it was my own skin. I can sense where people are, wherever they are. I know what they're doing."

"Do you know what they're thinking, too?"

Eloch shrugged. "Maybe. Possibly. But it's not interesting to me."

"What is interesting to you, Eloch?"

"Creating this ship. Transforming it into something more, something alive. Making it a part of myself. Expanding into the ship. Understanding it. Manipulating it. Making something that wasn't before."

"Ahhh."

After a period of silence, Eloch reached out with his other hand and pulled her close. "You're quiet. Am I frightening you?"

She curled into him and wrapped her arms around him. "No. Never. I'm trying to understand. Taking it all in."

"I am as well," he said. "Especially now the fear is gone."

"So," she said after a while. "It appears to me the *Valiant* has become your planet. And the more you," she paused, "mold it?

Manipulate it? Create it? the more it will take on your personality. Just like Spur. Or Entean."

They were quiet for a while.

"I suspect there will be more and more of Entean and Longwei in my personality," he said, stroking her back. "I feel myself battling between Entean's gentleness and Longwei's passion. I've noticed I'm more short-tempered."

"You are a creature of Entean, Eloch. You can handle your temper."

"I think I can, too. But there have been times over these past three years when I haven't wanted to. Grale can be very confrontational."

Wren snickered. "I can see how he might be annoying after a while."

Eloch snorted. "Not the word I would have used."

"And you can create life," she said, getting back to the business at hand. "You made prey for the Nuri. And the butterfly. And this landscape."

"If there is a need, it appears I can."

"There was a need for the butterfly?"

"To pollinate the flowers. And birds now, too. To keep the butterflies in balance."

"Birds, too? Interesting."

"Yes."

"Hmmm. I haven't heard any chirpings."

A bird chirped. Wren looked at Eloch, who smiled lazily. "Show-off," she snickered.

He waited for Wren to absorb what he had been absorbing during the many months she was asleep.

"What about us? Not you and me, per se, but Genji, Aiko, Wade...you know, the others?"

"I think," he said slowly, "I am beginning to feel toward them as one of the Sisters would feel toward their inhabitants. I love them. I care about them. I wish them to thrive. I will do all within my power to maintain them."

She nudged him, "Even Grale?"

"Even Grale," he chuckled.

She nodded. "This shift in your focus, this must make me your Champion."

Eloch shook his head and covered her mouth with his own. "You are so very wrong," he told her between kisses. "Not my Champion, Wren. You are my heart. Without you, I am lost."

"Then I must make sure you are never without me." Wren leaned into him again. "You know, Eloch," she said after a while, "you seem lost, a little unfocused. Not like the you I've known since we met."

Eloch stirred. "I am beginning to understand why the Sisters have Champions," he told her. "It is because Champions help Them concentrate Their attention outward. It is so simple to disappear into the making."

"Longwei—"

"Longwei has a Champion now, and before, She had her priestesses. It's the same thing."

"Are you afraid of disappearing into creating? Is that what you're telling me?"

"It's a possibility," he replied slowly. "I felt myself slipping into that state of mind, but Perin kept me from going there."

"I really must thank that woman," Wren said and lapsed into thought. "Well," she said, sitting up. "We've got five years together before my next sleep. I'm pretty sure we can sort this out. For now, I want to read all the vid-messages from Mouse that have piled up. And tonight we should have a big celebration now we're all awake and together again." She turned to him, "Think you can manage creating some Entean Ale and Longwei Ferment?"

He grinned. "Always up for that challenge."

"Good." She lifted her face to his. "And I want more of this," she said, kissing him. "A lot more."

"I'm up for that challenge as well," Eloch said, returning her kiss. But before it could deepen, he stilled. "The Nuri need wakening. I must help Mink." Eloch drew Wren to her feet. "Before we go," he said, "there's one other thing for you to think about. I know you just woke up, but I've been thinking about this for the past three years. I know I can keep you young and strong, Wren. Maybe you won't need to go into Cryo again."

Wren cocked her head at him. "To not be frozen. That's a very tempting offer," she said. "What about the others? Can you keep us all young?"

"I believe so."

Wren tapped her lip. "I think we should discuss this with everyone. Get their opinions."

~~~

For the next several years, life settled into a harmonious pattern with a comfortable balance of companionship and solitude. Wren noticed with satisfaction how the crew seemed to sense when one of their members needed to be alone and would respect one another's needs. Conversely, when she felt there was too much self-appointed solitude, she would organize a gathering where the ten of them could share their discoveries and what they had been up to.

She had discovered long ago that Eloch wasn't the only one who had a favorite place on the ship. She still ran the ever-expanding corridors that ran just inside the ship's perimeter.

Sometimes she ran them alone. Other times, Perin accompanied her. Wren also continued practicing with her knives or sparred with Aiko, who was almost always either in the gym or on the Navigation Bridge, staring out at the stars while she monitored the ship's vitals.

Grale and Wade had formed a friendship and could be found in the lounge, playing one game or another, and usually betting was involved. Mink, Spider, Kalea, and Genji were constantly in the science labs which, she was informed, had been expanded, courtesy of Eloch and his growing mastery of his power.

As for Perin, she could be found either on her garden bench or in what Wren called the Blue Room, a cozy music room with deep, comfortable furniture upholstered in a dark blue-green velvet, the color reminding Wren of the tide pools on Longwei.

Today, when she went looking, Wren found Perin in the Blue Room. "Knock-knock," she said, even though the sliding door panels would have alerted Perin of her presence. "May I come in?"

Perin turned her sightless eyes toward Wren and smiled. "Wren! Greetings." She set down the lute she had been strumming. "I've been expecting you."

Wren plopped down across from her. "You have?"

Perin nodded. "I had a True Dream last night. You and I were discussing Eloch."

"And so we shall," Wren said. "I'm going back into Cryo soon, and I'm a little worried."

"Don't be. He is finding his way, Wren. When next you wake, you will see a remarkable difference." She hesitated. "I don't mean this the way it will sound, but you have been a distraction at a time when he really needs to concentrate his will and creativity within."

"Uh-huh, I agree. That's why I elected to take the sleep when what I really want to do is stay awake this time." She shuddered. "I hate the whole Cryo process, and I love watching Eloch explore his boundaries." She paused. "I do feel better knowing you monitor him so he doesn't disappear into his creating. Thank you for that."

"You've already thanked me several times, but there's no need," Perin said. "I'm his Seer. I look after his welfare. I know this is a sacrifice for you and appreciate what you're doing, Wren. Hopefully, this is the last time you will need to distance yourself this way, but Eloch needs to fully understand what he is. For his sake. For all our sakes."

Wren leaned forward. "Have you seen something? Is Eloch in danger?" She paused. "Or does he endanger others?"

"No. Nothing like that. It's just that I sense his need to turn inward for a span."

Wren sat back again. "Good. That's a relief."

"Let me clarify something, Wren," Perin said after a pause. "As Eloch's Seer, I only see what needs to be addressed for his benefit and for the benefit of those he values. That's why I dreamed we were to meet today and have this conversation," Perin explained. "This conversation puts you at ease, which allows Eloch to relax and be okay during your next Cryo sleep. Our conversation benefits him."

"I get it, Perin," Wren assured her. "I do understand. But I want you to know it *really* puts me at ease while I'm in Cryo, knowing someone is making sure he's not always turned within, that he engages with the others from time to time. I know I've thanked you before and there's no need to, but I want you to fully understand how important it is to me. I'm not sure," she swallowed, "that I'd be able to do Cryo if I didn't know you'll be there for him."

Perin chuckled. "Of course. Rest assured, I will be watching over him."

Wren studied Perin's lovely face, noticing the signs of age around her mouth and eyes. Perin not been a young woman when she arrived on the *Valiant* nearly ten years ago. "You know, Perin, if you'd like, Eloch could make you young again."

Perin laughed, the creases around her eyes winging up. "I don't fear age." She hesitated, then smiled a secret smile. "Besides, I am sensing Eloch will be keeping me young with or without my consent. I think it's in his nature to keep us all thriving."

Wren flashed back on a memory of when Eloch, as Spur's Champion, changed Max back into a young man.

"No doubt," she said. "He's aching to do it, and I suspect he's already been secretly playing with my wrinkles. It's been subtle, but I think I'm looking a little more youthful than before."

Perin laughed. "The good thing about you being in Cryo is he will miss you while you sleep, which will motivate him to work harder on understanding and practicing all the ways in which he can use his power."

"Now, if he can only come up with a way of dealing with the boredom. I'm not bored yet, but we've many, many, *many* more years before we reach our destination."

"I'm afraid alleviating boredom is up to the individual," Perin said. She gently touched the lute resting quietly beside her. "Do you like music, Wren?"

"I love music. I just don't know how to play an instrument. Never had the chance to learn."

"You have the time now," Perin said. "I would gladly teach you."

"And I would gladly learn." Wren shook her head. "Growing up, I never thought I'd have time to ever worry about becoming bored."

"You never talk about yourself, Wren. I would like to know more if you would care to tell me."

"My life has been so different from yours, Perin. I don't mention it because my childhood was full of danger, pain, and violence."

Perin nodded, her expression sorrowful. "It made you strong, though," she offered.

"That it did. And determined to keep others from experiencing the same childhood as mine."

"Tell me, then, and I will tell you about myself. Although my childhood was an easy one, once I had a True Dream, everything changed."

"How so?"

"I was sequestered, shut away from everyone I knew and loved. None of my friends from my old life could visit." She paused. "Actually, I don't think they wanted to. I was different, after. I knew things. I saw things. And I was blind to normal sights, so I was helpless on my own. Although I was coddled and pampered, I felt I like was in a prison."

"Sounds lonely."

"Yes, it was. Thank you for understanding. I was surrounded by people and rarely left alone, but I was so lonely. My only confidante was Rayne, The Lady's High Priest. And of course, anything I told Rayne was discussed with The Lady or other priests. Therefore, I kept my own counsel as much as possible."

Wren touched her hand. "I hope you know you don't need to keep your own counsel with us. We're Kinfolk, here. A small band of Kin, and we look after our own."

Perin smiled at Wren, her eyes bright with tears. "Thank you, my friend," she said as she placed her hand over Wren's. "I've never felt free enough to express my loneliness before."

"Well, it's time then, isn't it?"

"Beyond time."

Wren gave Perin's hand another squeeze before she disengaged. "About this lute," she said, picking it up and holding it the way she'd seen Perin do. "Is it hard to learn?" She strummed it. "Can you show me a few chords right now?"

Chapter 7 – Eleven Years into the Mission

Eleven Years into the Mission...

When Wren opened her eyes and gazed into Eloch's, she immediately noticed the shift in him. He seemed calm, in control, more...focused.

This was the Eloch she remembered before Spur and Longwei had gifted him in such a careless, harsh manner with more power than his body could contain—so much power Longwei had to rebuild him, to strengthen him.

Now he gazed at her calmly, a trace of a smile on his mouth and around his eyes. Deep in his eyes, she saw the power—the knack— but its fires were banked and contained. "Wow," she said through chattering teeth as she reached for him. "You're back."

Eloch's chuckle rumbled through her. "I don't quite know what that means, but I'm happy to see you, too." He pulled her in, warming her, and tugged on the hood covering her coilmats. "I didn't tamper with the length this time," he said, smoothing his hand over the springy auburn masses.

Mink cleared her throat. "Back on the bed, Wren. You two can cuddle as soon as I check you out."

With a sigh, Wren did as she was told, lying as quietly as she could in spite of the shivering and chattering teeth while Mink ran the scanning wand over her. She pouted up at Mink.

Mink laughed. "Very nice sad eyes, Wren, but I think Grale has already patented that look." She checked her wand. "Okay, you're checked out. Go back to your cuddling." Mink turned to Eloch. "I will need you in about forty-five minutes to help with the Nuri."

Eloch scooped Wren up. "I will see you then," he said and carried Wren out of the med lab.

Wren wrapped her arms around Eloch's shoulders and burrowed her nose into his neck, inhaling his scent. When she felt his warmth begin to saturate her, she sighed. "The cold sucks."

"I've mastered a new process so you will never have to experience Cryo sleep again...unless, of course, you want to," he said with a twinkle in his eye.

She looked up. "Yeah?"

"I now completely understand how the body ages, and I can definitely prevent it."

Wren laughed, "You've been experimenting on Perin. She said you might."

"Perin and everyone else who wanted to be part of the experiment."

"Mink and Spider?"

Eloch nodded. "Mink and Spider, too."

Wren frowned. "I didn't notice much change in Mink just now, but then," she smirked, "truth be told, I wasn't really looking at her. How about Grale?"

"Um-hum. Grale."

Wren's brows shot up. "Grale? You don't say?"

"I do say. And he's now not as challenging."

"Really? You got on with him better this time around?"

"I did, especially after I let him win some of the games he likes to play."

Wren laughed. "You'll make a KinLord yet. So, we've solved the aging process. What about boredom of long flights? Although," she added, "I do like learning to play the lute."

Eloch grinned. "I've been making changes. I think you will find it difficult to be bored."

The panel to their shared quarters slid open, and Eloch carried her into their sleeping area.

Wren gasped.

Curled up in the center of the bed was a miniature sniffer.

The sniffer lifted her head and watched with intelligent eyes while Eloch set Wren down.

Wren looked at Eloch and back at the sniffer.

"She is not Little Sister, but I think she will fill that void," Eloch said.

"But I thought you could only create life when there was a need," she said, the whole of her attention remaining squarely on the sniffer.

"I think there is a need, don't you?" Eloch asked softly. He crossed his arms and surveyed the pair, looking satisfied.

Wren slowly extended her hand, and the elegant creature nestled her head against Wren's outstretched hand. As Wren stroked her ears, the sniffer began a deep rumble in her chest. "Such a big rumble from such a small body," Wren whispered. She looked up at Eloch. "A tiny Little Sister. She's perfect."

"She doesn't eat as much, either."

Wren laughed. "I would think not." Her voice was still filled with awe. "You *made* this sniffer? Created her from nothing?"

"Not from nothing, no. From aminos and other elements found on the *Valiant*. She is a part of the ship. This is her natural habitat."

"So she won't be unhappy like Little Sister would have been," Wren guessed.

"Exactly. Welcome back, Wren. Ready to take your shower and get warm? Your new friend isn't going anywhere."

"Little Wonder," Wren said.

"Little Wonder?"

"That's her name," Wren told him as she rose from the bed, already shedding the Cryo sleep suit as she headed to the bathroom. "Come with me," she said over her shoulder. "Didn't Mink say you have forty-five minutes? I'd like to begin to thank you properly." She winked before disappearing into the shower.

Eloch listened to the sound of running water and glanced at Little Wonder, who yawned, her pink tongue curling. "I think she likes you," he told the sniffer with a grin. His clothes dissolving, Eloch turned and followed the sounds of running water to join his mate.

~~~

Forty-five minutes later, Eloch left Wren sitting on their bed with a vid pad on her lap and Little Wonder curled up beside her. She had three years of messages from Mouse, and he knew she was eager to catch up with her friend. But before he left, he made her promise to meet him later at the Solar Farm. He was eager to show her how much it had changed since she last saw it and to share with her everything he had learned about his powers and abilities while she was in Cryo.

When Wren and Little Wonder joined him in the Solar Farm, no sooner had Wren settled herself beside him than the sniffer let out a hunting cry and disappeared into the undergrowth.

"I take it we don't need to worry about feeding her," Wren said, trying to see into the thicket where the sniffer had vanished.

Eloch chuckled. "She definitely can fend for herself."

"She's so much like Little Sister, although it's strange to have her shoulder at my knee rather than my waist," She sighed happily and tossed her coilmats over one shoulder. "I feel like I've bonded with her already."

"I'm glad, my love."

She peered around him, and behind them. "So what else have you created?"

"A lake. Fish." In the distance, there was a squeal, then silence. "More pigs for our Nuri."

Wren nodded toward the squeal. "Sounds like there's one less, although it must have been a smallish one." She tilted her head back. "It seems larger in here, too."

"I expanded some. Spider and Mink came up with a way to capture the space debris we come across. I can break it down to its basic components and use it to increase our size."

"Our size?"

"That's another thing that has happened while you were sleeping. I've completely bonded with the *Valiant*. We are one entity."

Wren's eyes widened. "Any repercussions?"

"None that I'm aware of," Eloch replied with a shake of his head. "Although if there are any, I'm sure Spider and Mink can find out. They've taken to studying me along with their other projects."

Wren laughed. "You've become one of their pet experiments?"

"It appears so," Eloch said, sharing a grin with her.

"Spider and Mink," Wren mused. She lifted an eyebrow at Eloch.

He nodded. "It appears to be so."

"Hmmm," Wren said. "Cozy."

"Hmmmm, yes. Cozy."

"I'm happy for them."

"You enjoy your vid messages?"

"There are so many, it's going to take me at least a month to watch them all. I think Mouse must have made them weekly." Wren smiled, then sobered. "They're getting older, Eloch. Max's brows are as bushy as when I first met him. And Mouse…"

Her voice trailed off. "But their children are lovely, and even though Little Brother and Little Sister are gone, they had more than one litter together. Sniffers are alive and well on Talamh." She sighed. "I've missed so much I would have liked to experience with Mouse and Max." She held up a hand, "I don't regret it at all, Eloch…you must know that…but I feel sad about it."

Eloch gathered her to him. "As do I. As do I."

Wren snuggled against him, wrapping her arms around his middle. "I love you, Eloch."

"And I you. Everything feels right again now that you're here with me." His arms tightened around her, and they rested quietly in each other's arms. After a while he said, "Would you like to explore my domain with me? I made some running trails for you."

Wren looked up and grinned. "More paths to explore! A creator after my own heart. What are we waiting for?" she asked as she hopped to her feet, hauling Eloch up with her. She called to Little Wonder, who came leaping out of the thicket. "Lead the way, Eloch."

For the next two hours, Wren and Eloch explored the world he had created.

The lake was a marvelous addition, with its sandy bottom and clear water. Wren made plans to swim in it later and have a picnic on the shore. The older trees had grown bigger, and there were plenty of saplings. Bees buzzed, and birds twittered and sang.

Eloch showed her where Perin had demanded a beehive near a field of clover to capture honey, and the field bordered a little stream that drained from the lake. Eloch explained that the stream fed into the lake as well, a closed system.

He showed Wren the new trails and paths that were already being used as shortcuts to traverse the length and width of the ship, pointing to the signs at the intersections that Grale made so no one could get lost.

"I was surprised," he told Wren. "Making those signs sounds more like something Spider or Mink would do, not Grale."

"Hmmm," Wren said, her brow creasing, "Perhaps there's another side to Grale he keeps hidden. I've always felt he was going through some heavy mental stuff, considering his teasing and acting out and all. I figured the best way to deal with it was just allow Grale to be who he was."

Eloch considered Wren with his deep, penetrating gaze. "You make getting along with people sound so easy. That's one of the things I admire about you."

Wren shrugged. "I think most people want to feel like they belong, and if they don't feel like they fit, they act out to draw attention to themselves. That's what I think Grale has been doing these past few years, you know? Of all of us, he's the one who has never quite belonged. The rest of us have had either common ground or a common history."

"Grale has history with us," Eloch countered.

Wren chuckled. "Well, he does now, that's for sure." She pointed at the signs. "And it looks like he's feeling like he fits in now, too. I'm sure you interacting with him these past few years helped. I'm glad."

"Me, too."

At the exit that led to the galley, they parted—Eloch and Little Wonder to welcome Genji and Kalea back from their Cryo sleep and Wren to search for Perin.

As she left the Solar Farm, Wren thought about her vids from Mouse and felt again the pang of loss.

~~~

Two weeks later, Wren was still wrestling with the feeling of loss. Spying Aiko when she went to the galley for a cup of tea, she paused and decided to visit with her. Perhaps Aiko had some deep wisdom that could lift her spirits. Or perhaps she'd like to spar with her to blow off some steam.

Tea in hand, Wren slumped down in the chair across from Aiko, sipped her tea, and then looked up at Aiko with a sigh and a half-smile.

Aiko lifted a brow. "You okay?"

Wren shrugged. "Thinking about the vids I got while I was in Cryo. So many of them, I couldn't finish them all at once. Mouse and Max...they're getting so old, Aiko." She flashed a grin. "Max's eyebrows are as white and bushy as when I first met him. And Mouse? It's surreal seeing her face looking old, you know? And their kids are so big. It really hit me that most likely I will never see them again. Didn't really sink in at first." She took another sip. "We're so far away now. It's hard."

Aiko nodded. "Just be glad we're not flying light speed. They'd be long gone by now." Aiko grimaced. "Speaking of which, Manabu died."

Wren reached out a hand. "Oh, Aiko. I'm sorry."

Aiko looked at her, allowing Wren to see the pain. "He's gifted the *Stardust* to Max and Mouse's oldest. She shows knack, he said."

"Nice. That should make you feel happier, knowing she's a wanted vessel."

"It does."

"Say, didn't Manabu rename the ship?"

Aiko grimaced. "Could never think of her as the *Aiko*. She'll always be the *Stardust* to me."

Wren nodded and took a sip of her tea.

The two sat in silence.

"I suppose," said Aiko after a while, "that's why shipmates get so much closer the farther out they travel. So much time passes at their old home base that they don't belong there anymore."

"I've never heard of any ship traveling so far that they never see their friends again at all."

"Neither have I, Wren. Neither have I."

Wren stood up abruptly. "I'm going to get something a little stronger than tea," she announced. "Want me to bring you some ferment?"

Aiko shook her head. "Can't. We're going through our first wormhole in a couple of hours. Unlike Manabu, I need a clear head to access my knack."

"Well, since I'm not flying, I'm going to have a small glass. Be right back."

When Wren returned, she held up her drink and clinked her glass against Aiko's mug of tea. "To those we left behind," she said.

"To the memories."

They both took a drink.

"Ahhhh," Wren smacked her lips. "Good stuff." She leaned closer, confidingly. "Know what I think, Aiko? I think we should have some sort of gathering. Now. Tonight, even. While we're all together before the next sequence of Cryo sleeps. Honor those who've died and those we'll never see again. I'm sure we're not the only ones who feel this way."

Aiko nodded. "Mink told me Kalea's mother died." She took another sip of her tea.

Wren nodded, the corners of her mouth drooping. "I know. Eloch told me. It's why Kalea and Genji haven't been around much since we all woke up."

"I am ashamed to say I just found out. Felt it important to spend these past few days on my own, remembering Manabu." She took another sip from her mug. "Just now feeling a little more social. Sad, but social."

"You did right, Aiko. People should take the time they need to take care of themselves."

"I agree." Aiko pushed her hair off her forehead and sat back. "It's a good idea, Wren, having the gathering tonight. It will help. We can comfort one another. Bring us all together, if anything."

"And we can celebrate going through our first wormhole, too."

Aiko set down her tea. "It's a brilliant idea, but now I'd better head on up to the Bridge. Keep Grale company, begin the system check run-through." She rose and reached for the mug.

"Leave it," Wren said. "I'll clean up, and then Eloch and I will meet you up there. Don't want to miss the wormhole ride."

Aiko smiled. With a nod, she left Wren to her thoughts.

~~~

"No," Aiko cried. "No. No. No. No! Eloch, stop! You don't know what you're doing."

"I do, Aiko," he said calmly while his power flowed from him in waves.

"You don't. I'm sorry, but you do not. I've had nearly forty years' experience with flying through wormholes."

Grale's head whipped around. "You're that old, Kitten?"

She scowled at him, waved his comment away. "I've got the knack, Eloch. Your coordinates are off. Please. Trust my knack."

"Eloch," Wren said before he could say anything. She touched his hand and waited until she had his attention. "Give the controls back to the pilots. We're a team on this ship. We take advantage of our individual strengths to make us stronger."

"The ship is me," Eloch said. "It's a part of me. I know exactly where we are in relation to the wormhole."

"But you've never taken her through a wormhole before, have you?" Aiko asked.

"Aiko makes a good point," Grale said. "It's one thing to know where you are in relation to that," he pointed out the viewing panel at the mammoth vortex of energy, "but flying through it is a whole other kind of relating. One mess-up and we're all just a memory...if that."

"I need to learn and understand how to take myself..." he caught himself and paused. "Take the *Valiant* through one. How can I learn if I don't try it?"

"By watching us, Eloch," Aiko replied. "We've got knack, Grale and I. We were born to do this, Eloch. Were you?" she challenged, then sucked in a breath when she saw his expression.

"Eloch!" Wren said sharply.

He glanced at her, confused.

She tugged his hand. "Cool your temper. You may have some Longwei in you, but you are *not* Her. You don't need to own that planet's temper." She waited for the fire to leave his eyes. "Give the pilots back their Bridge, Eloch," she said quietly. "Learn from them."

He took a deep breath and nodded, covering Wren's hand with his own. "My apologies, Aiko. I overreacted." He glanced at Aiko and Grale. "Take us through. Teach me how."

Aiko nodded and took a deep breath to quiet her nerves, not wanting to show how much Eloch had unnerved her. She closed her eyes, opened to her knack, and looked at Grale. "Ready to hand over the controls?" she asked, glad she won the coin toss for the first jump.

Grale smiled and flipped a switch. "All yours, Kitten. Make it clean and mean."

Aiko shot him a fierce grin, already pulling her knack and lining up the coordinates. "This one's for Manabu. Gonna be perfect." She glanced at Grale. "Make the announcement to lock in."

Grale pinged the crew. "Land and lock, people," Grale said through the ship's PA system. "We're taking our jump. Get ready for a smooth one. Aiko's promised perfection."

And it was. As soon as Aiko locked the coordinates in place, she let go of her breath and allowed the vessel its head as the *Valiant* was pulled into the vast vortex.

"Now the light show!" Grale shouted as he fist-bumped with Aiko.

The ship surged forward, and Wren clung to Eloch. "I forgot to strap in!" she squeaked.

Eloch wrapped an arm around her. "I've got you," he said calmly, while his eyes lit with power as he watched the viewing screen.

Wren was about to say more, but the words died as she watched Eloch. He stood like a pillar, rooted as he was to the floor. The arm wrapped around her felt more machine than flesh. His eyes, bright and burning, were flickering back and forth, gathering data while he observed.

In that moment, she understood what Eloch was. He was more than just a Champion, yet he wasn't what the Sisters were. Those things she had acknowledged and understood. But what she hadn't truly understood was that *Eloch was the Valiant and the Valiant was Eloch.* She had thought Eloch understood the ship, could create, recreate, and transform parts of the ship because of the power bequeathed to him by the creative Sisters. But he could do that only because he had *become* the ship, just like the Sisters were both the spirit of their planets *and* their planets.

Just like the Sisters.

Pain squeezed her chest when complete understanding smacked into her. Her breath hitched.

Entean's spirit could never leave her planet. Neither could Spur or Longwei, or any of the planets' spirits. Eloch would never be able to set foot on another planet again. Eloch could never be separated from the ship.

She bit her hand to stifle the sob and looked to see if anyone heard. She needn't have worried. All three were riveted on the viewing screen as they hurtled through the wormhole.

While the three concentrated on the viewing screen, she focused on Eloch, all the way through the wormhole.

~~~

"Show's over," Grale announced. "Well done, Kitten. Next time, it'll be my turn to strut my stuff."

"Doubt you could do as well, Cowboy," Aiko grinned.

He sobered. "Perhaps not," he said. "Perhaps not."

Eloch grinned at Wren, but his smile quickly faded when he saw her expression. "You understand," he said.

Wren wiped her eyes with the heel of her palm. "What did They do to you?" she whispered.

His arm, once again warm and pliant, held her close as he brushed her hair off her face. "It's not too bad," he said. "Come, let's talk."

Aiko watched the pair exit the Bridge.

"What was that about?" Grale asked.

"I have no idea," she answered, shaking her head. "But it sure scared the crap out of me."

"Me too, Kitten." He ran his fingers through his hair, making it stand up straight, then pinged the ship's intercom "The Kitten's pulled us through, gang. Time to unbuckle. See you all at the party." Grale glanced at Aiko. "You up to scanning the stars for the next jump?"

He had to say her name twice to get her attention.

"Yeah. I'm up for it." Her eyes sparkled when she grinned at him. "We're officially in uncharted territory, Cowboy. Think we're the first people to see these stars?"

~~~

Eloch took Wren to the Solar Farm, to their grassy hill overlooking the lake. "We should name this Eloch's Domain," Wren said.

Eloch shook his head. "I like Solar Farm. It's amusing, don't you think?"

"Because it's so much more than a few rows of greenhouses? Yeah, it's amusing. We all think so."

"I know you have things to say, Wren," he told her. "I tried to tell you what I have become, but Perin said you would have to understand at your own pace. She said this would be difficult for you at first. So take your time. I'll wait."

She looked at him and tried to gauge her emotions, feeling a flash of annoyance that Perin and Eloch had discussed her. But then, as Eloch's Seer, wasn't that Perin's role to be his confidante? "I'm feeling a little jealous of Perin right now," she told him.

Eloch put an arm around her. "Perin said you'd feel that as well," he said, looking down at her. "But then she said you'd soon see that you have no reason to be jealous, without me saying a thing. So I'm not saying a thing."

Wren laughed and settled herself against him so she could look up and study his face. He had returned his attention to the vista, his creation.

She loved his profile, the straight nose, the firm full mouth, and the square jaw ending in his pointed chin. His features aligned so beautifully. She could see his strength, his intelligence, his compassion, his playfulness, and tenderness. Within his features, she could read all the qualities that set him apart from other men, that made him the leader—the Champion—and now would make him become something more.

"It's true, isn't it?" she said. "Now you and the *Valiant* are one in the same, you can never leave the ship."

Eloch looked away from his creation and down at her. In the depths of his dark, forest-colored eyes, she saw his love for her. It emanated from him. Nobody had ever looked at her the way he did. Nobody ever would.

"Yes, love, it's true."

"Are you okay with that?"

He snorted. "Does it matter?"

She shifted so she could take his face in her hands. "Of course it matters." She searched his face and waited.

Eloch covered one of her hands and kissed her palm before replacing it on his face. "I mourned the idea of never stepping foot on Entean again," he said. "I mourned that loss before, as you know. But it was like an old wound had been reopened and hope was lost."

Wren felt her eyes filling. "I am so, so sorry I wasn't there for you."

He smiled at her. "It was something I needed to do on my own. I shut myself away from everyone, even the Seer, and I reached out to Her. To Entean."

Wren stroked his face.

"It was difficult. We are so far now, and I have not learned to master the range like the Sisters. Not sure if I have that much power." He swallowed. "She called me *Brother* and not *Champion*, and I knew then."

Wren pulled him to her, held him, stroked his back as he buried his face in her hair. "You must know this is not a prison, Eloch," she whispered softly. "This is a home. Our home. And our home is very beautiful. I love it only a little less than I love you."

Eloch sighed. "Thank you," he whispered.

~~~

Grale slouched down beside Aiko. "Not much of a joiner, are you?"

She glanced up at him and took a sip from her glass before answering. "My years of piloting, I suppose. Captain has to be a little standoffish to command."

"True, but you're really not the captain here, Kitten."

She shot him a glance. "Neither are you."

112

"Hey, no need to get your panties in a bunch. I just mean that he's in command here," Grale said, pointing his drink toward Eloch. "So you can relax. Socialize more."

"Not really feeling like socializing much tonight, Cowboy." Aiko sighed. "Sorry to lash out."

"Ahh. I hear ya. Me neither, come to think of it." He held his glass toward her. "Truce?"

She looked at him, returned his smile. "Sure, why not?"

They clinked glasses.

"Look, Kitten," Grale said after a few moments. "I know I can come off..." he hesitated.

"Rude and harsh?"

He snorted. "Yeah, that. I haven't been too happy about being forced to be here, and I suppose I've taken it out on you. You know, to distract myself from being out of control."

Aiko raised an eyebrow. "You starting to be nice to me now?"

"Let's just say I'm beginning to not be *not-nice*."

She laughed at that. "Good. Don't want you getting soft or anything." She took a sip of her drink and then looked at him. "What do you mean about being out of control?"

He held up his forearm, exposing the black handprint on it. "Well, Longwei didn't give me much choice about coming with you all on this crazy...what do you even call what we're doing?"

Aiko shrugged. "I like to call it a quest. Following the Knack Man."

"Knack Man?"

"Yeah, Eloch."

Grale barked out a laugh. "Knack Man," he repeated, shaking his head.

"So Longwei didn't give you a choice?"

"Not much of one. I could remain on Her planet or," he paused, "follow the Knack Man. Probably just as well. Would have gambled all that beautiful crystal money away by now."

"Or have gotten killed blowing up some asteroid while mining for more."

"Or that," he agreed, thinking about Jocko and hoping his friend had had a long, fruitful life. He raised his glass. "To old friends and new ones."

"To old and new friends."

~~~

Wren leaned against Eloch and threaded her arm through his. "What are you thinking?"

He smiled at her, and she basked in the warmth of that green gaze, happy that they were on the other side of mourning what Eloch had become. "My double on Entean. I was wondering if he is aging by now."

"Do you suppose he's still Champion?"

Eloch shook his head. "No. Entean has had two other Champions since him."

"You don't say?" she said. "How long do Champions remain Champions?"

"Depends upon the planet. Spur is enjoying Flick, and he seems content to be Her Champion for the remainder of his days."

"Oh."

"You seem sad about it."

Wren shrugged. "I was hoping Flick would be a grandfather by now."

Eloch unthreaded his arm and drew Wren close. "Flick is fulfilled."

Wren nodded against his side and listened to his heart beat, slow and steady. "Do you talk with them very often? The Sisters?"

"I tell you when I do, Wren."

"Not so much, then."

"Like I said, I'm still learning how to contact Them. They have a much easier time reaching me, but They are busy with their work—maintaining the balance of Their creations. And of course They're concerned about what is happening in Vela Kentaurus. They are impatient for us to get there and stop whatever that *something* is that's coming for Them. Whenever I reach out to Them, I hear the same questions and feel the same impatient frustration. And so," he said after a pause, "why bother?"

"Why bother," Wren agreed. "The waiting is always the hardest."

"It's good our comrades have other interests so they aren't struggling with impatient frustration."

"True," Wren said. "You as well." She straightened and pulled back a little so she could look up at his face. "Which reminds me. What if something were to happen to you? How could we control this ship now?"

"What could possibly happen to me?" Eloch chuckled.

"Probably nothing, but you know me. *Caution First*. Makes me nervous without a safety net." She took a sip of her ale. "Mmmm, Entean ale."

Eloch shook her head. "Nope. This is my ale."

Wren grinned. "Elochean Ale? What's next? Elochean Ferment?"

He winked. "Perhaps. The men and I are talking about making some honey wine from Perin's beehives."

"I'd like to sample some of that. Sounds sweet and tasty. But let's get back to *Caution First*. Both times I've come out of Cryo sleep, there's been less and less for us to tend to. You're doing it all. You going to start breathing for us, too?" She glanced at him. "That's a joke."

"I knew that, Wren. But me controlling the ship is what I do, what I need to do. The ship is my creation." He saw her frown. "Why is that a bad thing?"

"We don't want to take too much responsibility away from our people, Eloch. Like the wormhole jump, even though I now know you could do it too. But Aiko and Grale are pilots. We don't want them to feel useless.

"And remember *Caution First*. Every aspect of life support, all navigation, it's all being controlled by you now." She shrugged and looked up at him. "It doesn't mean you can't continue to do so, but I'd be a lot happier if there was a backup plan. Just like how we're all trained to do more than one thing on this ship, and we all know how to bring someone out of Cryo sleep. It just makes sense, is all."

He nodded thoughtfully. "If it would make you happier, then I will create a switch that takes the *Valiant* out of my control and puts it back into yours."

Wren sighed. "Thank you, Eloch."

"Of course, my heart." He was silent for a moment. "It's done."

She blinked. "That fast?"

"It was easy enough. The switch is in our sleeping area, on the table on your side of the bed. It will recognize only your touch."

"But—"

"Only you," he repeated. "You are the only one I trust to make that choice."

Wren nodded, and, after a while, she turned to him and cupped his face. "I need to explain something to you because what happened when you created that switch just hit me."

She brushed her lips over his. "When I see you, Eloch, I see Eloch. You. My wonderful mate. And you're more than that, but I'm still wrapping my head around the fact you're actually this ship, too. It just never crossed my mind what it really meant...the ramifications...when I asked what I just asked. I feel...I feel...humbled and...honored to be trusted."

"And who is more deserving of my trust than you?" he asked softly, covering her mouth with his.

~ ~ ~

"Refill?" Mink asked, holding a pitcher of ale in one hand and a pitcher of ferment in the other. She nudged Spider with her hip.

He glanced up, and she dimpled at him.

"Please! Ferment for me," Kalea said and held up her glass, which Mink immediately refilled. "For all of us."

"You think?" Genji asked reluctantly.

Kalea giggled. "Isn't this ceremony for remembering all our loved ones who have passed? This is what Nuri do. We drink." She took a long swallow. "Then we dance."

Genji held up his glass to Mink. "She said dance. I think I'll need more if I'm going to dance."

Mink laughed, filled up Genji's glass, then raised an eyebrow at Spider. "You? Ready for more?"

Spider held up a finger, drained his glass, then held his glass out for Mink to fill. "Ale, please."

"Wade?" Mink asked as she gestured toward him with her pitchers, "Ferment or Ale?"

Wade shook his head. "I'll pass."

"How about you, Perin?" Mink asked their Seer. "A little more?"

Perin hesitated, uncertainty flickering across her expression.

"Have a little more, Perin," Kalea urged. "Then we will all dance." Her expression sobered. "I will dance the most beautiful dance for my mother. A queen deserves a beautiful dance."

Genji squeezed her hand.

"A little more ferment then," said Perin. "Please."

Mink poured for Perin, refilled her own glass where it sat at her place, and set the pitchers down on the table where they had gathered. "Scoot over, Spider, you're sprawling," she said, sitting down as he hastily made room for her.

Spider glanced down at Mink, who was leaning against him. "Look who's sprawling now," he muttered. "I don't envy you that hangover you're working on.

She hadn't heard him. She was looking at Kalea. "Only you dance, Kalea," Mink was saying. "Only you can honor your mother with dance."

~~~

"Look," Aiko said, propping her elbows on the table and her chin in her hands. "Kalea is dancing."

"So she is," Grale said.

"Beautiful," Aiko murmured.

"Yes."

They watched as the Nuri swayed her hips, her graceful arms and hands telling a story.

Grale took a sip of his drink. "She's so much like her sister."

Aiko nodded. "Her twin. I remember."

"Back on Longwei," Grale hiccupped, "spent more time with Makini." He snorted. "Tried to seduce me once."

Aiko shot him a glance. "She did? What happened?"

"Told her I didn't do virgins is what happened. So, nothing happened."

"Hmmm."

"Hmmm? What do you mean by 'hmmm?'"

"Didn't realize you were such a nice guy, Cowboy."

Grale snorted. "Nothing nice guy about it, Kitten. Virgins are a lot of trouble. They cry."

"Hmmm."

"Stop with the 'hmmm.' They do cry, and that's the trouble."

~~~

Mink studied Kalea's graceful gestures and foot and hip movements. "I know this dance," she whispered, then glanced across Spider at Wade.

Wade nodded. "The Dance of the Dead," he said.

"What is that?" Perin asked softly, her eyes following the energy trails left by Kalea's dance.

"It is danced on the planet Longwei to honor a loved one," Genji

119

said. He moved closer to Perin. "Let me describe it for you."

She nodded. "Please."

Quietly, so he wouldn't disturb the others, Genji described the moves and the hand gestures, painting a picture for Perin as Kalea, his mate, danced. After a time, his throat closed and he couldn't go on. "I'm sorry," he whispered.

Perin touched his arm. "What you have described makes sense of the light streaks I am seeing as your beloved moves. It is beautiful, and I thank you." She sucked in her breath. "Oh! She's shifting."

"Yes," Genji said. "Excuse me."

~~~

"You've got this?" Wren asked dreamily, surrendering to the warm, fuzzy, soothing effects of the ale.

"Yes," Eloch said gently, cocooning his adorably woozy mate while he enlarged the doorway, ceiling, and halls to allow passage for two Nuri, wings unfurling on their way to the Solar Farm.

~~~

Grale drained his glass. "Well, show's over," he said setting his glass down. "May I escort you to your cabin, Kitten?"

Aiko narrowed her eyes at him.

He laughed, his eyes glittering. "Nothing more than an escort. I don't do kittens, either, Kitten. They've got claws and like to dig in."

Aiko knocked back her drink and accepted his outstretched hand. At her cabin door she paused and turned toward him. "Thanks for the escort, Cowboy."

"No problem, Kitten." He held out his hand. "Friends?"

She reached up and smoothed back a wild curl from his brow. "Hmmm," was all she said, then disappeared into her room

For several moments Grale stood where he was, staring at the closed door. Then he laughed, shook his head, and found his way to his own cabin.

CHAPTER 8 – SIXTEEN YEARS INTO THE MISSION

Sixteen Years into the Mission…

Perin sat straight up in bed, eyes wide. "It's coming," she whispered and reached for her robe. Using her fingers as her guide, she hurried to where Eloch and Wren slept.

Eloch met her halfway.

"It's coming," she told him.

"I know," he said. "I felt it. But we have time. Let me take you back to your room. Sleep."

She nodded and took his arm, allowing him to guide her back down the corridor to her room. "This is what we have been seeking. It seeks us, now, Eloch. It seeks *you.*"

"I know," he said softly.

"You are in great danger."

"It will be all right, Perin. Here we are. Can you find your way around your room?"

"Yes, of course. But Eloch, you are in very grave danger. Remember the True Dream so many years ago? I just dreamed it again. Only this time I understand it. I'm afraid for you."

"It's late, and we can discuss this in the morning. We'll hold a meeting. Sleep now." Her door panel slid open.

Perin nodded and paused before she entered her room. She turned to him, fists clenched at her sides. "I will Dream for you, Eloch," she said fiercely, "I will Dream a way out of this, I promise."

~~~

"Listen up, people," Wren said. "We've got some news."

They were gathered around the large rectangular table in the galley, Eloch next to Wren, she and Perin flanking Eloch. Across from them sat Aiko, Wade, Genji, and Kalea.

"This sounds serious," said Wade. "Do you want me to wake the other three?"

Wren hesitated and looked at Eloch.

"It's not necessary. Maybe later, when we know more."

"Know more about what?" asked Genji.

"Are you talking about the anomaly the ship's sensors picked up last night?" Aiko asked.

"*Anomaly!*" Genji exclaimed, his pupils slitting. "When were you going to inform us of this anomaly?"

Kalea touched his hand. "Calm your Nuri, Genj," she whispered. "It senses your anger."

"I'm telling you now," Aiko answered. "I just noticed the readout, told Wren, and Wren called this meeting, so I figured I'd tell you all now." She glanced at Genji, "Didn't mean to excite the lizard," she added dryly.

Kalea snorted.

"Simply put," Eloch said, interrupting the banter, "the thing we're seeking is seeking us."

The room fell silent.

"I think I should wake the others," Wade said.

Eloch shook his head. "It's not necessary. It's still far away."

"How far?" asked Genji.

Eloch looked at Aiko.

"Hard to say," she said. "It comes and goes from the sensors. But it's still far enough away that I can't get a clear read." She shrugged. "I'm guessing maybe two to three months?"

Genji sat back. "Plenty of time for analysis. It may not be out there. It may be faulty readouts." He looked at Wade. "I'd like to do some systems checks."

"Sounds like something we should be doing," Wade agreed.

"That's it? Do we have any more of a plan?" Kalea asked.

"We'll sit and wait for it," Eloch said.

"Set up an orbit?" Aiko asked.

"Yes."

"Eloch is in danger," Perin blurted. "I have Seen it. A True Dream from long ago."

"Have you dreamt that dream lately?" Wren asked.

Perin nodded. "Just last night. The danger exists. I sense it." She looked at Eloch. "We both sense it."

"It feels like I'm being hunted," Eloch acknowledged.

This time Genji put his hand on Kalea's. "We have time to study the anomaly, Kalea," he told her quietly. "We will be able to protect

Eloch."

"Do you need help, Genji?" Wren asked. "Should we wake Spider and Mink?"

"It's better for the sleepers to remain in their cycle," Wade said. "Less stress on their bodies."

Genji glanced at Wade. "I think Kalea, Wade, and I can handle it for now. With two additional people, we might just get in each other's way. It's happened before."

Wren nodded. "Well, if you do need extra help, don't hesitate to wake them up."

"I'd like to set up a watch," Aiko said, looking at Eloch for approval. "I don't like how the sensors sometimes pick up the anomaly and sometimes don't."

"It could be just the distance, like you said," said Genji.

"That was before Perin said Eloch is in danger. I think it's prudent to set up the watch." She glanced at Wren. "*Caution First* and all."

"It could be the solar winds are messing with the sensors, too." Genji said.

"It could be a lot of things," Aiko said.

"I'll take the first watch," Wren said. "You guys start gathering your data." She looked at Eloch, "And you will be...?"

"I will be where I'm most needed," he replied. "For now, I'm going to the Solar Farm."

"Great, then you can take Little Wonder with you. She could use a good prowl."

He grinned and headed for the hall, Little Wonder loping to catch up.

"And we need a name other than Solar Farm to describe that expanding world you're creating in there," Wren called after him.

"We will vote on it at the next meal gathering," he said as he strode from the room.

Aiko rose. "The Knack Man has spoken," she said. "You can find me on the Bridge."

"I'm right behind you," Wren said. "Right after I have a conversation with Perin." She reached over to Perin and touched her hand. "Will you come with me so we can talk?"

"Of course," she said. Reaching for her tapping stick, she got to her feet and strode beside Wren.

~~~

The serenity of the Blue Room always calmed Wren. Over the years, it had become one of her favorite haunts when she wanted to be quiet and reflective. Often she found Perin quietly playing her lute, which added to the peace. Sometimes she joined her, but often she would simply sit and soak in the atmosphere created by Perin's music.

Once, Wren asked Perin how she knew when she needed peace and quiet, Perin told her it was the colors she saw when she looked at a person. Normally Wren's colors were bold and bright. When Wren was troubled, they became dull. "It's the same with everyone," Perin said. "Eloch is the easiest to read because he is so blindingly bright to begin with."

Today the Blue Room didn't calm Wren, but it was where she gravitated nonetheless.

"Have a seat, Perin," she said. "I'm sure my colors are pretty dull at the moment," she added as Perin settled in her usual spot in the chair where her lute leaned within easy reach. "Don't bother trying to play me into a peaceful mood. I think a run is more what I need," she said as she paced in front of where Perin sat. "Good thing the Navigation Bridge is so far from here. I can jog over there when I join Aiko."

Perin sighed. "I can imagine how you must feel, knowing Eloch is in danger."

"Can you tell me about this dream?"

Perin hesitated. "What I saw doesn't seem possible," she finally said. "That in itself is troubling because True Dreams show events exactly. And if it's impossible, then I must interpret this one as a metaphor, you see."

Wren stopped in front of Perin, studying the woman's upturned face. "I don't understand. Why would this True Dream be any different than the hundreds you've dreamed in the past?"

"I don't know, Wren. All I know is what I saw is impossible."

Wren folded her arms, cocking her head to the side. "Define impossible, will you? Maybe I can help."

Perin sighed and rubbed the knuckles of one hand. "I saw two ships occupying the same space. One was ours and one was..." she hesitated. "A ghost ship? I don't know. It was seemed solid enough, but we couldn't see them and they couldn't see us."

She paused again. "That's not quite true. I saw the others on the ship, and one person on that ship saw me." She shook her head. "The ghost ship had a weapon which they fired straight at Eloch's heart. He collapsed."

Wren slowly sat in the chair facing Perin. She cleared her throat. "Did he die?"

"I don't know. But Wren, True Dreams are sent to me to help. We can alter these events."

"How?"

"I don't know." She turned her sightless eyes toward Wren, "Somehow?"

Wren chewed her lip. "*Caution First*," she said at last. "Where did these events take place?"

"I-I'm not sure, but from what you've described to me, I think it was the Navigation Bridge."

"Okay, then we don't let Eloch out of our sight, especially when he's on the Navigation Bridge. For now, that's the best I can come up with. At all times, someone is with Eloch."

Perin brightened. "That might help. In the True Dream, you were there, Wren. You were right by his side."

"And now I know what might happen, maybe I can do something about it," Wren said, "At the very least, I can push him out of the way."

"Do that, Wren. Be ready to push him then, because it *will* happen."

~~~

The ship's intercom pinged. "The anomaly is back," Aiko announced from the Bridge. "And it's coming our way. I've cut the engines. Would appreciate some company."

Feeling a thrill of anticipation, Genji glanced at Kalea. Returning her grin, he slapped the com panel. "On our way," he said. "Wade?"

"I'll stay here and watch the readouts. This may be important to document," Wade replied. "Go! Shoo!" he said when they hesitated. "It only takes one to record the data."

When the pair reached the Bridge, Eloch and Wren were already there, gathered around an instrument panel. "As you can see on the viewing screen, there's nothing there," Aiko was saying. "But there's definitely something out there."

"Another ship that's cloaked?" Wren asked.

Aiko shook her head. "No. I still would be able to get a ping response, and I got zero when I pinged. It's heading right toward us. We should have visuals."

"Think it's wise to be standing still?" Wren asked with a frown. "Shouldn't we get out of their way?"

"But there's nothing there," Akio replied, her hand sweeping across the viewing panel. "See for yourself. Nothing. Just empty space."

"I sense energy building," Eloch said. "I'm going to put a shield around us."

"Shields are already up," Akio told him.

"Different kind of shield," Eloch told her.

"Are you recording all this? Wade is, too. I'm going to want to compare the data," Genji said.

"Already on it, Genj," Aiko said.

"I'm feeling something, too," Kalea said and hissed.

Genji touched his mate's hand, his eyes glued to the readouts in front of them. "Easy, Kalea. We're quite safe. Eloch's got this. Look here,. He pointed at the readouts. "There's a spike in the data."

~~~

Perin burst out of her stateroom. The need to be with the others was overwhelming—irrational.

Yet she felt driven to get to the ship's Navigation Bridge. There was no other option in her mind. Trailing her fingers along the sides of the corridor and sweeping her stick in front of her, Perin ran as fast as she could. Streaking around a curve, she quickened her pace until she stopped, panting, in front of the door where she knew she'd find the others.

Something was happening. What, she did not know.

She fumbled at the door panel. It refused to budge. She took a breath to steady her trembling hand and tried again. It slid open. Caught off guard, she lurched into the room, mindful that the floor sloped down into the center of the room. She lightly touched the railing to get her bearings and calmed her breathing. Now that she was here, the urgency was gone. She waited, worried, sightless eyes scanning for energy patterns.

The outline of another ship punctured the *Valiant's* bulkheads.

Perin gasped. Her heart began to pound so fast she thought she might black out.

The ghost ship from her dream! But this time she was *not* dreaming a True Dream. She was awake and *this was happening!* This was *real!* Her heart lurched when she understood she was helpless to stop the rapidly unfolding events.

Horrified, Perin followed the ghost ship's path as it slowly and silently sailed through the *Valiant's* sides.

Not a ghost ship.

It was just as real as the *Valiant.* Just as solid. And there was the uniformed crew, slightly exotic with their slanting, expressive eyes and creamy skin.

The people paid no attention to her, exactly as it had happened in her dream. Nor did it appear her companions saw the exotic people as their ship drifted through the *Valiant's* hull.

How can this be? How could these two ships be in the same place at the same time *without being aware of the existence of the other?* This was no collision, no rending of metal, no attack. Yet there it was.

Just like in her Dream.

And even though it was happening, she still didn't understand what she was seeing. Both ships shared the same space, just as she had described to Wren, and only she could see them both.

She could actually, simultaneously see them both!

That knowledge struck her with such force, she put a hand out to steady herself against the railing. How could she, who was blind, see both ships?

Was it her vision that was doing the seeing?

She looked around, recognizing her companions by their energetic signatures and now she saw faces, like an overlay.

It must be the vision that was doing the seeing. It must be because she saw their faces. Their expressions.

And there, in the middle of the Bridge, bending over an instrument panel with his mate, was Eloch, his light so bright, so very much like The Lady's, so brilliant she could barely see his features within the light.

And there, on the other ship, just like in her vision, were the others, preparing that deadly weapon, the weapon that at any moment would puncture Eloch's heart. And there was Eloch, unaware of this attack.

Surely, he must sense *something!*

Shouldn't he?

The vision said not.

"No!" she gasped.

She couldn't let it play out like the vision.

She could not.

She *would* not.

This was why The Lady had sent her on this voyage. By saving

Eloch, she was saving The Lady, for surely, this other ship was *The Something That Was Coming.*

"No!" she shrieked. "Eloch, duck down! Duck down! *Please!*"

Wren looked over. Her eyes widened when they locked gazes.

"Push him, Wren! *Do it now!*"

The weapon fired, and Perin screamed, covering her eyes.

For one brief moment, time stood still.

Her ears rang.

The vision was dissolving. Her sight was changing back to vague outlines of energy, except, she remembered, there was one more thing. One more thing she needed to do.

Lowering her hands, she turned, watching the enemy ship sail past on its ghostly course. She studied the people, searching for the one. Yes. He was there, eyes wide as he looked *directly at her.*

Their gazes locked. Held. She felt a current run between them, palpable and real.

Something else to do, she knew.

Something important.

She put a hand to her heart and spoke her name. "Perin."

"Jon," he replied, as clear as day.

There. It was done. She owned his name.

With a soft sigh, Perin slumped to the floor.

~~~

"Eloch, duck down! Duck down! *Please!*" Perin shouted, her voice shrill.

Wren looked up, locked gazes with Perin. Perin? Seeing?

"Push him, Wren! *Do it now!*" There was real panic in her voice.

Wren shoved Eloch in his chest.

He staggered back with a twisting motion, but with such force Wren was momentarily confused. Had she hit him that hard? She squinted at him. He seemed confused. "Eloch?" she said, resting a hand on his forearm. "You okay?"

"Perin!" Kalea exclaimed.

Wren looked away as Kalea rushed to the fallen woman's side. The Nuri hoisted her up and turned to Genji, "I'm taking her to the med lab, Genji."

"Right behind you," he answered and studied the instrument panel in front of him. "Looks like the anomaly is gone. I'll want to study the recordings." He looked at Aiko, "Can you make a copy for me?"

"Already done," she said with a smile. "Go see what's wrong with Perin."

"Wait! Genji, help me!" Wren grunted. "He's too heavy."

"Good god!" Genji exclaimed and rushed forward.

~~~

When Wren looked back at Eloch, he had the distant expression he got when he was turned inward.

"Feel funny," he said, absently rubbing his right shoulder, "like too much ale." His hand went up to his forehead. "Dizzy."

"Here, Eloch, let me help you sit down," Wren said, guiding him to one of the two pilot chairs.

He slumped into it. "Strange," he mumbled. "Feel strange.

Something is happening."

His voice was slurred.

"Eloch!" Wren grabbed at him when he pitched forward and called out to Genji for help.

With Genji's help, they strapped Eloch into the chair. His head lolled as he tried to focus on Wren. "Wh-where am I?" he asked and smiled weakly.

Wren knelt beside him, stroking his hand. "You're aboard the *Valiant*, Eloch. Sitting on the Bridge in the pilot's chair." She glanced worriedly over at Genji and mouthed, *What's going on?*

Genji knelt down beside her. "Eloch? You okay?"

Eloch squinted at Genji. "Thaif? Why aren't you on Entean? I don't understand," he said woozily.

"We need to get him to the med lab, Wren."

She nodded, and the two unbuckled Eloch and braced him between them. "Glad you're a strong Nuri," she huffed while they supported Eloch's stumbling footsteps.

"I'm coming, too," Aiko called after them. She turned to her control panel and flipped on the Bridge recordings. "Going to mark these coordinates and put us in a slow rotation around them," she said. "Genji's going to want to take readings," she added to herself as she cut the engines to save the thrusters. As a precaution, she strengthened the shields. Before she left for the med lab, she snatched one of the remote ship-to-captain control devices and instructed the ship to contact her if anything else out of the ordinary occurred.

CHAPTER 9 - TROUBLE

Grale had been in Cryo sleep before. This was nothing new. In his long career as a rock pounder, it was the only way to travel and maintain muscle mass necessary to do the labor-intensive job of gathering iron ore, aluminum, and the like from the asteroid belts scattered throughout the galaxy. In fact, he enjoyed slipping into his tank, a little soft around the middle from planet leave, only to wake up several years later with a rock-hard gut.

But not this time.

He was in the shower, washing off the grease they used to make sure the Cryo didn't freeze you to death, when he noticed his flat abs were missing. What had happened? Some malfunction? He definitely remembered asking Wade to double-check the muscle stimulators, making sure he was harnessed in. Wade had winked as he assured him he was good to go. His smirk was the last thing Grale remembered before he drifted into the oblivion.

Grale stood under the steady stream of heated water, waiting for his teeth to stop chattering. The cold was his least favorite part about going into and coming out of the sleep. *Hate this freakin' cold.* The warmth felt good, and after a span he began to relax under the steady spray. He stretched, popping his joints to get the kinks out, and soaped his middle again, frowning that he'd need to get his abs back the old-fashioned way, which meant work.

He paused. There could be another reason his abs hadn't hardened. Maybe he hadn't been under all that long. A couple of months, maybe, rather than three years as planned.

He paused in his washing. It was Aiko, not Wade. She brought him back online. The sleep always made him groggy, but he was coming back pretty quick now that he was warming up.

So Aiko brought him back online, which meant he was needed for something. Some equipment malfunction she couldn't handle? He snorted. Bet that had gotten her good, her with her "I'm-a-colonizer-scout-pilot-and-you're-nothing-but-a-rock-pounder" attitude. He was going to enjoy teasing the Kitten about this one.

The shower had done its job, and he waved his hand over the on/off panel, suddenly hungry, in need of a cup of coffee, and grateful Kalea had insisted they bring plenty of coffee beans and baby coffee plants from Longwei. He quickly toweled off. Flinging the towel onto the drying rack, he dressed in loose-fitting clothes, exited his cabin, and hustled toward the galley.

Over the years, the Knack Man had expanded their ship, even beyond the size it was when they acquired it. Grale didn't mind. There was plenty of space so people wouldn't get on each other's nerves, which could easily happen on long journeys like this one.

And what a difference from his own ship, where people's modular cabins were a third the size as the ones on this ship, which had been built for the UpperUppers. Nothing was too good for the colonizers, that's for sure. Lots of comforts on this vessel. No wonder he'd gotten a little soft! Couple the comfort already built into the design with the constant tweaking Eloch was doing, and Grale was surprised he hadn't become a butterball.

The three-year Cryo sleeps were good, too, for giving people their space. Wren did good when she scheduled them so there'd be overlap times. Important for cohesiveness of the crew. He'd done the same thing with his ship.

Yeah, he felt pretty good with this crew. It had taken him a while to get over resenting that he'd been pushed into going with them, but he liked them all. They all had their quirks, sure, but they all shared the same sense of adventure he had and, he decided, if he was forced to spend gods-knew-how-long on this strange quest they were on, he was good with all of them.

Not sure if they were as good with him—especially Kitten—but didn't that just add to the fun? He liked the banter. His thoughts drifted back to the party they had after the first wormhole jump. He liked her, too, and not just the banter, although he'd never admit it to a soul.

The galley was empty, and he took his time with his meal before heading back to the med lab, where Aiko had told him meet her when he was ready. Long ago, he found out the hard way that it wasn't good to rush your digestion with your first meal, so he took the time to savor the flavors. By crossing through the Solar Farm, he could knock twenty minutes off, so he took those twenty minutes to finish his meal.

The sterile greenhouses were long gone, replaced by Eloch's creations and landscapes, but everybody still called it the Farm. As he followed the path by the brook, there appeared to be less water flowing, and he wondered what Eloch was up to next. The man lived to create.

Not that Grale was complaining. The more Eloch played around with the *Valiant,* the less it felt like a ship and the more it felt like a place to live.

Grale exited the Solar Farm and headed toward the med labs, blowing off any concerns about getting back into shape. All he needed to do was stop taking shortcuts and walk the ship. Sparring with Wren, Aiko, or Wade in the gym would help, too.

Kalea smiled at him when he entered. He nodded at Genji and Aiko. The blind girl turned her opaque eyes toward him. Those sightless eyes followed him as he joined the group sitting around a table laden with instruments and tech screens. He suppressed a shudder as he pulled out a chair and sat by Aiko. For someone who was blind, that woman sure saw a lot.

He watched them silently for a few moments as he got his bearings. Abruptly, he straightened, alert. "The ship," he said to Aiko when she glanced at him,. "Are we dead in space?"

She shook her head. "Cut the engines. Stopped, is all."

"What for?"

"Let's wait for the others."

He nodded. "Did you wake us all up?"

"Yeah."

"I might have something," Genji said, and Kalea leaned over him to gaze at the info console he'd been working on, their heads together and deep in conversation.

"What gives?" Grale asked Aiko.

She shook her head. "You'll know soon enough." She glanced down at his fist. "Relax. The ship is safe. We're safe enough."

He nodded and spread his palms out on the table before him. "How long have I been in the Cryo tub?"

"'Bout a year."

"That long, huh?" His hand stole to his soft belly. Maybe there *was* something wrong with his tank after all.

Aiko watched him and smirked.

"What?"

She looked pointedly at the hand on his middle and back up to his face, grinning.

He felt his face pull into a frown. "*What?*" he said again, stressing the word.

Genji snorted, and then he noticed they were all looking at him, grinning like fools, even the blind girl.

Grale looked back at Aiko.

She started to laugh, and he felt his face heating up. "Awww, no. Tell me you didn't," he said.

140

She nodded. "Oh, but I did," she laughed.

Kalea burst out laughing, and the blind girl giggled. Genji chuckled. Wade shook his head with a snort.

"And you all knew about it," he accused them. He pointed at Wade. "You went along with it."

Wade's snort turned into a laugh.

He watched them while they hooted and guffawed, keeping his expression blank. Finally, he shook his head and glanced at Aiko. "You know this means war, Kitten," he told her, giving her his best wicked grin.

~~~

"I heard laughter. What's happening?" Spider asked as he entered the med lab.

The room fell silent.

"Sit," Aiko said. "We'll wait for Mink."

"I'm here," Mink said, and she squeezed past Spider and sank into the only empty seat at the table. She shot him a grin. "Hey, Spidey. You snooze, you lose."

Spider made a face, snagged a lab stool, and wheeled it in beside Mink. "Where's Wren?" he asked.

Aiko nodded toward a door panel that led into one of the med rooms, "In there with Eloch."

Spider raised his eyebrows. "And Eloch?"

"That's why we're all here and awake," Aiko said. She looked at Genji. "Why don't you tell us what happened, Genj? Since you were monitoring it."

Genji nodded and glanced around the room. "There was an

141

anomaly," he began.

"An anomaly?" Spider asked with a scowl. "What kind of an anomaly?"

"Something we didn't feel was serious enough to warrant waking you all up for," Genji replied.

Grale snorted, "Yet, here we are, all awake."

"Exactly!" Spider said. "This has to do with Eloch, we all know that. I think that's pretty serious since we've become so dependent upon him for our very survival."

Genji glared at the two, his pupils beginning to slit as he hissed softly.

"Okay, okay," Aiko said, raising her hand. "Calm the lizard down, Genj. Let's all take a breath here. The anomaly was just a blip on our readouts that moved in and out of our sensors' detection. We determined it to be more of a curiosity than a threat. In fact, we weren't even sure whether it was real or some glitch. We really couldn't tell."

"But what we could tell," Genji said, taking up the narration, "was that it appeared to be moving in our general direction."

"At a leisurely pace," Aiko added. "Again, no cause for concern."

"We had a meeting," Genji said. "And we decided to set up an orbit, wait, and collect data."

"Eloch said he felt hunted," Aiko said.

"And you still didn't think to wake us?" Spider asked.

"It was discussed," Aiko answered. "We believed we had it covered, and why disrupt your cycle if we didn't need to, right?"

"Yesterday," Genji said, "Kalea, Wade, and I were running through our systems when Aiko called us from the Bridge to tell us the anomaly was back. When we arrived, Eloch and Wren were already there. According to the readouts, the thing was right on us, but there was absolutely nothing on the viewing screen."

"Cloaked?" asked Grale.

"No pings," Aiko said, shaking her head.

"Kalea and I were watching the readouts, following its path, when—pow!—Perin shouts for Eloch to duck and Wren pushes him. Eloch staggers like he was smacked into by one of us in Nuri form. Perin faints, then Eloch collapses. We bring them both down here and pull you three out of Cryo. And that's all we know."

Genji looked at Spider, Mink, and Grale. "We've waited for us all to be together before we try to science this out." He put a hand on Perin's shoulder. "We've scanned Perin here, and she's medically sound. Eloch is another story. He's groggy and appears to be in some discomfort. Yet we can't find a reason."

"Why did you tell Eloch to duck, Perin?" Spider asked, turning toward her.

Perin's hand fluttered to her face, where she brushed at a stray strand of hair. "It was my True Dream," she said. "I saw everything through my True Dream's vision." She looked at them, her eyes shining. "I could see. The way I used to, with my eyes. For the first time since I became a Seer for The Lady."

She turned toward Genji and grasped Kalea's hand. "I saw you. I saw both of you." Her head whipped around toward Aiko. "And you, Aiko. Not your energy signatures, but how eyes see others." She shook her head at the memory. "You are all so beautiful."

She paused and took a deep breath. "But the vision showed me more, some things I can't understand and don't seem possible. Yet I assure you, they were very real."

Kalea squeezed Perin's hand. "What else did you see, Perin?"

"I can only describe it as a ghost ship. I saw a ghost ship."

"A ghost ship? What do you mean?" Spider wondered.

"A-a ship. I don't know what else to call it. Smaller than ours. Much smaller. And it moved through our ship. Like a ghost, only I could see people on it—uniformed people—and they were as real as you and I. Just as solid."

Aiko looked at Genji. "The anomaly?"

Genji shrugged. "Possibly. Likely, but how?"

"I may be able to answer that. Something I was studying way back on Spur, but let's let Perin finish telling us what she saw," Spider said.

Perin nodded. "Okay. Next, I saw what the people on the ghost ship were intending. I shouted for Eloch to duck, and Wren pushed him like we'd planned. Because Wren pushed Eloch, they weren't able to kill him, but they still wounded him badly."

"How did they wound him?" Grale asked sharply.

"They shot him with...a...I don't know what to call it...a spike? It is shaped like a long spike, and it flashes."

"And you can see it?" Genji asked.

Perin nodded. "If it's still in his shoulder, I will be able to see it, yes."

Mink glanced at Wade, eyebrows raised.

With an *I don't know* shrug, Wade said, "I helped stabilize Eloch, and there is no flashing spike sticking out of him, although he keeps reaching toward his right shoulder and he's favoring it when he moves."

"That's the side," Perin said. "That's where the flashing spike is."

"A ghost spike?" Aiko asked. "No, I'm not making a joke." she said when she saw the others' reactions. "I'm just saying, wouldn't ghost ships shoot ghost spikes?"

Genji raised a brow at Spider. "Something you want to add?"

Spider nodded. "What Aiko said may not be as far-fetched as it seems," he said. "Back on Spur, in university, there was a great deal of speculation about parallel worlds, of other sentient beings living within different dimensions. Different vibrational frequencies, if you will."

Grale snorted. "Seems far-fetched to me."

"Yeah? Well, do you have another explanation for what Perin's describing?" Mink shot back.

"I spoke with one of them," Perin said.

All eyes turned to her.

"Go on, Perin," Genji said softly.

"As the ship drifted through our ship, one of them saw me as clearly as I saw him," she said. "I gave him my name, and he gave me his." She paused. "Jon. His name is Jon."

"Did Jon happen to tell you why they singled out Eloch for attack?" Wren asked, leaning against the doorway between the two rooms.

"Wren!" Spider half-rose. "How are you?"

"I'm dealing. Thanks, Spider."

"Have you gotten any rest?" Mink asked softly.

Wren shook her head. "'Fraid not. Nor do I plan to until we can science out what's going on with Eloch. So, get used to the dark rings and bloodshot eyes." She snorted. "I, fortunately, don't have to look at myself. How's it going, guys? Anything yet?"

"We've got another issue with Eloch's condition," Genji said. "I've been monitoring the *Valiant*, and if Eloch doesn't come back to us soon, we're going to be in trouble."

"How so?" Grale asked.

"Eloch is so tied into this ship that whatever affects Eloch, affects the *Valiant*. If he declines, it's safe to assume all the ship's systems will begin to decline, too."

"I think that may be happening already," Grale said, rubbing his chin. "I noticed things looking a little wilt-y when I cut through the Solar Farm comin' over here."

"Yeah?" Spider asked. "Me, too, now you mention it."

Wren sighed. "Just keep monitoring, Genj," she said and ran a hand down a coilmat. "If things get worse, there's a fail-safe."

Spider lifted an eyebrow. *"Caution First?"*

"Always," Wren answered with the briefest of smiles. "Perin, why don't you come see Eloch? Maybe you can see the spike."

Everyone rose and waited expectantly.

"Okay, okay," Wren said. "Let's *all* go find out if Perin can see the spike. But just don't crowd, all right? Wade, would you check Eloch's vitals? I haven't noticed any changes, but I want to make sure." She turned to go back into the room but paused, causing Genji to nearly collide with her.

"Brace yourselves, people. This isn't the Eloch you're used to."

CHAPTER 10 – MORE TROUBLE

Aiko held back and observed the scene from the doorway. She hadn't expected Eloch to be so restless, as if he was in the middle of a feverish nightmare. She swallowed hard. "Oh, Knack Man," she whispered softly.

"Does he recognize you, Wren?" Spider was asking.

Aiko wished she could compartmentalize her feelings the way Spider did. Only when flying, she thought, or captaining her own ship. But as this journey progressed and she'd allowed Wren and Eloch to control their destination, she'd changed.

"He goes in and out of consciousness," Wren said. "When he's awake, I know he knows me, but he's confused. I don't think he really understands what's happening to him."

"Like dementia," Spider said.

"Like the infected Sisters," Genji said suddenly, his eyes on Eloch.

"What?" Mink asked.

"Does anyone notice the similarities between Eloch's behavior and what Entean, Spur, and Longwei have been describing? I think we've just discovered what that *something* is when They tell us, 'Something is coming.'"

"The flashing spike?" Perin asked, her eyes fastened on Eloch's right shoulder. "There," she said, pointing. "I can see it. It is lodged between his shoulder and his body on the right."

"Here?" Wren asked and she touched his collarbone. She drew her hand back sharply when Eloch groaned. "We have to get it out," she said fiercely. "Genji? Spider? Any ideas?"

"How do you pull something out that's invisible and only a blind woman can see?" Wade asked hesitantly.

Kalea looked at him, and hope drained from her expression.

Aiko glanced at Grale, who looked slightly paler than usual. "Why don't Grale and I go up to the Bridge, keep an eye on the systems, and monitor for returning anomalies," she suggested. "That way all the scientists can work on what they do best, and we'll focus on what we do best."

Not even sure if anyone heard her, she nodded to Grale and they exited the room. "I was beginning to feel a bit claustrophobic back there," she said as they headed for the Bridge.

"Yeah. The Knack Man not looking so good made me not feel so good," Grale replied. "Don't like feeling helpless."

"That's why we're going to do what we're good at and leave the others to do what they're good at. At least he's alive. I've seen him in much worse shape."

"Yeah? When?"

"When I first brought him to Spur. Genji and I believed he was dead. But turned out he'd slipped into a coma. Hibernation, Eloch called it. Whatever. By the time we got to Spur, he was nothing but sinews and bones." She grinned and glanced at Grale. "Took him to the Board of Colonizers and they laughed at him. Called him a Bone Puppet."

Grale barked out a laugh. "No!"

Aiko giggled. "Yes. And he endured, Grale. He endured and became more and more powerful. Sure, he looks bad. Sure, I don't want to see him like this, but I've seen him worse, and I'm not losing hope."

148

"Then neither will I, Kitten. Neither will I."

~~~

Spider tugged on his lip. "I think," he said slowly, "we first need to stop that flashing light Perin described. Deactivate the signal somehow."

"I see where you're going with this," Genji said. He looked at Wren. "If the signal is deactivated, then Eloch won't be under its influence any longer."

"And once Eloch is Eloch again, perhaps he will know how to pull it out himself!" Kalea exclaimed, the hope flooding back in.

"That would be the best case," Genji agreed.

"Worst case, we've got him stabilized and will have more time to create a miracle," Spider said.

"Let's revisit your parallel worlds suggestion, Spider," Genji said. "Can you tell me more about it?"

Spider gave him a crooked smile. "It's more theory than science...late night University speculations with fellow students, if I'm going to be honest, but the concept always fascinated me."

"How so?" Mink asked.

"It's proven that there is only so much our eyes can see. We call that the visible spectrum, and it's only a small portion of the electromagnetic spectrum. And what we're seeing are vibrational wavelengths. It's also proven that the whole of the universe is made up of energy vibrating at different frequencies. So who's to say that the frequency my reality is vibrating at is the only vibration? And who's to say that Perin can or cannot see into other vibrational realities?"

"So Perin can see what we cannot because her eyes see beyond a normal person's visible spectrum," Wren guessed.

149

Spider smiled. "Exactly. And this Jon person could be living in a reality that vibrates at a frequency different from ours. Not better or worse...just different. So what we need to do—"

"—is develop a way to tune into the frequency that matches the vibrational wavelengths of Jon's reality, and then jam that frequency," Genji finished.

"Only all our equipment is designed to study interstellar frequencies," Spider said. "Not—" he gestured toward Eloch, who groaned again, his head tossing from side to side.

Wren swallowed hard, placing her hand on his forehead.

"Something is happening to the spike," Perin said as she stared fixedly at a place on Eloch's right shoulder area.

"Can you describe it?" Genji asked.

"It's..." she looked more closely. "There's a small panel that I can see now. It wasn't there before, and something is unfolding...blooming...like a metal flower." Her sightless eyes widened. "Now it's moving and...there...it stopped." She gasped. "Light is coming out of it."

Eloch cried out. The *Valiant* shuddered. Lights flickered.

The ship's intercom pinged. "Brace yourselves. The ship is losing its integrity," Aiko said as the ship groaned and shuddered again. "We'll redirect the life support systems as best we can."

Eloch moaned and clutched at his shoulder.

The ship convulsed, the accompanying grinding of twisted metal so loud, Wren was forced to cover her ears. "Aiko! What was that?" she shouted into the intercom.

"That was a chunk of the *Valiant* tearing off. She's falling apart!" Grale said. "Aiko's doing what she can to keep us alive, but I don't know, people."

"I'm going to activate the fail-safe," Wren said, already in motion. She stumbled out of the room, slamming her shoulder against the door frame when the ship lurched again. She ignored the pain, gave all her attention to maintaining her balance as she raced past the Cryo beds and out into the main corridor along the perimeter of the ship. Despite the pitching and rocking, she managed to reach the access door to the Solar Farm fairly quickly.

It took her three attempts to open the Solar Farm access panel, and the lake was sloshing out of its bank. Wren nearly toppled into it as she ran full tilt along its shore.

There was another shudder, and she found herself sprawled on top of wilting vegetation. Alarms blared. The ship lurched. As she struggled to her knees, a huge wave of water rolled over her, carrying her in its surge, along with uprooted vegetation which buffeted and bruised her. The water finally withdrew when the ship tilted the other way.

On her knees, Wren choked and gulped air, pushing her dripping coilmats out of her eyes. She collapsed again when the ship shuddered, regained her balance, then staggered to her feet.

Dizzy and disoriented she looked around, trying to get her bearings. Luck was in her favor. The wave had washed her closer to the other side of the Solar Farm. Arms windmilling for balance, Wren dashed toward the exit panel, which kept opening and closing, opening and closing. She pushed herself harder when she saw that every time the panel opened, the opening was narrower. Reaching the exit, she shoved her way through just as the ship lost gravity.

Wren's momentum slammed her against the outer bulkhead. It bowed under her hands, rivets straining. Terror lanced through her. If the ship's hull didn't hold, they'd all be dead in an instant.

Her fingers found purchase on the seams, and she pulled her body along the corridor, legs trailing behind. The flickering lights made it difficult to see. The alarms made it difficult to think. "Keep it together, Eloch!" she shouted, projecting her thoughts toward him, sending the force of her will and the fear driving her efforts to connect with him.

For a brief moment, everything went still. She paused and held her breath. Had she somehow reached him through his confusion and pain?

The ship lurched sideways.

Her fingers were torn away, and she was thrown against the inner wall, ricocheting up toward the ceiling in a head-over-feet tailspin, making her dizzy. She pressed off from the ceiling toward the floor.

Like a cat, she twisted her body so the momentum pushed her down the corridor toward her stateroom. It was visible now, and she focused on it with every ounce of her being, willing herself to go faster. But she was slowing! Twisting her body had had a counter effect on her forward momentum.

"No! No! No! NO!" she screamed, stretching as far as she could until her booted feet touched the inner wall. Hoping it would be enough, she pushed off with her toes, arms outstretched and reaching.

Wren sailed toward their stateroom, her hand slamming the door panel. It slid open and jammed halfway, but Wren was small enough to wedge herself through.

She was greeted by Little Wonder, floating over the bed, paws splayed, yowling in confusion.

"Hey LW," she crooned over the noise. "Let me work a miracle here, and then you'll be safe."

Wren pushed away from the door and used her momentum to maneuver over to her side of the bed, hand reaching toward the fail-safe switch Eloch installed there. The lack of gravity made it difficult for her find any leverage. She swore as she stretched and batted at her table by the bed until she could see the switch. Nearly within reach.

The table floated away and she swore again.

"Think, Wren, *think*," she muttered. "I can do this." She took a deep breath, calming her ragged breathing, went still, and studied her surroundings. Little Wonder's pillow drifted by. She grabbed it and threw it away from her, which made her coast a little closer toward the table, but still not enough to grab it.

"My knives!" she exclaimed, catching a glimpse of the helpless sniffer floating nearby. "Hang in there, Wonder. Thank the gods old habits die hard."

Slowly, Wren unsheathed a throwing knife and threw it at the wall behind her. She shot forward and slammed against the opposite wall, winding her.

Little Wonder let out a plaintive yowl when the ship shuddered again.

"I'm hurrying," she said and maneuvered her feet around so she could launch herself toward the floating table.

This time she reached it and, with a sigh, pushed the fail-safe switch.

Nothing happened.

She pushed it again.

Still nothing happened.

"WHAT NOW?" Wren shouted.

The ship groaned...shuddered...then went eerily still.

Little Wonder squeaked.

"Oh, girl, I'm sorry," Wren said. She abandoned the fail-safe button to glide over to the overwrought mini-sniffer, scooped her up, and reached for the closest intercom by the bed. "Aiko?" she asked.

"We've regained ship control, Wren," Aiko said. "Grale is putting a field around the whole ship to maintain its integrity. Will get the gravity stabilized after that. So get yourself in a safe position and hang on. You did it, Wren. I'm going to contact the others in the med lab."

Wren cuddled the trembling sniffer in her arms. "Hear that? Gravity soon, and lucky us, we're floating only a couple of feet over the bed. Now, if we just don't move, we should land okay."

Little Wonder began licking her face and didn't stop, even after they landed on the bed.

Wren rolled off the bed, threaded her way around the debris, and picked up her knife and sheathed it before she tapped the ship's intercom located near the half-opened door panel. "Aiko, can you hear me?" she asked.

"The Kitten's scrolling through our systems doing a double-check," Grale said. "Looks like we can patch things up a bit more," he said.

"Good. I'm going to make my way back to the med labs. Can you maintain surveillance on me?"

"Can do. I'd recommend taking the corridors. Initial visuals on the Solar Farm area show lots of downed trees. Looks pretty muddy, too. Like some sort of tidal wave went through there."

"Yeah, I was there. The lake decided to take a solo and flooded all over. I'm going to get some dry clothes on and will ping you when I'm heading out."

"Also think about picking up some portable food and water from the galley. Lots of broken stuff and possible contamination in the labs."

"Will do. Eloch?"

"Safe. They buckled him in."

Wren heaved a sigh of relief. "Can you patch me in?"

"Sure thing, kiddo. Later."

There was a brief pause. While she waited, Wren began to peel off her wet clothing. Underneath, she was a mass of bruises, and she wished she had the time to indulge in a long, hot soak.

The intercom crackled.

"Wren? You okay?" It was Mink.

"Yeah." Wren snatched up a towel and began to gingerly blot herself dry as she talked. "You?"

"We're all safe. It was tough going there for a while. I'm still shaking." A pause. "I think we're all pretty shaken. You saved us, Wren. Thanks."

"Thank my knives," Wren said.

"What was that?"

"Never mind. I'll tell you when I see you. I'm heading back. Going to check on the galley first and bring some food. What's happening with Eloch?" She flung the towel on the bed and shimmied into dry clothes, tucking her knives into their places.

"We're back to sciencing out how to scramble that signal. Spider and Genji are on it. Kalea and I are cleaning up. It's a mess here. Wade's monitoring Eloch while Perin's watching the spike. Says the metal flower is still shooting out light."

"Okay, I'll be there as soon as I can. Taking the long way 'round."

Chapter 11 - Stopgaps

"We need to science out how to access the spike's frequency and stop it before it does any more damage to Eloch," Genji said, turning toward his info console

Wade glanced over his shoulder. "What about all our portable planetside scanning equipment? Could be something there."

Genji raised a brow at Spider, who scrambled out of his chair to open the cabinet where the planetside equipment was stored. An avalanche of paraphernalia slid out and clattered onto the floor. Spider knelt. "I'll start sorting," he said.

"Here, Kalea, take this." Mink held out a hair fastener. "Tie up your hair. It's so long, it could fall into something nasty."

"Thanks," Kalea said and stood looking down at her covered feet. "But I can just do this." She gathered her hair, twisted it a few times and put the end through, forming a tidy bun.

Mink shook her head. "I envy you. My hair never did that. One of the reasons I cut it all off. Take these gloves, too," she said, holding out a pair of thick gloves. "I know Nuri have thicker skin, but still, we don't know what these chemicals are, and I want to get them cleaned up ASAP."

Kalea snapped the skintight gloves onto her hands. "Eloch would have cleaned all this up before I even got my hair tied."

"Not only that, he would have broken all the chemicals down and reused them for...I don't know what. Fertilizer, perhaps, for his forest." Mink scrunched up her face. "I don't think it really occurred to any of us how dependent we've become on Eloch," she said with a grimace. "Not until we have to clean up the old-fashioned way, anyhow." She knelt down and started sifting through the scattered debris.

Kalea frowned while she considered Eloch lying prone on his pallet and sighed. She squatted down beside Mink, who was gingerly picking through spilled canisters, vessels, and other receptacles. "Show me what you're doing and how."

Mink looked up and smiled. "I'm gathering all the broken pieces and safely disposing of them. While I'm doing that, why don't you pick out any containers that are still intact, clean them up, and put them on that clean counter over there?"

Kalea began working. "This shouldn't take too long," she commented. "Fortunately, most of it was strapped into cabinets."

"And hopefully not in the same condition as the planetside equipment."

Kalea chuckled, then sobered. "I hope we can help him soon. Wren—"

"Wren is fine," Wren said, entering the med lab with Little Wonder draped over her shoulders. "Where is a safe place for the food I brought?"

"Any of the counters where Perin is sitting," Mink said. "I've already cleaned and disinfected them all. Glad to see Little Wonder safe and sound."

"She's surprisingly all right," Wren said, setting the supplies on the counter next to Perin. "Hi, Perin, glad to see you're not hurt. No, don't move. You're fine where you are. I'm using the other counter," Wren said, then continued answering Mink. "So, yeah, Little Wonder is just fine, although she was pretty unhappy when I first found her. She's settled right down, now, though, haven't you, LW?" Wren asked, stroking the sniffer's front paw.

Little Wonder butted Wren's hand and churruped.

158

Mink smiled and returned to her sifting.

Having deposited her supplies, Wren crossed to the room where Eloch lay. She watched everyone in silence, then cleared her throat. "I don't want to interrupt anyone, but I could use a status report," she said, moving to Eloch's side.

"Eloch is holding his own, although he is in pain," Wade said. "In fact, whatever that fail-safe switch was, when you flipped it, Wren, it seemed to take some of the stress off Eloch."

Wren nodded and rested her hand on his forehead. "Not surprised. That switch released his control of the ship and gave it back to us."

Genji's head shot up. "You don't say? Don't you think we should all have known about the switch and its location?"

"Nope," Wren answered, eyes remaining on Eloch. "I'm afraid its location is classified and will remain so. I promised Eloch I would tell no one."

"But—"

Wren shook her head. "No buts. Not ever. This ship is Eloch, and Eloch is the ship, as you all, I'm sure, are aware of by now. He only created that switch because he loves and trusts me. Can you see what an invasion of his privacy it would be if we all knew where it was?"

"But all of us are dependent on the health of this ship for our survival," Genji pointed out. "We should have access to that switch. What if something had happened to you, too?"

"We can't let that happen, then, can we?"

"I don't like it," Genji said.

"I'm sorry you don't, Genj, but that's the way it is," Wren said kindly. "Look, think of the *Valiant* as our little planet. Like Spur. There's no fail-safe switch on Spur, is there?" Wren said.

Genji reluctantly shook his head, rubbing the back of his neck. "No, there is no fail-safe switch on Spur. And you are correct, Wren. The *Valiant* appears to be taking on more and more characteristics of a planet."

Wren nodded. "It's taken me a long time to understand this. And," she thought for a second, "it requires a lot of trust in Eloch. However, the sooner he's healthy, the sooner we can all breathe easier, because you know darn well Eloch will create a way to protect us if he ever does become incapacitated again. And without the need for a fail-safe. So, what's the status?"

Little Wonder moved from her perch on Wren's shoulders to curl up by Eloch's side.

"I'm checking through data while Spider is sifting through the planetside scanners to see what we can do to cobble something together," Genji replied.

"A spectroscope," Spider said, holding up the portable spectroscope. "It converts incoming waves into a frequency spectrum."

"Perfect!" said Genji, reaching for it.

"And a polychromator," Spider said with a grin, holding up his other hand.

Genji laughed. "Where'd you find that antique?"

"Luck," Spider answered. "All the equipment no longer used was stuffed in the back and fell out last when I opened up the cabinet. So it was all on top of the mess. Which one do you want?"

"I'll take the spectroscope," Genji said, reaching for it. "We're going to have to merge their readouts to get the info we want."

Spider nodded and stood. "You'll be able to do that, easy."

The two joined Wren around Eloch's pallet. "Let's see what we've got here," Genji said. He turned on the scope and pointed it toward Eloch's right shoulder.

Wren gasped. "Perin's metal flower," she whispered.

"You can see it?" Perin called from her perch on the counter in the adjoining room. "It is real?"

"Very real," Genji answered. "It appears to be some sort of transmitter, and whatever it's transmitting, I will speculate that it is being powered by Eloch's knack."

"Get it out of him!" Wren hissed.

"That's our first task, Wren," Genji said calmly. "What's your readout, Spider?"

"It's some sort of high-energy frequency," he said. "Looks like gamma rays."

"What does that mean?" Kalea asked rising to her feet.

"The spectrum of light says we're dealing with gamma rays," Genji explained. "Something our bodies aren't capable of withstanding, but what a planet is quite capable of processing, so in that respect, although he's weakened, this situation will not kill Eloch."

"But Eloch isn't one hundred percent planet," Wren said, her brow crinkling.

"Then perhaps that's what is causing him the discomfort."

"So," Wren said after a moment, "you're saying Eloch won't die, but that part of him that is human might if we can't fix this."

"I'm not going to commit to that, Wren," Genji said. "We don't know enough to come to that conclusion."

"I think I can jam it," Spider said excitedly. "Come here, Genji, and see what you think."

The two rushed to the monitor where Spider began entering

equations.

Unable to follow their conversation, Wren reached for Eloch's hand, stroking it. She stiffened when a pair of arms wrapped around her, and she automatically went for a knife, causing her to let go of Eloch's hand.

It thumped lifelessly at his side.

"Have faith in Genji and Spider," Kalea said gently, hugging her tighter. "They will heal him, Wren."

"Those two can science out anything. You know this," Mink said. "We're all in this together, and we're all very, very good at what we do."

Wren sighed, released her grip on the knife, and leaned into her friends. "Thanks. I just hope it's not too late," she whispered. "I hope he doesn't lose any more of who he is."

Abruptly she reached for Eloch's hand again. "Hold on Eloch," she pleaded. "Just hold on. And come back to me. Come all the way back to me."

~ ~ ~

The pain was intense. He could feel parts of himself burning away. He knew if he let that part go, the pain would be less. It would be so easy to just let that part go.

But then, through the pain, he felt something. Something important to him.

Her.

It was Her. She called.

Wren.

For Wren, he could endure.

For Wren, he would endure.

~~~

"We've got it!" Genji exclaimed. "We've got it, Spider!" He reached out with both hands and kissed Spider on the top of his head, his big hands all but burying Spider's face. "I'm pinging Aiko. Need those coordinates, Spider," he said and released Spider to ping the Bridge.

"Yes?" Aiko asked through the intercom.

"I want you to send out a pulsar flare using the coordinates Spider is going to read to you."

"Okaaay," came her reply. "But why? It's just a big burst of light."

"It's more than that," Genji told her. "It's payback. We're going to jam their invisible signal right down their invisible throats," he growled. A wisp of smoke emerged with his breath.

Spider hooted and leaned toward the intercom. "I love it when the Nuri gets the better of him. Can you hear me, Aiko? I've got the coordinates."

"Give them to Grale. He's better at this than I am."

~~~

Up on the Bridge, Aiko turned to Grale. "They want to send a pulsar flare. I told Spider you'd handle it."

"That I can, Kitten," he said and raised his voice so Spider could hear him. "I'll take those coordinates whenever you're ready.

Spider read them off as Grale punched them into the flare's settings. "Flare going active in three, two, one," he said and flipped the switch at "one."

A band of light shot out into the vast expanse, flared bright, then faded.

Grale glanced at Aiko. "Why are we doing this?"

163

Aiko shrugged. "Something about feedback. I think we're trying to jam the signal that's attacking Eloch." Aiko pinged the med lab. "Anything happen?" she asked.

"Again," Genji said. "Same coordinates."

"You heard the man," Aiko told Grale. "Maybe set it for a longer flash?"

Grale nodded and repeated the flare, but for several seconds longer.

After a few moments, Aiko pinged the med lab. "Anything?"

"We're going to hold with that and see what happens. Standby," Spider said after a brief pause.

"Copy that," she responded and closed off the intercom. She folded her arms and looked over at Grale again. "Now we wait."

"And while we're waiting, I'm going to continue assessing the damage."

Aiko shivered. "We almost didn't make it," she said.

"Yeah, I know. I don't think the others realize how close we were to breaking apart."

"I think Wren knows. She's been roaming around a lot."

"Brave lady."

"She is. She always talks about *Caution First*, but I've seen her do some pretty crazy things when it's necessary. Did I tell you how she risked her life to save her Kin back on Spur? Led a whole pack of sniffers on a chase to give her Kin time to escape when a hide went wrong."

"I've heard that one. That's when she lost the leg," Grale said. "Like I said, brave lady." He squinted at her, "Reminds me of you."

Aiko barked out a laugh. "Me? You've been pounding too many rocks, Cowboy."

"Seriously. It takes a brave pilot to go on scouting missions for the colonizers. Many of those scouts never returned. You risked your life all the time. Most pilots would pick an easier life."

"Yeah, well...maybe my life wasn't really worth much, except for risking it."

"Come on, Kitten," Grale growled. "You don't really mean that."

She shot him a sad look. "Don't I? All I know how to do is survive and fly. I've got a goodly amount of knack and that's about it. If life is supposed to be about happiness and prosperity, well, I guess I missed that memo." She waved a hand. "Don't look at me like that. I don't want your pity. I'm just stating facts. I've made peace with the way my life has turned out. And now—"

The intercom pinged, and Spider's jubilant voice filled the Bridge. "We did it! It worked! The signal's been jammed, and Eloch just fell asleep."

Grale and Aiko shared a smile.

"The Knack Man..." Grale said.

"...is back," Aiko finished. She pinched the bridge of her nose and let out a sigh. "I'm going to find a place to sleep, Grale. I've been up for too many hours, my eyes are blurring, and I'm having trouble concentrating."

She stood. "You've got this, right? Eventually that anomaly will be back. Once they see the signal is down, they're going to want to investigate. I want to be alert for that."

Grale nodded. "Smart. Sleep when you can. I'm fresh. I'll make sure we don't break apart while you're dreamin'."

Aiko snorted. "Okay, then, I'm heading out."

"Going to keep surveillance on you like I did Wren until you're safe in your room."

"Not necessary. Going to be bunking close to the med lab where everyone else is."

"It's necessary. *Caution First*." He paused, watching Aiko staring out the view panel as she swayed. "You're asleep on your feet. Go, Kitten. You know I've got this."

She pinched the bridge of her nose again. "Yeah, yeah. I think you might be right. I've really smacked into a wall. Must have been the relief at hearing Eloch's okay." She turned and left without a backward glance.

Grale watched her make her way down to the med lab. "No one should ever feel as alone as you do," he said softly. "Especially you, Kitten. Especially you."

Chapter 12 – On the Offensive

Eloch winced as he shifted positions.

He was still in the med lab, but they moved him to a more private room once Genji confirmed the spike embedded in his shoulder was no longer sending and receiving. He lay propped up in a bed that adjusted and contoured to his every move. Little Wonder was nestled on one side of him, Wren on the other. He looked down at where she lay with one arm across his middle and the other cradling her head. He reached over and fingered one of her coilmats.

Wren sighed and slowly opened her eyes. "Hi," she said with a smile.

"I heard you," he said.

She sleepily threaded her fingers with Eloch's. "Was I snoring? Did I wake you?"

He smiled and gave her hand a squeeze. "Little Wonder sleeps louder than you. No, when I was unconscious. I heard you talking to me, telling me to come back to you. It...helped."

"Thank you for telling me. I felt pretty useless, Eloch." Wren sat up, and Eloch winced again at the sudden movement. "Oh, Eloch, I'm sorry. It still hurts, doesn't it? That invisible thing."

"Yes, but not a physical pain. Hard to explain."

"We've got to get it out of you."

"Nothing I'd like better. But as long as it's not affecting me and I don't move, I can learn about it."

"We do, in fact, already know quite a lot about it." Wren yawned. "Think I need to get some tea. Brace yourself. I'm going to move again." She eased out of the bed and quickly redressed. "Do you need anything?"

"Just you, here, with me."

She smiled down at him. "Then I'll be back as soon as I can. We've all basically moved over to this side of the ship, galley and all, so I won't go far."

Wren took the time to relieve herself and wash her face and hands before collecting her tea in the makeshift galley. There she found Spider and Genji in deep conversation with Perin.

"Hello," Wren said. "What's happening?" she asked, helping herself to a steaming mug of tea.

All three looked up.

"Perin had another vision last night, and we're trying to decipher its meaning," Genji replied.

Wren lifted her brows. "Interesting." She looked at Perin, who seemed a bit pale. "I want to hear about it, but first, bring me up to speed."

"How's Eloch?" Spider asked.

"He's awake. Aware. I don't think the experience has affected him permanently, but it's a little soon to tell that. He's uncomfortable with that spike still in him. He seems to be coping, though, and is curious about how it works."

"May we go see him?" Genji asked. "Spider and I made a new gamma-ray readout device that should give us a better visual. We want to try it out."

Wren nodded. "Let me go check on him first, but I'm sure it'll be fine." She touched Perin's shoulder. "I want to hear what your True Dream was about. Why don't you come with us to see Eloch, and then you and I can find a private spot?"

"Of course," Perin answered. "Spider will you guide me, please? Who knows where my tapping stick is anymore?" she said mournfully.

"I'll make you another if it's lost," Spider said, helping her up and following behind Wren and Genji.

"What's up with the others?" Wren asked Genji, eyes on her mug. She'd filled it rather full.

"Wade, Kalea, and Mink are checking the Cryo beds and continuing with the cleanup," he said. "Aiko is sleeping a couple of rooms down. Grale is still on the Bridge, monitoring systems both inside and outside the ship. There is quite a bit of external damage. The robotics are analyzing and repairing what they can, but Grale said he may need to take a space walk. Take a look for himself."

"If he's up to it, I'm sure Eloch can take care of the ship's skin," Wren said, pausing at the entrance to Eloch's area.

Genji nodded, "But we don't want to tire him out so soon after his ordeal. He needs to take care of his own skin right now."

"You've got a point," she said and tapped on the doorframe before peeking in. "Up for some visitors, Eloch?"

"Yes," Eloch said, smiling.

Wren smiled. "You look like you knew I was returning with guests."

"I'm reconnected to the ship, so, yes, I knew." He smiled at them. "It's good to see you all."

Wren looked at the others. "Grab a couple more chairs and come on in," she told them. "Perin, take my arm and I'll guide you to a chair already here. Wait, my other arm. The mug's pretty full. Here, I'm going to take a couple of sips first." She blew on her tea, then sipped enough to keep it from spilling when she helped Perin.

Mug in one hand, Perin's hand in her other, Wren settled the Seer near Eloch's bedside.

Perin's face lit up. "You're much brighter," she told him, "And the metal flower is not flashing." She cupped her hands, mimicking what she saw.

"'Metal flower' is a good description for it," Genji said, setting down his chair and taking a seat. "It looks like a small sending-and-receiving disk. Which, I might add, we can now see quite clearly, using this." He held up the handheld unit he and Spider created.

Eloch reached for the device to examine the screen as Wren settled down beside him. She took a sip from her mug, then set it down to help hold the device so Eloch could angle his head in order to see the image as it scanned his shoulder. "I think I could replicate this so you can actually see and hold it. Will that help?" he asked.

"You can do that?" Genji asked, glancing at Spider.

Both Spider and Genji leaned forward.

"I believe so."

"It was a spike before it flowered," Perin said.

"I see where it unfolded," Eloch said. He studied the device's screen for a few moments longer, then handed it back to Genji and focused on his outstretched hand. A spike materialized in Eloch's hand.

Wren sucked in a breath.

"You should be used to this by now," Eloch told her with a grin.

She shook her head. "Never. It's always magic."

Genji and Spider held out their hands, but Eloch turned toward the Seer. "Perin, what do you think?" he asked. "Here, hold out your hand." He winced as he placed it gently into her upturned palm.

Perin's fingers danced lightly over the device. "It's longer than this," she said. "The tip more pointed."

"Other than that?" Eloch asked.

Her fingers tripped the catch near the spike's tip and the small dish unfolded from its housing. "Other than that, it's the same," she said.

"Good. Thank you."

She smiled and held out the device toward the colors that were Spider and Genji.

Genji took it. "I'd like to analyze the device." He looked at Spider.

"And I'll finish upgrading the ship's scanners so they can literally see the ship next time it returns. No more ghost ships."

"The anomaly. Is that what you ended up calling it, a ghost ship?" Eloch asked.

Wren nodded. "How you managed to get that device into you was the vision Perin kept seeing. She described a ghost ship that occupied the same space that the *Valiant* occupied," Wren said.

"Can you tell me what happened? I remember Perin telling me to duck, you pushing me, Wren. I stumbled back with a sudden pain in my shoulder. Where I was shot, I presume. After that, it's all very confusing."

"Well, you acted like you'd been drinking too much Entean Ale and started to collapse. I called to Genji, and he helped me get you down here to the med lab. Then somehow that stake was activated and the ship started falling apart. I had to use the fail-safe so Grale could put a field around the ship to keep it together. Then Genji and Spider stopped the stake from sending out its signal, and here

171

we are, with a little time to figure things out."

She looked up at Genji. "Want to add anything, Genj?"

"We believe the ship and crew are real, but are living in a different vibrational dimension from where we are," Genji explained. "To them, we are the ghosts. Spider knows more about this than I do."

"There is one on the other ship who can see us," Perin said. "Jon. I spoke with him."

Eloch cocked his head at her. "These people. What do they look like?"

"Like us, only very pale, with slanting dark eyes. They are very beautiful, and all looked the same to me, although I'm sure they are all very different from one another."

"And you said one could see you?" Eloch asked.

Perin nodded. "Yes. Jon."

"She had a True Dream about Jon last night," Spider announced.

"Is that what you three were talking about earlier?" Wren asked.

"Yes," Genji said. "We were trying to understand what she saw." He shrugged. "We didn't get very far."

Wren considered Perin while the Seer twisted her fingers together. "Let me help you, Perin. Would it be okay with you?" The relief she saw on Perin's face provided the answer even before Perin nodded.

"Thank you," Wren said to her. "As soon as we figure out how we're going to know when the ghost ship returns, you and I will go someplace private and discuss your True Dream."

"I will sense when it's returning," Eloch said. "We won't have too much time and must make the most of it. I want to remove this spike and then find a way to deflect the one they will most likely try to shoot at me again, although I still don't understand why I'm the target. How can they even know we're here if they're living in a different vibrational dimension?"

"They think you're a planet, Eloch," Genji said. "We believe this device and the people on the ghost ship are what the Sisters have been so afraid of. We think they're what has been attacking the planets in Vela Kentaurus. If we can stop them, we can keep our planets safe."

"I think it's more than they're attacking Sisters, Genji," Eloch said. "I felt my power draining from me. It was being used for something. If we can find out why they are draining the Sisters' power, then we can stop them. It's important to understand why they need all that power."

Wren put a hand on his arm. "Speaking of power, is yours back? Can we return the *Valiant* back to your care?"

Eloch covered Wren's hand. "Thanks to you, there still is a *Valiant*."

She smiled softly. "*Caution First*. Always. Thanks for trusting me."

He returned her smile. "I will always trust you, Wren. And yes, I've already taken my ship back into my care." His eyes grew distant, "We are both healing." He glanced around the room. "I promise you this will never happen again, and I thank you for your care."

"We all love you, Eloch," Wren said. "Of course we will take care of you."

"And it's not over until we get that spike out," Genji said, standing. "I'm going to excuse myself and get to my analysis."

"We've all got things to do," Wren said. She drained the last of her tea and slid off the bed, leaning over to kiss Eloch. "I'm going to discuss Perin's True Dreams with her. Little Wonder can keep you company."

Eloch smiled. "It's good to be awake," he said, sliding his hand down Wren's arm. It came to rest on Little Wonder's head.

The sniffer lifted her head with a churrup.

Wren smiled. "It is good to be awake. Stay with Eloch, LW. Let's go, Perin. Let me guide you back."

Before she left, Wren glanced one more time at Eloch. He wore the distant, inward expression he got when he was reaching beyond what she understood. She bet he was already learning how to remove the device the ghost ship had implanted in his shoulder region.

CHAPTER 13 – PERIN'S TRUE DREAM

"You must be relieved," Perin said as Wren lead her down toward their makeshift galley.

"Beyond," Wren said. "I'm not going to lie, Perin. I was terrified. I have never seen Eloch out of control—out of his mind—like that. I hope to never witness it again. No wonder the Sisters are so frightened. Look what happened to our ship. Can you imagine what would happen to a planet?"

Perin shuddered. "I don't want to imagine that."

"We've reached the galley. There's no one here, but is this private enough for you? Would you prefer somewhere else?" Wren asked.

Perin hesitated. "The stateroom where I slept last night is close by. I would rather go there."

"Not a problem. Let me refill my tea mug and we'll head over there. Would you like some tea as well?"

"That sounds nice. Thank you."

Wren left Perin standing near a table and filled two mugs before returning to the Seer. "If you hold onto my arm, I can guide you and carry our tea," she said.

Perin nodded. "It's only two rooms down on the left. I counted forty steps."

"Okay, let's go."

"I miss my stick," Perin said.

"We'll have to find you a replacement."

"That would be nice."

When the two women reached the stateroom, Perin felt for the panel and it opened at her touch.

Wren giggled. "You've made your bed! You're a much tidier person than I will ever be," she said. "There are two chairs over in the sitting area, let me guide you there," she said.

"Not necessary," Perin said. "You bring the tea." She gracefully crossed and sat, relaxing into her chair as it formed itself around her contours.

Wren handed Perin her tea and settled into the other chair. They briefly talked about music and sipped their tea before Wren changed the subject.

"So, you had a True Dream last night, did you?"

Perin nodded. "I should have known better than to mention it to Spider and Genji. They wanted to know all about it and," she blushed, "parts of it were personal. I tried to stop before that point, but I'm not good at lying. I think they sensed I hadn't told them everything that happened and were starting to insist that I tell them the dream again." She took a sip of her tea. "I was so relieved that you came in right then."

Wren smiled and shook her head. "Those two...they really aren't good at reading signals are they? Like sniffers chewing bones. Not going to let go until the final morsel is gnawed off and the marrow sucked out."

Perin laughed. "That's it exactly."

"Are you comfortable telling me about your vision?"

"Of course. It was personal, but not something I wouldn't share with a woman friend."

"Then please share whenever you're ready," Wren said.

"The True Dream did not last long. They never do, really, usually just a series of images. It's the details that are so important," Perin explained.

Wren nodded. "Go on."

"I was on a ship, and it didn't feel familiar. I don't believe it was this one."

"I see."

"I believe I was on the ghost ship. That's the important part, you see, and that is all that I wanted to tell Genji and Spider, but they wanted more details."

"Such as?"

"What did it look like, who was I with, were we conversing, what about, and so forth. Details."

"And?"

Perin blushed. "Well, I was with Jon, and we were in an embrace, and he was kissing me. He asked me not to go, told me to stay with him, be with him always." She smiled softly at the memory.

"That's very romantic."

"Yes, it was," Perin agreed, a smile tugging at the corner of her mouth. "But don't you see what this means?" She reached out and grabbed Wren's hand. "It means we somehow connected with the ghost ship. I actually *traveled* to the ghost ship. I was actually standing on the ghost ship. And I could *see*! The way I used to. Somehow, it is all going to happen."

"Forgive me for asking, but I must, Perin," Wren said, squeezing her hand. "Could this dream of yours just be that? A dream?"

"No, Wren. I swear by The Lady, it was a True Dream."

"By the gods, Perin," Wren breathed. "And you only saw Jon, nobody else?"

Perin shook her head. "No, no one. But surely I didn't get there on my own."

Wren tucked a leg underneath her and took another sip of tea. "What I find so interesting is you could understand each other, and you could breathe the same air. That's correct, isn't it? I didn't overlook anything?"

Perin nodded. "I've learned there are translation devices, so perhaps we were communicating through one of those. But I was not wearing any breathing apparatus. In fact, I was wearing what I usually wear." She chewed her lip. "It's important information, but I really don't want to tell anybody I was kissing Jon."

"Totally understandable. And it isn't really necessary. We just have to figure out a way to tell the facts while keeping the personal stuff out of the telling." She set down her mug. "Let's imagine you are back on Talamh. What parts of the dream would you tell your High Priest?"

Perin pursed her lips, then began to describe what happened, gathering momentum as she continued. "I would tell him I was on board the ghost ship. I could breathe without any apparatus, and I could easily communicate with the people. I only saw one person, Jon, the individual from the prior True Dream. I knew he was my friend. To me, the dream means we will be able to establish a relationship with the ghost ship and that Jon is the key."

Wren clapped her hands. "Well done, Perin. And that is exactly what you're going to say."

~ ~ ~

Eloch relaxed in the bed, absently toying with Little Wonder's ears and listening to Grale, Mink, and Spider work together. He extended his senses, found Kalea and Wade cleaning up debris and scanning the Cryo beds. Extending farther, he found where Aiko was sleeping, where Wren sat with Perin, and where Grale worked on the Bridge, diligently scanning the ship and the outlying area while they maintained their orbit.

Then Eloch extended farther and became his ship. He felt the hulls and checked for tears in the skin. Remembering Wren's advice, he allowed Grale to monitor the robotics and make most of the repairs. Eloch worked on the external repairs and gathered the parts of the ship that had broken off and were floating away. He reshaped them and bound them back into his ship's framework.

Satisfied, Eloch turned his attention to the Solar Farm. He paused in dismay. Without his ongoing attention, many of the plants had withered, some had died. Trees had been uprooted. Water had overflowed its channels and pooled in unlikely places. His creatures had died as well. He could not find one butterfly.

He did what he could to stabilize his forests and meadows, and those who had perished he reabsorbed into the ship.

Later, after the emergency was taken care of, he would recreate each and every one of his plants, creatures, and waterways, vowing that never again would something like this occur. Never again would Wren be forced to activate the fail-safe she had so wisely begged him to create.

Satisfied for the moment, Eloch turned his attention toward a more pressing matter, the object that had wounded him. All this damage, he thought, caused by the small mechanism invisibly lodged in his body. It chilled him to imagine what would happen if such an object were to lodge itself in his beloved Entean or in any of the Sisters, for that matter. They had reason to be afraid.

He made another vow. He would end this.

Eloch wrapped his senses around the spike, recalling what he had seen through the instrument Genji and Spider made. Perin was right. The stake's shaft was much longer, lodged deep within his body...or at least some form of his body that vibrated at a different frequency than he had ever encountered.

179

Accustomed to the way a planet experienced her surroundings, Eloch was very familiar with gamma rays. He could feel the gamma energy on the *Valiant's* skin as his ship slid through space. It was powerful and harmful to life.

Yet Genji had suggested that not only was the spike vibrating at the gamma ray frequency, but that those who created it vibrated at that energy frequency as well. What kind of species would they be? Perin said the people on the ghost ship looked just like them, like everybody on the *Valiant*. How could that be? What was he missing?

He continued probing the spike and wondered if he was concentrating too much on the destructive qualities of the gamma ray frequency rather than seeing it as a frequency, an energy, or, as Genji and Spider had explained, a faster-moving wave of light. Obviously, there was a part of him that was already vibrating at that frequency or he would not be as wounded as he was.

What if he allowed his entire body to vibrate at that speed? What then?

~~~

Genji sighed. "We're just running in circles," he said through clenched teeth. "Let's take a break. Eat something. My Nuri needs to stretch his wings."

"I think it's a good stopping place," said Mink. "While you stretch your wings, Spider and I can install the new sensor on the Bridge."

"And eat," said Spider. "I'm feeling rather peckish myself." He groaned. "And stiff. I've been sitting hunched over this screen for too long. What, Genj?" he asked, having noticed Genji's sudden stillness.

Genji didn't answer. Looking wide-eyed at something behind Spider, he half rose in his seat, nostrils flaring.

Spider cautiously turned to look. "Oh," was all he could manage.

Little Wonder darted out of the area where Eloch lay on his pallet, hissing and growling, then paced stiff-legged in front of the entryway. Light pulsed brighter and brighter, so bright it nearly burned, forcing Spider to shield his eyes. Suddenly, the light was gone.

Spider glanced at both Genji and Mink. "D-did you two see what I just saw?"

All three lunged up out of their seats and scrambled to the opening to peer in at Eloch.

"Where did he go?" Spider whispered.

Mink scooped Little Wonder up off the floor and smoothed her ruffled fur.

Genji stood silently, his brows drawn together.

Wren came tearing into the med lab, her eyes wide. She gasped when she saw the empty bed. "I felt him...and then I didn't anymore," she said and reached for Little Wonder, taking her from Mink. "What happened?" She held the sniffer close.

"I believe Eloch was experimenting with frequencies," Genji said. "There can be no other explanation."

"What can we do?" Wren asked him.

Spider raced back to his work area and snatched up the makeshift frequency scanner. He held it up in front of the bed, looked at the screen, and gasped. "Look!" he said, holding it so the four of them could watch through the viewer.

Through the screen, they saw Eloch sitting up on his pallet, examining his right shoulder. He had splayed the fingers of his right hand around the spike, hand flat on his chest, thumb holding his shoulder still. With his left hand, he gripped the device and slowly pulled it out of his body.

"It's so much longer than the copy he made for us," Genji said and winced.

Through the viewer, they saw Eloch slump against the pillows.

Wren gasped, took half a step toward the empty bed. Mink touched her shoulder. "Wait, Wren," she whispered calmly.

Gripping the spike, Eloch slowly lowered it down to his lap. With his other hand, he shakily rubbed at the area where the spike had been.

"Interesting," Genji said, leaning forward to touch the rim of the scanner.

Through the viewer, they watched Eloch study the device, turning it this way and that. He wiped it on the bedsheets, apparently cleaning it. Looking down at his chest, he wiped the injured area as well before easing himself back against the bed. For several moments, he was still. Then his image began to fade from the viewer.

"Wha—?" Wren began.

"Close your eyes!" Genji shouted as light again flared into the room.

When they opened their eyes, Eloch was back in the bed, grasping the now-visible device. He nodded at them and held up the spike. "I did it," he said as the color returned to his face.

"Can you explain what just happened?" Wren asked, trying to decide if she was relieved or angry or both.

"Since something was in me that could be seen on Genji's scanner, I wondered if I could take all of me to that place and then pull it out." He held up the device. "And apparently I can."

Wren handed the sniffer back to Mink and reached out to take the device from Eloch. Without shifting her gaze away from Eloch, she handed it to Genji. "Will you all please leave so Eloch and I can have a moment of privacy?" she asked, her voice flat. She waited, arms folded, until they had shuffled out.

When it was just the two of them, Wren climbed onto the bed, covering Eloch's body with her own. He was so big she could stretch out flat if she wanted to. Instead she curled around him until she felt Eloch's arms wrap around her.

As he gently stroked her back, she laid her cheek on his chest and listened to his heart beat. It was steady and strong, just like him. She sighed, allowing herself to relax into the moment.

Finally, she lifted her head and gazed into his deep green eyes. "I can take a lot, Eloch," she said, "but losing you?" She shook her head. "That would destroy me."

Eloch pushed back Wren's coilmats and took her face in his hands. "You will never lose me, my heart. You are my home."

She sighed and rested her cheek on his broad chest again. "Does it hurt?"

"Not really. Just a slight twinge."

"You wiped it. Was there blood?" She shivered.

"I don't know what it was. Some clear, viscous matter. I started healing as soon as I pulled the stake out."

"And now?"

"I'm continuing to heal."

"Good," she sighed.

Chapter 14 - Decisions

Since a meeting was scheduled in an hour, Grale took it upon himself to wake Aiko. She'd been sleeping for six hours, so he figured she was rested enough. Even if she wasn't, he knew she'd be spitting mad if she slept through a meeting.

He knocked softly on the door to her cabin and waited a few moments. When there was no response, he waved his hand across the activation panel. It slid open, and he called her name in a low voice. When there was still no response, he went in.

In the dim light, Grale could barely see her where she was all curled up in a ball on the bed. He stood at the foot of the bed, watching her breathe, her chest rising and falling, her hands tucked under her pillow.

Aiko's face was relaxed, and he tried to remember the last time he saw her that relaxed. Then he wondered if he had ever seen her that way. He wasn't sure. Maybe at that party about three years ago. That time he thought that maybe...

He stomped on his thoughts. Didn't matter what he thought. Nothing happened, so he squashed that hopeful "what if" dream before it could overtake him again.

No, he decided, he had never seen Aiko look relaxed. When she was awake, she was all focus. It surprised him, but he liked that about her. Truth was, there was a lot about Aiko he liked. It just seemed like there was never the right time to tell her what he liked about her. It was beginning to eat at him.

They'd been flying together for nearly twenty years. That was longer than he'd known anyone else, ever. And the thing was, he felt like he'd just scratched the surface of getting to know her. And he really did want to get to know her.

Without thinking, Grale moved to sit beside her. She was sleeping so soundly the sag from his weight didn't even make her stir. So he reached out tentatively and stroked her hair.

It slipped through his fingers like water.

He leaned forward and inhaled. She smelled fresh, a little like flowers and a lot like Aiko. Feeling foolish, Grale straightened. She was so small, he thought, in her tiny ball, just like his nickname for her. That made him grin.

"Kitten," he said as he stroked her head. "Time to wake up."

Aiko was instantly awake. She shot up fast, giving him no time to move out of the way.

They collided.

"My nose!" he cried out, cupping his face. "You smashed my nose!" he moaned and ground out a string of swear words.

"Sorry," Aiko said, still a little groggy. She rubbed her forehead. "Ouch," she muttered. "That *hurt.*"

"Is it bleeding?" he asked, his eyes tearing up.

"Let me see. Move your hands, I can't see."

Grale lowered his hands.

She peered at his face, "No, no blood. Lots of snot, but no blood."

Grale cupped his face again. "That's good. Hurts like a son of a bitch." He blinked at her through his tears. "You sure know how to kill a moment," he groused.

She stilled, very much aware she was wearing nothing but a T-shirt.

"What are you doing in here, Grale?" she asked, eyes narrowing.

"There's a meeting in ten in the galley...the usual one, not the makeshift one. Didn't think you'd want to miss it." He gingerly felt his nose. "You sure it's not broken?"

Aiko grinned. "Who knew the Cowboy was such a big baby? No, it's not broken. You may end up with a couple of black eyes, but it's not broken, I can assure you."

She leaned closer to him. "How about my forehead? Am I starting to get a bruise?"

He took her head in his hands and turned it toward the little bit of light leaking from the bathroom. "Might be a bump there." He grinned wolfishly, "Want me to kiss the booboo?"

Aiko refused to acknowledge the burning in her cheeks. "No, thank you. A meeting in ten, you say? Will you leave, then, so I can get ready?"

"Yeah, of course, your ladyship," he said, rising. "You're going to need plenty of time to disguise that nasty bump." He paused at the doorway and turned to look at her. "If I ever need to I wake you again, I think I'll poke you with a stick or something."

Aiko laughed. "Go blow your nose before the meeting, Cowboy, and thanks for waking me."

~~~

Aiko had been worried she was late but, to her surprise, Mink was the only one in the galley when she entered. She blew out a breath, happy she could relax and grab a cup of coffee, glad the galley was back online and she didn't have to wait long.

She filled her mug and took a seat by Mink, sampling the rich brew. She glanced at Mink and smiled. "I can never decide which I like more, the flavor or the scent of a good cup of coffee." She took another sip. "This one's got both."

187

Mink gave her a smile. "You're looking more rested than the last time I saw you."

Aiko nodded. "Feel more rested, too. Those were an intense forty-eight hours. You get any rest?"

Mink shook her head. "But I think I'll be able to soon. Curious to hear why Eloch called this meeting. It was pretty wild what happened earlier, removing that spike and all."

Aiko felt her brows rise. "The spike is out? I thought the only thing we could do was jam the signal."

"That's all *we* could do, but Eloch could do more." Mink summarized what transpired at the med lab.

Aiko was silent for a few moments, taking another sip of her coffee, nodding to Genji and Kalea as they entered the room and found their seats. "I wish I had seen that," she told Mink.

"Seen what?" Grale asked as he joined them. Perin was on his arm, and he gently guided her to a chair. Then he settled in beside Aiko as Spider and Wade strolled in and headed to the beverage dispensers.

"Mink was telling me how Eloch managed to extract the spike from his shoulder."

Grale nodded. "I wished I could have seen that one, too."

She studied him as he spoke. There was a little blackening under his eyes, and she felt a twinge of guilt. "How's the nose?"

"Hurts. But like you said, it's not broken. And your forehead?"

She smiled. "There's a small bump. Doesn't hurt. I'm sorry you got clipped."

He shrugged. "Wasn't your fault." He looked at her half-finished coffee. "That looks like a good idea." He rose. "Want a refill?"

"Thanks," Aiko replied, handing him her mug. She watched him move away, then turned to the group. She sensed a shift in her friends. Everyone felt nervous and skittish. She did as well.

But they had survived. That thought flooded her with a deep sense of satisfaction. They had survived. They had protected Eloch. They had all leaned on each other's strengths, and they'd survived.

Genji glanced at her. "What is it, Aiko?" he asked.

"I was just thinking how well we all work together in a crisis. I was thinking how good that feels." She took the mug Grale held out to her. "Thanks, Cowboy," she said. When she looked back at Genji, he was smiling. They all were.

"Yeah," Genji said. "It does feel good."

"What feels good?" Wren asked as she and Eloch entered the room.

"We survived. We pulled together and survived," Aiko said. "Good to see you back with us, Eloch. And," she said squinting at what he was holding, "what is that in your hand?"

Eloch held it up. "The reason we're here," he answered. "It's what was in me, and it's also the *Something That Comes*, the thing Entean and Her Sisters are so afraid of." He paused. "They have just cause," he added. "This must end. Now."

As one, Eloch and Wren sat. Genji held out his hand, and Eloch gave him the alien device in it.

Aiko blinked. "It's much bigger than I thought it would be."

Eloch nodded. "It was buried pretty deep inside my body."

"Mink told me how you pulled it out." She grimaced. "Must have hurt."

"Not as much as you'd think. But I'm not sure why," Eloch mused.

"Perhaps everything vibrates at such a faster pace in that frequency?" Spider guessed.

"Maybe."

Genji carefully probed the device, muttering, "Can't wait to dismantle this and find out how it works."

"I want to know what it's for," said Spider.

"I'm not sure we will know what it's used for until we can discuss it with the ones who did this to me," Eloch said.

Everyone around the table went silent.

Eloch looked at Wren, who nodded and leaned against him.

"As you all know by now," he said, "in order for me to rid myself of this device, I had to match my frequency to its frequency, to where it originated. Then, after its removal, I slowed both it and myself down so I could again return to this frequency. I believe if I can do that, then I should also be able to do the same thing with the *Valiant* and everything within it, including all of you."

Aiko scanned the faces of the group, knowing beyond a doubt that her face expressed the same skepticism she saw on those around her.

"The *Valiant*," Grale said into the silence, "is quite a bit larger than that stake Genji's holding."

"Yes and no," Eloch said and glanced again at Wren. "Over the years, this ship has become more and more a part of me. I'm sure you're aware of that."

"Well, if we weren't, we sure are now. It nearly fell apart while you were under the influence of that thing," Wade said, nodding at the device still in Genji's grasp.

Eloch nodded. "And because the ship *is* part of me, I can move the *Valient* to that frequency as easily as I can move myself."

"And us?" Spider asked. "Can you move us along with the ship?"

"We're going to find out," Wren said, "when Eloch takes me there."

"It should be me," Perin said, raising her voice over the commotion.

"We can't ask you to risk your life like that, Perin," Wren said quietly.

Perin shook her head. "We know I will get there. The True Dream told us that. And since I will get there, Eloch must have brought me."

"She makes a valid point," Eloch told Wren.

"I need to go, Eloch. I don't want to be separated from you again," Wren said. "Not ever again."

Aiko had never been jealous of Wren and Eloch, but in that moment, the look they shared did something to her. *That look,* she realized. *I want that. I've always wanted it.*

"Then it will be the three of us," Eloch said.

With a nod, Perin sat back, arms folded.

"How's this going to work?" Aiko asked.

"That's why we're all here," Eloch. "We have to make some decisions."

Wren nodded and sat up straighter. "We're at a crossroads, and we each need to decide what's next for us as individuals," she said.

"My mission is not your mission," Eloch said. "I must continue forward. I must speak with these higher-frequency people and somehow get them to stop interfering with the Sisters of Vela Kentaurus, as well as keep them from expanding into our galaxy."

Spider raised his hand. "I know this is just semantics, but let's come up with something to call these people. Something other than 'higher-frequency people.' It doesn't sit well with me. There's nothing higher about them, other than the dimension in which they're living, and it's just about wavelengths. They're living in a different place, and that's all. No better than us, no worse."

"So you're objecting to the word 'higher,'" Genji said.

"Yes, I am," Spider responded. "Makes me feel lower. And I'm not lower. That's the point I'm trying to make. We're living in the same place, only in different frequencies. They're ghosts to us, and we're ghosts to them."

Grale leaned over to Aiko, "I kind of liked the ghost ship idea. Ghost people. Ghosts." He waggled his fingers and made a face. "Boo."

She covered her grin with her hand.

"How about our Frequency Neighbors?" Mink asked.

"They are more like Frequency Neighbors," Wade agreed.

"If they're ghosts to us, and we're ghosts to them, perhaps they're unaware of the destruction they are causing," Perin said.

"Good point," Wren said.

"I like Frequency Neighbors," Eloch said.

"So do I," Genji said.

"Works for me," Wren said.

"Anything is fine by me," Grale said.

Aiko lifted her hands. "No opinion."

"Spider, you good with Frequency Neighbors?" Wren asked.

"Can we shorten it a bit?" Spider asked sheepishly.

Grale rolled his eyes. "Freak Neighs?"

Spider laughed. "I know I'm being a little anal. Frequency Neighbors sounds nice, but it's a mouthful. Can we just go with the initials? FN?"

"FN," Wren said. "Everyone good with that? We've got more to cover."

"I'll say," Genji said. "Like what will we do when the FNs return?"

"And, more importantly," Eloch said, "who wants to continue on with me, and who wants to go home?"

"There's a choice?" Kalea asked, straightening.

"Of course there's a choice," Eloch replied.

CHAPTER 15 □ CHOICES

"How?" Wade asked. "How can some of us go home and others go with you? Are you going to split the ship in two?" He smirked.

"That's exactly what I'm prepared to do," Eloch said. "Maybe not quite in two."

Aiko raised a brow at Grale.

He shrugged, mouthing *Knack Man*

"I know we were all prepared for this to be a long journey," Eloch continued. "Maybe even a journey we wouldn't return from. But like Wren said, we're at a crossroads, and I think it's fair to make it possible for those who wish to go back to do so." He looked at Kalea, "Don't you think that's fair?"

Kalea lowered her eyes. "Very fair," she whispered.

Genji looked up from the stake he'd been studying. "This technology is fascinating." He glanced around, his enthusiasm dimming. "I've missed something, haven't I?" He glanced at Kalea. "What am I missing?"

She kept her eyes lowered and shook her head.

"Look," Wren said, "Why don't we take a break and think about it? Right now, I think it's important simply to know it's possible for those who want to go home to go home. Nobody here had any idea there was such a choice. And now Eloch has offered it, so let's just mull this over and see what happens."

She clasped her hands on the table in front of her. "In the meantime, let's all grab a quick meal, then get busy. We need to plan how we're going to face the FNs, and we need to see how that," she grinned at Genji, "*fascinating thing* works. And of course, Eloch, Perin, and I need to practice traveling between Frequency Neighborhoods.

"Aiko, can you, Grale, and Wade check and double-check the new tech that was installed? We'll want to see more than an anomaly next time."

"Give me an hour to wash up and eat something, and I'll get right on it," Aiko said. "I literally crawled out of bed ten minutes before this meeting began."

Wren smiled. "I'm sure we've got time for that. Do you need longer?"

Aiko finger-combed her hair. "Nope, I'm good."

Wren nodded. "Genji, Kalea, Spider, and Mink, you four want to analyze the device? See what it can and cannot do?" She laughed when she saw Genji and Spider's expressions. "Okay, think I hit the sweet spot with that one."

She got to her feet and turned to Perin and Eloch. "Perin, Eloch, I've got some questions for you both before we begin our neighborhood stroll. Shall we go to the Solar Farm with a picnic and relax a little bit while I ask the questions I've been saving up?"

Eloch stood and wrapped an arm around her shoulders "You won't get an argument from me."

"Nor me," Perin said.

"Great!" Wren said, "I'll put the picnic together and meet you both in Eloch's special spot."

~~~

"Spider and Mink, I'm skipping lunch and going back to the Lab," Genji said.

"I'll go with, Genji," Kalea said.

"Sure, see you in a few," Spider said. "Don't try to do it all on your own. Save some of the fun for me."

"There will be plenty of fun left for you," Genji said with a laugh as he and Kalea left the Galley. "Let's hurry," he said, taking her hand, his enthusiasm quickening his pace. "I want to take this device apart ASAP, try to understand how it works and what it's used for, because I doubt that it's used solely to capture the energy of a planet.

"I agree with Eloch. There must be a valid reason for why they need so much energy. And assuming we're ghosts to them as they are ghosts to us, then perhaps they don't even understand that they're draining planets of their life force. Perin thinks so."

He glanced over at Kalea and froze. "What is it, love?"

"Kind Genji, my beloved mate," she said quietly, eyes searching his face. "I wish to go home."

"Oh." He sucked in a breath. "Oh, I see."

"My Nuri wishes to fly free in Longwei's skies. I willingly left, Genji, to follow you and explore. I did. And I don't regret a single moment. But," her eyes sparkled, "Eloch says there's a choice. And now all I can think about is the smell of the salt air and flying high above the volcano, playing in the thermal spirals."

Genji flashed to a memory of Kalea taking a swan dive off a cliff and transforming into her Nuri form, soaring and spinning in the air currents. He remembered how it felt, skimming through heated air saturated with the moist, heady fragrances of a thousand tropical plants.

Genji reached out and gathered Kalea to him, felt her arms wrap around his waist, their mirrored tattoos blending. When was the last time she had let her beautiful hair tumble all around her? He looked at the spike still in his hand. "I can take things apart and learn from them anywhere in the universe, Kalea," he said. "But there is only one Longwei, and that is where you and I truly belong because we are Nuri." He drew back a bit and gazed into her

197

luminous eyes. "Shall we go home, love?"

~~~

Eloch had done a great deal to repair his world within the ship's hull, and he was pleased with the results. The uprooted and destroyed foliage was beginning to grow, reminding Eloch of springtime after a long Entean winter. He led Wren and Perin down to the lake, once more back in place, and the three settled near its shore.

Wren guided Perin to a blanket Eloch created for them, and when she was settled, Wren handed her a plate of fruit and cheese Eloch also created for them. She took the second one and began to eat.

Between bites, she and Eloch took turns describing Little Wonder's antics to Perin. The mini-sniffer was thoroughly enjoying all the sights and smells, racing around, leaping high in the air and rolling in the sweet grasses. When she had worn herself out, she returned to the trio. Wren allowed the tired sniffer to curl up on her lap.

"So, Eloch," Wren began as she wiped her fingers on her napkin and set it down beside her. Fingers cleaned, she stroked the sniffer's soft fur, smiling at LW's rumbles of pleasure. "If you took us to that higher frequency, where would we end up? Floating in space?"

Eloch shook his head. "I don't believe so. When I took myself, I was still in the same place, on the ship, in bed in the med lab."

"I don't understand." Wren picked up her napkin and tossed it onto her plate. She giggled when the sniffer's paw darted out to swipe as it sailed past. "We were also on the ship and saw you disappear. The *Valiant* didn't disappear around us. You did. So if you disappeared, but you said you were still sitting in bed…"

She shook her head. "How can that be?" She chewed her lip. "Unless, since this ship is a part of you, some of the ship travelled with you? Or maybe part of the ship is already vibrating at that level? But then wouldn't the FNs have seen that part? Spider said we're ghosts to them."

198

She tugged on a coilmat, frowning. "I don't get it. If we do manage to travel to the FN frequency, what will they see? A whole ship? A part of a ship? Three people suddenly visible, bobbing around in space?"

Eloch sighed. "Let's leave the science to Genji and Spider, Wren. I honestly don't have an answer for you," Eloch told her. "Besides, do we really need to know how it works as long as I can make it work?"

"And it will work," Perin said. "I have seen it."

Wren threw up her hands, jostling Little Wonder. "You're both right, of course," Wren said. "But it's hard to do *Caution First* when I have no idea what's going to happen or how it will happen."

Little Wonder gave her a disgruntled look and moved off her lap and onto the picnic blanket between Wren and Eloch.

Wren watched the sniffer resettle herself. "Okay then, if it works, it works, and that's what counts," she said, putting an apologetic hand on Little Wonder. "And how we get onto their ship doesn't really matter right now anyway. We haven't even reached their neighborhood."

Perin chuckled.

"But we know we'll get there because Perin had a True Dream," Eloch commented.

"I did," said Perin.

"Let's do this now," Wren said suddenly.

"Now?" Eloch asked.

"Why not? This is your favorite place on the ship. I'm thinking it would be the easiest place for you to practice. I'm ready. You ready, Perin?"

"Yes," she said. "I don't like putting things off if it's not necessary."

Eloch got to his feet. "Okay, then." He paused, frowning. "I'm not sure how to begin. Let's see... Why don't we all three stand and join hands?"

"Shouldn't we have a witness?" Wren asked as they stood.

"Not this first time, if you don't mind," Eloch said. "I don't want distractions until I get comfortable with the process."

"It will be well," Perin assured Eloch. "Your light shines bright." She held out her hands.

"I appreciate your trust, Perin," he said, taking her hand, grasping Wren's with his other. When they were joined, he took a breath. "You should know that when I traveled there, I became very heated. It was nearly unbearable. I will do my best to keep you both safe, but if it is too much for either of you, squeeze my hand and I will stop immediately."

"Got it," Wren said.

"And close your eyes until I say you can open them," Eloch said. "Close your eyes now, and I will begin on the count of three."

Eloch waited. As soon as their eyes were closed, he silently counted to three and focused on repeating what he had done the previous time.

~~~

The heat was intense, and flashes of colored lights danced against Wren's eyelids. It was like being plunged into the middle of a one of Longwei's lava pits, and she was sure her skin was turning as black as her animated leg.

She gasped and held tightly to Perin and Eloch's hands, refusing to signal for Eloch to stop, even though the heat was becoming intolerable. Just when Wren made the decision to squeeze Eloch's hand to make it stop, the heat ceased.

"We're here," Eloch said, his deep voice a salve to her frayed nerves.

Wren opened her eyes and looked into Eloch's. His eyes still sizzled with power, deep green embers gazing back at her.

Wren sucked in a breath. "Ouch," she said.

Perin's knees buckled, pulling Wren down to the picnic blanket with her. She landed on her knees beside the Seer. "Perin?" Wren scrambled over and helped her sit up.

Eloch squatted down on the other side. "Steady," he said, a hand on Perin's shoulder.

Perin ran a hand over her face and took a breath. Letting her hand fall to her lap, she took another deep breath and opened her eyes, blinking. "Wren!" she said. "I can see you! Just like my True Dream. I see *you*." She looked over at Eloch. "And you. I see you, too. Not just energy, but real." She held her hands out, her mouth forming a silent O as she turned them palms up, then palms down.

Wren looked at the blanket where they were seated. "Where's Little Wonder?"

"Back in that other dimension, I assume," Eloch replied. "I didn't bring her."

Wren looked up and gasped. Arching high above them was a web of energy, pulsing in different colors and hues. Beyond that, she saw only black space dotted with stars. "What is that?"

"I'm assuming that dome is what our ship's hull looks like in this dimension," Eloch said. "When I traveled here before, I was concentrating on removing the stake and didn't look up. It's quite beautiful, isn't it?"

Wren nodded. "Reminds me of a vid Spider showed me a long time ago." She swept her hand above her. "Brain neurons look just like that."

Perin stopped looking at her hands and looked up. "That's not what I see."

"What do you see?" Eloch asked, standing and helping the two to their feet.

"I see you, Eloch," she answered. "I mean, I see the energy...the light...that I see when I look at your body back in our dimension." She squinted up at him. "Here, when I look at you, I can see your features overlaying the light. And above is only the light." She gestured at the blanket, "This blanket is just a blanket, but the trees surrounding us all are overlaying the light that is you."

She looked at Wren and smiled. "You, with your eyes all wide looking at me, have a different light spilling out of you. Different from Eloch's."

"Huh," Wren said, and looked around. "I see the neuron-looking things in the shape of trees. I can still see trees and the lake and all that, but the neuron-looking things are all there, too." She looked down. "The blanket still looks like the blanket. Maybe everything that isn't Eloch will still look like what we normally see," she mused, shifting her gaze to Perin. She beamed. "And *you*, Perin, look like yourself, only your eyes aren't cloudy white. They're the most beautiful blue."

Perin beamed back. "I think I like it here. I feel..." she searched for the right word. "Normal. I feel normal here."

"Interesting," Eloch said, his voice hushed. "One thing you are both saying which stands out to me is how connected I am to this ship, this world I've created. It really *is* me. Everything I have created is an extension of myself."

Wren nodded. "We knew that, Eloch, but now we *know* it."

They stood in silence, looking up. "It's so beautiful," Wren breathed.

"Ready to return?" Eloch asked. "I want to think about this, figure out a way to make the transition easier for us if possible."

"The heat," Perin and Wren said in unison.

"Fortunately, the heat isn't nearly as intense on the return." He stretched out his hands, and they clasped his like before.

Perin looked around one more time. "I love being able to see this way," she said. "It's been so long. I look forward to coming back here."

Wren squeezed her hand.

Eloch nodded. "For now, we go. So close your eyes again, and count to three like before."

The transition was nearly instantaneous. Wren opened her eyes and looked up at the ceiling. "We're back," she said and looked down. "And there's Little Wonder again, still asleep." She laughed, then clutched her stomach. "I'm feeling kind of funny," she said.

"Me, too," Perin said. She made a gagging sound.

Eloch rested a hand on each of their shoulders, sending them healing warmth. He waited until the color came back to their faces before he removed his hands. "Better?" he asked.

"Yes," they said in unison.

"But I think I'd like to sit and rest for a little bit," Perin said.

"Me, too," agreed Wren. She took a deep breath and blew it out. "That was a wild ride," she exclaimed. And then, staring into the distance, "...a wild ride."

~~~

Longwei.

(A pause.)

Greetings, Brother. It has been several days.

(A pause.)

Yes. It has become harder for me to reach you.

(A pause.)

I see. I will reach out to you. What news have you?

(A pause.)

I was wounded by That Which Comes.

(A pause)

And have you recovered?

Sufficiently, yes.

And have you stopped That Which Comes?

Not yet, but we are close. We have found a way to neutralize the threat and are making plans to negotiate.

(A pause.)

The other Sisters, our neighbors from Vela Kentaurus, are still unwell, yet no further deaths.

Good. If negotiations fail, we will still be able to free them, and they will recover as I did. It will take many more years, but it will happen.

(A pause.)

I am pleased. I will relay the information.

I am returning Kalea and Genji to you.

(A pause.)

Are they dishonored?

No. In fact, Genji—

Kalea's Mate.

Yes, Kalea's Mate, saved my life.

I am pleased. Kalea chose well.

Yes. Kalea's Mate will be bringing back the weapon that wounded me. He will learn from it and devise a way to better neutralize the threat. With his knowledge, You will have even greater protection against That Which Comes.

And I will have My beloved Kalea with Me once more.

Yes.

(A pause)

Longwei?

Yes, Brother?

I plan to alter Kalea and her Mate. It will be nearly twenty years until they arrive. With Your permission, I will make it so they remain young.

(A pause)

You have my permission, Brother. I appreciate your asking. I will keep Kalea's remaining family young as well.

That will bring her much joy, although it is You she yearns for.

This pleases me greatly.

I am also returning to You Wade of the Ancestors. He is unhappy. If he chooses, I will also help him remain young.

Understood.

(A pause)

Where I go, I do not believe I will be able to communicate. This may be the last time we will converse. Tell Entean, my planet, tell Her....

(A pause)

Entean knows, Brother. We all know of the sacrifices you have made. We trust Our gifts, the power We have shared with you, have eased some of the sorrow.

Yes, Longwei. I am grateful.

I look forward to seeing My Kalea and her Mate. They will be treated as great warriors for the rest of their days.

Thank you. They have earned the right.

Chapter 16 - Plans

Genji reached for Kalea's hand, "Kalea and I would like to go home, back to Longwei," he told the group as they sat together around the galley table. "Our Nuri will be happier."

Eloch nodded. "Understood," he said.

"You don't seem surprised," Genji said.

"I'm not," Eloch said with a smile. "And Longwei is looking forward to your return. She told me you will be honored as great warriors."

Kalea peered at Eloch. "You already told Longwei we were returning?" she accused.

Eloch shot her an apologetic shrug before replying to Genji. "After you and Spider have analyzed it and understand its purpose, take the device with you. Perhaps you can create a defense for the Sisters in case our mission fails."

"*Caution First*," Wren said with a grin. Then she sobered. "I know you need to go home, but I sure will miss you both."

"Likewise," Genji said. He was about to say more, then shook his head.

Kalea squeezed his hand.

"I want to go back to Longwei as well," Wade said. "I know the ship," he shrugged. "Or I did before Eloch started playing with it, but I can help with the wormhole jumps, and I'm good at troubleshooting. And," he added, "I've been on this rust bucket for

207

a thousand years. That stint on Talamh wasn't nearly long enough. I would like to end my days dirtside somewhere."

Mink sucked in a breath. "Wade! You can't," she pouted. "It won't be the same." She reached out her hand.

Wade gripped it hard. "You'll get by, Mink. You and Spider have each other."

Mink glanced at Spider and smiled. "I don't know what I'd do without Spider. But you're my Cryo partner. We've kept shifts together for so long, it's like... I don't know." She released Wade's hand with a sigh. "It's going to be hard, is all."

Wade grinned and gave her a friendly arm punch. "I'm not gone yet."

"I'm going, too," Aiko said.

Grale made a strange choking sound.

She looked quickly at Grale. "What? They're going to need a pilot."

"No, we won't, Aiko," Genji said.

"But you don't have the knack to line up the wormholes," Aiko protested.

Genji shook his head. "I'm not going to let you make this sacrifice, Aiko. I know how much you want to continue with this journey. How many missions have we been on together? How many times have I watched you line up for a jump?" He paused, waiting for an answer. When none came, he continued. "That's right. Countless times. And I'm smart. I may not have knack, but I've got my brain and keen observational skills."

"And he's got me," said Wade.

"And the ship will know what to do," Eloch said. "I, too, have keen observational skills, and since I feel what the ship feels, I can train the second ship to know when it's lined up to make the jump without any problems.”

Aiko rested her hand on Genji’s arm. “I just want you to get there safely, Genj,” she whispered.

Grale leaned over to her. “Trust the Knack Man, Kitten,” he whispered. “Your words, not mine.”

She glanced at him and nodded, raising her hands in surrender. “Okay, okay. Just get him home in one piece, Eloch. That’s all I ask.”

“I love him, too, Aiko. I love all three of them. They will get home safely, I promise,” Eloch said. He looked at the others, studying their faces. “Anyone else want to go home?”

“Not a chance,” Grale said. “We live in a traveling planet. Best of both worlds in my book. Best home I can think of.”

“Best of both,” Spider agreed. He looked at Genji, “Going to miss your brain, buddy.”

Genji grinned. “This is an opportunity to stretch yours, Spider. I think you’re going to surprise yourself at how smart that noggin is.”

Spider snorted.

“When is the best time for us to go?” Kalea asked Eloch.

“I would appreciate it if you stay until we know what exactly we are facing and we’re prepared for when the FN return.”

“Gladly,” Wade said.

“Wouldn’t miss it,” Genji said.

“That feels complete,” Kalea agreed.

“I also need to create the ship for you,” Eloch said.

Wade straightened suddenly. “What about the Nuri? Only you can put them to sleep and wake them up in Cryo."

Eloch smiled. "I thought of that." He looked at trio. "I can make it so you three will not age. That way there will be no need for Cryo."

Wade's mouth pulled into a frown. "But it will take nearly twenty years to get to Longwei. I don't want to be awake for twenty years. I prefer Cryo."

"I can provide a Cryo bed for you, Wade," Eloch said.

"And we can wake you if we need you," Genji said. "We're trained."

"Will you two mind being awake for nearly twenty years?" Eloch asked. "Frankly, I don't see any other alternative."

Kalea grinned shyly at Genji. "I know Genji will love having the time to study the stars, especially the parts we missed coming here. And," she looked at Genji again, "we wish to start a family, and this will be the perfect time."

"A Nuri nursery!" Wren exclaimed happily. "I love it!"

"Better make it flameproof then," Grale said.

"With plenty of room for them to stretch their wings," Mink added.

"I would have liked to have seen the baby lizard things," Aiko mused. "Genji and Kalea's children."

Grale snorted.

"Me, too," Perin said. "Children are such a delight."

"It will be nice to think about," Wren said. She looked at Eloch. "Is there a way they can send us vids?"

"It's possible," Eloch said and lifted a brow at Spider.

"I'll figure something out," Spider promised.

"The sooner we make our plans, the sooner this can happen," Eloch said. "Genji, what have you discovered about the device?"

"Spider, Mink, and I have pulled it apart and put it back together several times," Genji replied. "We know how it functions. We also know how to activate it, although we won't prove that to you, Eloch," he added with a grin.

"Gods, I hope not," Eloch said.

"I'll second that," Wren said.

"Best of all, we know how to jam it. If the FN do not agree to power down these devices, you can do it yourselves and free the Sisters of Vela Kentaurus, although that would mean traveling to each planet that's been affected." He rubbed his chin, "If we only knew their function. There must be a reason." He cocked his head at Spider.

"Mink and I have been analyzing data," Spider said. "Now we know what we're searching for and our ship is finally close enough, we're starting to locate exactly which planet is affected in Vega. Not all planets have received the implant. There is a pattern, a trajectory."

"Can Aiko and I take a look at what you've got?" Grale asked.

"Sure," Spider said. He slid a portable viewer across the table to where Aiko and Grale sat, where Grale positioned it between them. The two bent over it, squinting at the screen and occasionally whispering together.

"Since not every planet is affected, I don't think it's for malicious purposes," Wren said.

"Neither do we," Genji said. "We feel there is a scientific explanation for why they need to draw so much power."

"Looks like a flight pattern to me," Grale said, studying the portable view.

"You're right," Aiko said. "Maybe. It does seem to have a direction." She looked up. "Have you taken readings from beyond Vela Kentaurus?" she asked.

Spider shook his head. "We haven't. We will, as soon as this meeting breaks up."

"Why don't we ask them what it's for?" Eloch suggested.

"How are we going to do that?" Wade asked, "Kidnap an FN?"

"Exactly."

Wade laughed. "You're kidding, right?"

"No, I'm not kidding," Eloch said. "I've thought about this. I could access their ship when they return, take one, and bring them back. We've got the equipment to communicate with one, so there will be no language issue. In fact, I can make this whole ship so everyone can understand each other."

"But how do we kidnap one?" Wade asked.

"And how do you know he or she can live in our environment without some sort of life support?" Mink asked.

"They can." Perin said. "I have *seen* it."

"You've seen us kidnap an FN and bring them back here?" Wren asked, leaning forward.

"Not that," Perin answered. "But I've *seen* that I was on their ship, and I was breathing their air without any sort of special life support."

"Okay, assuming we can do this, who do we take?" Grale asked. "How do we know they all have the same working knowledge of what the spike does? On mining ships, not all the crew knew how to mine."

"That's true," said Aiko. "People are specialized."

"We take Jon," Perin said. "Jon will know."

"Jon," said Wade looking around the group. "Who is Jon?"

"He is the individual from the FN ship who Perin saw and who saw Perin," Eloch said. "That makes sense," he said to Perin. "Since there is a connection already, he might be easier for me to bring through."

Perin nodded. "And I will go with you to point him out."

"And I will go to protect you, Perin," Wren said. "Also because where Eloch goes, I go."

"Well, that's decided then," Eloch said with a chuckle. "Moving on, let's set our priorities. We don't know how much time we have before our Frequency Neighbors return."

"I've put together a list of priorities," Wren said.

"Of course you have," Grale said with a grin, sliding the portable viewer back to Spider. He looked at the others. "Doesn't she always?"

Spider grinned and nodded. "That's our Wren. Always two steps ahead of us."

~~~

Grale found Aiko on the Bridge in the pilot's chair. She appeared deep in thought as she gazed out the view port at the wide expanse of space. When he cleared his throat, she looked up.

"Hey," she said. "Didn't hear you come in."

He sat in the copilot chair next to her. "Yeah, you looked pretty engrossed. See anything out there?"

She shook her head. "But that doesn't mean the FNs aren't out

213

there and heading this way."

"Think the new scanner system will work?"

"With Spider and Genji's ingenuity behind it? Without a doubt." Aiko toyed with the seam of her chair's armrest. "I'm going to miss Genji. He's been my right hand for so many years." She sighed and glanced at Grale with a wistful smile. "But nothing stays the same. I should count my blessings for having had him for so long."

They were silent for a few moments, lost in their individual thoughts. The silence was broken when they both spoke at once.

Grale laughed.

"Sorry, what were you going to say?" Aiko asked.

He swept a hand and bowed toward her. "You go ahead. Age before and all that."

Aiko snorted and swiveled her chair to face him. "I was surprised when you didn't volunteer to pilot Genji and Kalea back to Longwei. I'd think this...what'd Wade call it? Rust bucket?...is cramping your style."

Grale gave her a crooked smile and ran his big hand over his hair. "I thought about it when Eloch first gave us a choice. But where would I go? Rust buckets are what I'm used to. I've lived on spaceships more than I've lived on dirt. And this one...well, it's got the best of both, doesn't it? There's a whole world within this vessel, and I don't see Eloch calling a halt to his expansion any time soon. No, this rust bucket is my home now."

He cocked his head at her. "'Sides, I'd love to see what this thing looks like when it's as big as a world."

"You think it will get that big?"

"I dunno. I hope so. Wouldn't that be something, Aiko? Piloting a ship as big as a planet?"

214

"Yeah," she agreed and smiled. "It'd be fun. But your freedom. You like things your way. You like being the captain of your own ship."

He laughed. "And don't you know it, Kitten. I made sure you knew it."

She grinned and waggled a finger at him. "But I gave as good as I got." She nodded at his softened belly with a sly grin. "And don't you forget it."

Grale patted his middle. "I have to admit that was a cheap shot. Hit me right square in my ego. But I would have done it to me, too, if I'd thought of it. Knock myself down a notch or two."

She laughed at that. "No doubt." Aiko leaned back and crossed her legs, relaxing. "So, what were you going to say?"

Grale hesitated.

"You forgot, right?" She smiled again. "And you'll most likely remember in the middle of the night. Tell you what, if you do, write it down. Don't you dare ping me and wake me up."

"No," Grale said with a shake of his head. "I didn't forget." He rubbed his face, glanced around the room, squared his shoulders, and said, "Look, this is going to be awkward, so just hear me out. And...don't interrupt. Deal?"

She sat up straight, searching his eyes. "Sure," she said quietly.

"Okay, then." Grale paused and blew out a breath. "So, Aiko. It's not only the ship that makes me want to stay." He reached for her hand. "It's you."

Her eyes widened, but she allowed her hand to stay in his.

He laughed. "I know. Took me by surprise, too, and I've been trying to figure out what to do about it. But when you volunteered to pilot those guys back to Longwei, it hit home that I'd better make my move now or I may never have another chance."

He took her other hand. "I know that in your eyes I'm just a rock pounder, a spaceport bar trawler, wisecracking womanizer and," he shrugged, "I guess I am. Or I *was*. I'm not anymore because you've gotten to me, Aiko. You made me want to be a better man so you'd take another look at me."

She opened her mouth to speak.

"I'm not finished yet," he said, cutting her off, giving her hands a shake for emphasis. "You promised not to interrupt. Look, I know we're out here in the middle of nowhere, and you may be thinking it's the lack of spaceport bars that's made me..."

He paused. "Well, let's just put it out there—horny, lonely, in need of some good lovin'. And the gods know it's true. I mean it has been fourteen years, Aiko, and I've never pretended to be a saint. Please, don't interrupt. You're making it harder."

"Just loosen your grip a little, and I won't interrupt again. My hands are getting numb."

Grale jerked his hands away, but Aiko reached out and twined her fingers with his. "Keep going," she urged gently.

He looked at their joined hands and back up to her face. "I think that's it. I *am* a rock pounder. I am a womanizer—well, used to be one—and I think that second part's important to take note of. But I'm also a damn fine pilot, and I want to be a damn fine man. Your man. So, Aiko..." He paused.

"Wait." He paused again. "Yeah, there's more." The rest poured out in a rush of words. "I want kids. I know that may come as a surprise, but I always have. I want to be a good father and give them things I never had. I want to teach them how to use their knack. I want to bust the balls on these FNs so we can get on with our lives. I want to see what else the Knack Man does to this rust bucket. And I want to do it all with you, Aiko. Only you."

Grale took a deep breath. "So, Aiko, do I have a chance? Will you take another look at me?"

She blinked, and a tear rolled down her cheek. "On one condition."

His face lit up as he gently wiped the tear away. "Anything. Anything at all."

"Just don't stop calling me Kitten, Cowboy."

Chapter 17 – Jon Gaylord

Jon Gaylord could not sleep, or so it seemed. He could fall asleep. That wasn't the problem. The problem was managing to stay asleep because when he slept, the dream came. The same dream.

The advent of the dream usually woke him. After that, it wasn't worth trying to get back to sleep because, in trying to go back to sleep, all Jon did was recount what happened in the dream. If he wasn't dreaming about it, he was thinking about it. That had become his new nighttime activity.

With a groan, Jon threw back his sleeping cot covers and flipped on the light in one seamless movement, born of a thousand repetitions. He stomped into the WC, something else he'd done a thousand times, and tried to relieve himself. But a full bladder wasn't the reason he was awake, so why pretend it was?

With a sigh, he turned on the faucet, splashed cold water on his face, and stared blankly at his reflection, which was staring blankly back at him.

He used to think he was quite good-looking, glad he took after his father's side of the family. He was taller than average, had an athletic build, deep-set brown eyes which one girlfriend had dubbed smoldering, and a chin another girlfriend had called manly.

But now his smoldering eyes were bloodshot and shadowed with lack of sleep, and his manly chin was rough with stubble. Jon rubbed his chin, wondering whether to shave or not. The time was 0230, so his stubble would be back by 0600.

Not worth the effort.

Jon left the mirror and surveyed his sparse little cabin, looking for something to put on. He tugged on a loose-fitting shirt and athletic pants, and flopped into his desk chair. Deciding he could function with four hours of sleep, he turned on his personal data processor and opened up his private files.

At first, Jon thought he was hallucinating, some odd flashback from his days of debauchery, those last weeks of defiance before his father gave him an ultimatum. He had hoped it was a hallucination. But once the dreams started—the one dream, he corrected himself—he began a journal, and did his best to research the phenomena with the limited resources the ship's computer provided.

The closest he could discover was something called *remote viewing*, although it didn't really fit what happened. Plowing through a transparent ship, shooting the fission generator wand into a man, and locking eyes with a beautiful woman seemed much more like a hallucination than a remote viewing session.

He had even exchanged names with the woman. What kind of name was *Perin*?

He then began to research space sickness, only to discover he had none of the symptoms. Dementia was the only other explanation, and he considered it a last resort. In fact, he had pushed that explanation so far away he finally decided to forget about it.

Then two things happened.

First, the fission generator wand stopped functioning. And then it disappeared. Vanished. It was his responsibility to maintain the thing, so it was his fault it had gone missing.

When asked what to do about it, the only thing he could suggest was to reverse course and try to solve the mystery at the site of the wand's last known coordinates.

The second thing that happened was the dream. The same one, again and again and again. He attributed the dream to either anxiety or fear. Anxiety over the upcoming re-insertion of a new wand if the old one was definitely missing, or fear that by returning to the same coordinates as his hallucination, it would cause another. Which made sense to him.

It had been rather shocking. After all, he had pushed the button that lanced a highly technical and dangerous device into another human being.

Jon yawned and eyed his cot warily. *God, I am so tired.* Perhaps he should request a sleep aid, although they left him groggy the next day. But at least he could sleep.

He glanced down at his fingers, still poised over the keyboard. Hadn't even typed a word. "Damn," he said, shaking his head. He shut down the equipment and shuffled over to the cot, not bothering to strip off his clothes. Lying prone, at least he would be more comfortable. Even if he didn't sleep, his body could rest.

But he did sleep.

And he dreamed.

The man he shot and the beautiful woman—Perin—and another woman appeared out of nowhere and pulled him off his ship before he could even lock onto the power signature's coordinates.

Jon woke, momentarily disoriented.

Someone was pounding on his door.

He sat bolt upright.

"Navigator! You awake?" a voice demanded.

"Yeah," he said hoarsely.

"Say again, Navigator?"

Jon cleared his throat. "Yeah, I'm awake," he said more forcefully, more annoyed than usual about how they never used his name and never used the door chime. He glanced at the clock. 0600. He needed to be awake by now anyway.

"Admiral wants to see you in twenty."

Jon heard the footsteps fade away without waiting for a reply. He finger-combed his short hair as he threw back the covers and headed to his WC. Twenty minutes wasn't too bad. He even had time to shower and shave. Someone must be a good mood, he thought drily. The crew generally only gave him ten minutes.

~~~

The door panel to the admiral's suite was open. Jon paused and knocked on the panel frame.

"Enter," a deep voice called from the other room. "Close the door behind you and help yourself to some tea. I'll be with you shortly."

Jon entered the spacious room and sat on one of the twin sofas that faced each other, helping himself to a cup of tea from the silver tea service on the coffee table. Leaning back on the sofa, he crossed his leg, resting his ankle on the opposite knee while he sipped his tea and waited.

The room was very much like the admiral: well-appointed, clean, comfortable furniture, but nothing fussy and nothing out of place.

The admiral strode in, adjusting his uniform cuffs. He nodded at Jon. "I see you've made yourself at home. Good," he said. He sat across from Jon and poured himself a cup of tea.

"I did, thank you," said Jon.

The admiral took a sip and scrutinized Jon over his cup's rim. "It's the least I could do since I called you here so early. You look tired."

"I am tired. Haven't been sleeping well."

"I'm sorry to hear that, Son."

Jon drained his cup and poured himself another. "It is what it is. Why am I here, sir?"

The admiral was silent for a brief moment. Then he quickly and efficiently placed his cup and saucer down on the table and clasped his hands together. "Do you know why I asked specifically for you to go with me on this mission?"

Jon snorted. "Hardly for a father/son bonding adventure, that much I know."

For a brief moment, pain and something else...regret?...flashed across the admiral's face. "I asked for you because, in the whole of my career, you're the best damned navigator I've ever come across. And I wanted the best."

Surprise rushed through Jon, and he nearly choked on his tea. "I see," was all he could manage in response.

"So why is it that the best damned navigator in this whole fucking Navy cannot locate a damaged fission generator wand?"

Jon set down his cup and sighed. "I haven't a clue, Father, and am just as baffled as you. It simply vanished. Gone. The best I can do is take us back to where we fired the implant. If it's there, it's there. If not..." He lifted his hands and shrugged.

The admiral scowled. "Not what I wanted to hear."

"Not what I wanted to tell you." Jon watched his father's scowl deepen. It was like looking at himself thirty years in the future. Why couldn't he have taken after his mother or at least have something recognizable of her in him?

"Do you always need to be so sarcastic, Jon? It's an expensive piece of equipment and extremely dangerous. We can't afford to lose even one. And if it ever got into the wrong hands—"

"I know, I know," Jon said, suddenly weary of the conversation. "I honestly don't know what to tell you. As you said, I'm the best damned navigator, and I've never witnessed anything like this." He fell silent for a moment. "Look, I've set the course for the last known coordinates. We should arrive some time tomorrow morning. And we won't know what we're going to find until we get there."

His father set down his cup and stood.

Jon followed suit.

"I suppose time will tell," the admiral said. "I really wanted this mission to go without a hitch," he said shaking his head. "This was to be my grand opus, so to speak. My final legacy before I retire."

"For the record, Father, I tried to tell you that the energy frequencies of this location felt off to me. They were too unstable for my liking. Couldn't maintain a firm location. Coordinates shifting. I did advise searching for another source for the star gate."

"I remember. But this sector, our outermost boundary, was the perfect place to assemble a fleet in the event one was necessary. From here we could use that particular star gate and go anywhere within our galaxy." He paused. "I didn't tell you, but I've been in planning sessions with HQ. They wanted to build a space station here, an entire floating city, and this star gate is critical. But now the wand is missing and the gate can't be opened."

Jon nodded, still mystified why this position, with its irregular energy source, would make the perfect spot. "Surely, you can find another position," he said as he made his exit. "There's a lot of empty space surrounding our galaxy."

His father called him back.

"I apologize, Son, if I have been brusque. This situation is beyond frustrating. I am especially concerned about the fission generator wand going missing. Yet there is not another ship in sight, so where is it?" He fisted his hands. "I won't rest until there is a positive resolution."

Jon took a deep breath before he answered, squashing the ready retort. "I appreciate your apology, Father. This is beyond frustrating for all of us. Like I said, I've never experienced anything like it. The wand was working perfectly before that energy surge, and then it simply stopped working." He paused. "And then it simply vanished. I've spent hours, on duty and off, trying to locate it."

His father nodded. "Does this give you enough time to test and prepare a second wand? The star gate's position is too critical to let it go."

"The second wand is already online and tested." He hesitated. "Although I would think you'd want to locate the first wand and ensure there won't be a repeat performance."

"We can search for it while we wait for the second to stabilize. The sooner a gate is created, the sooner we can complete this mission and go home."

~~~

Jon watched his hands shake as they skimmed over the control panel, locking the settings in place.

He could no longer ignore the toll his lack of sleep was taking. He hoped to all the heavens that once they inserted this second wand, found the lost one, and went home, he'd resume a normal sleep pattern.

But for now, he did what he could, using sleep aids to quiet his mind and stimulants to wake him up. The prescribing ship's medic told him he would report to the admiral that he had given Jon the drugs, which he had obviously done already, because Jon kept seeing his father glancing at him with an odd expression. Made him even more jumpy. He thought maybe the way his father looked at him had even more of an effect than the prescribed stimulants. He caught himself grinning and quickly suppressed it before anyone noticed. The crew already thought he was odd.

"Coordinates locked, Admiral," he said.

"Start the countdown," his father ordered.

"Setting for ten," he said, "nine, eight, seven—" A shiver ran through him and he looked up from his reader.

He gasped.

The dream! It was happening!

It's actually happening!

One minute they weren't there. The next they were. Three of them. *Right in front of him.* Just like in the dream, and he knew what was coming next.

"Oh, fuck me!" he shouted. He flung out his hands to ward off the trio. "NO! Help! No! Don't!" he pleaded.

The big man he had stabbed with the fission generator wand calmly grasped his arm and tugged. The atmosphere shimmied and shimmered around him. Pain wracked him as his surroundings began to fade.

The last thing he heard was his father calling his name. The fear in his father's voice matched his own.

CHAPTER 18 – KIDNAPPED

Pain.

An ocean of pain and nausea.

He couldn't move. He couldn't speak. He couldn't even breathe.

I'm dying! Jon thought, and he didn't want to die. He wanted very much to live.

So very much.

Soft hands gently probed his face. So light they felt like butterfly wings.

"What's wrong with him?" a voice asked. Female.

"I need to stabilize him," a deep masculine voice replied.

Another hand touched his shoulder. This one heavy, strong, and warm energy flooded through him, dispelling the pain.

He gasped, drawing in great gulps of air. *Sweet powers that be. Sweet, sweet powers that be.*

He was alive.

"How are you feeling now?" the deep masculine voice asked.

Jon opened his eyes slowly. He was lying on his back with a familiar man and two women bending over him.

He gathered his scattered thoughts, eyes on the man, trying to place him. Then memories surfaced. This giant was the man from his dream. The man he had shot with the wand. The man who had just materialized out of thin air and grabbed him.

Galvanized by fear, Jon struggled to sit. The big man helped him. His eyes darted around the chamber, trying to understand. He had been lying on a pallet of some sort. The room had the definite look of a medical facility. He swallowed, felt disoriented. "Where am I? What happened?"

"You are on board our ship, the *Valiant*," the big man said quietly. "We have questions we are unable to answer, so we brought you here to answer them for us."

"You are quite safe," one of the women said. She was petite, attractive, with a mass of auburn coils snaking around her. "We'll put you back as soon as we have our answers," she said, dark blue eyes wide with sincerity.

"Jon."

His head whipped around.

It was her.

The blond angel.

"Perin?"

She smiled.

Her eyes. Something was wrong with them. *What is going on?*

He closed his eyes, shaking his head. Too much. It was too much. The dreams. The reality. Both blending together. Merging. Nothing seemed real.

His breath came faster. "I don't get it," he gasped. "I don't...I can't...what's happening?" He buried his face in his hands, wishing it would all disappear, wishing he could wake up.

Perin reached out and drew him to her. "Hush now," she whispered and stroked his back. "Slow down your breathing. It's okay, Jon. We won't hurt you. Just breathe. That's it. That's good." She was smaller than he was, but he felt safe in her arms. He allowed her to soothe him, resting his forehead against her shoulder. She smelled good. In fact, he could stay there forever. Safe. Relaxed.

"I need to sleep," he said.

"Then sleep. I'll stay with you."

She helped him get settled on the pallet. When he noticed the others had left the room, he studied Perin leaning over him. "Your eyes."

She smoothed back his hair. Her hand was cool.

"I am blind in this world."

"But—"

"I am not blind in yours. Hush, now, Jon. Sleep. When you're rested, we will talk. All is well."

For some inexplicable reason, he believed her and closed his eyes.

She stroked his head, her hand soothing and rhythmic. He didn't think he could remain awake even if he tried.

~~~

"Poor guy," Wren said as she and Eloch exited the med lab. "I think we came on a little too strong."

Eloch nodded and grinned. "In his shoes, I would certainly have found it unnerving."

"Perin's got him, though. There's some sort of connection there."

"Definitely." He reached for her hand. "How are you after two crossings?"

"Better than the first. One, I knew what to expect, and two, the burning pain was less this time."

"Good. I'm working on stabilization, helping your body adjust more rapidly."

"One thing I noticed both times is how hungry I get. Ravenous."

"Is that why we're racing toward to the galley?"

"Yep."

"I forgot to mention," he said as they hurried along, "I created the universal translator I was talking about, the one for the whole ship. As long as we're on board, we can all understand Jon and he can understand us."

"Clever." She frowned, then laughed. "Of course you did. I just realized Perin and Jon *were* communicating just fine. The gift Spur gave me...well, I've learned to take it for granted that not everyone can communicate without a translator in their hand."

"And now they can."

When they reached the galley, Wren went in search of food while Eloch pinged the Bridge to update the others and hear their report.

"We're monitoring the ship," Aiko told him. "It's dead in the air. All engines have been cut. Genji and Spider are observing them. A second spike was activated, then deactivated. Our pulsar flare is armed. If that spike is reactivated, we'll be ready." She chuckled. "No worries, Eloch. We're sitting pretty. We can monitor them, and they don't even know we exist."

"Well done, Aiko," Eloch said. "When we make contact with them, we must bear in mind that they will be frightened and jumpy," Eloch mused. "After Wren finishes her meal, we'll join you on the Bridge to wait for Perin." He broke the connection.

"I'm nearly finished, Eloch," Wren said. "I gobbled like a starving person."

He sat across from her. "We've got time. Our guest is sound asleep."

Wren nodded, dabbing at her mouth with a napkin. "Best thing for him."

"Perin will help him adjust."

"Yeah, she will. That connection. What do you think it is? It seems so convenient, don't you think? Our Seer and her dreams…Jon…" she shrugged.

"I have a theory about that," Eloch replied. "Perin was a gift from The Lady, and Talamh is a planet of visions and dreams, yes?" At Wren's nod, he continued. "Well then, doesn't it make sense that The Lady who created Her people to be guided by dreams and visions is Herself guided by dreams and visions?"

"Hmm." Wren cocked her head. "You think Talamh saw all this, and that's why She gifted Perin?"

"In truth, I don't know, Wren. But I wouldn't be surprised."

"This universe is a strange place."

"It most certainly is," Eloch agreed.

~~~

Jon woke slowly, and for the first time in a long while, he felt rested. For a moment, he felt disoriented and kept his eyes closed, listening to the strange hum of—

This isn't my ship!

He shot up, bracing himself as the memories came flooding back. Eyes darting around, he found Perin, still sitting by his side as she had promised.

231

She smiled serenely, hands folded quietly in her lap.

"Oh. Hi," he said.

"How do you feel, Jon?"

He took three deep breaths, calming himself. "Better. Hopefully, more able to cope."

"It must be very strange to you."

"It is and it isn't," he said. "I think the strangest part is that it isn't. Strange, I mean." He hesitated, then plunged in. "I've dreamed for several days about being kidnapped and brought here. So when it finally happened, it was almost a relief..." his voice trailed off. "You must think I'm crazy, me dreaming all this. I nearly thought so, too."

She shook her head. "No. It answers many of my questions. You are a Seer, Jon. As am I."

"A Seer?"

"Yes. Your dreaming. Was it the same dream over and over again? Did it seem so real that when you awoke you weren't sure what was reality anymore?"

He straightened. "Yes. Exactly. How did you know?"

She smiled. "My people call that a True Dream. Those of us who dream True Dreams are called Seers. We see visions of what is to come so we can guide others."

"But I've never dreamed like this before," he said, rubbing his chin, noticing his beard stubble had grown.

She cocked her head at him. "Are you sure about that?"

He thought back over the years and remembered that he had, indeed, experienced occasional recurring dreams at pivotal times in his life. "I guess I have, now you mention it. But never anything as dramatic or as frightening as this one."

She nodded. "They can be like that, especially if you are untrained. Even trained, you can still be frightened by a True Dream. I dreamed of the merging of our two ships before I had even set foot on a spaceship. I dreamed your ghost ship would shoot Eloch with the metal stake that bloomed like a flower. And because I didn't know what I was Seeing, I was very frightened. Like you, I thought I was going mad."

"The metal stake that bloomed like a flower," he repeated. "Oh! You must be referring to the fission generator wand." All at once he felt more animated and less frightened. "Yes! I saw it penetrate a man—the man—the one who kidnapped me. I was sure I was hallucinating. It was the only logical explanation."

Perin laughed, a bell-like sound. "You were not hallucinating, Seer. It is the way of things." She smiled at him. "I also Saw we would exchange names."

"This will to take some time for me to process," Jon said after a while.

She nodded, her sightless eyes studying his face. "For someone who has not been properly trained, I imagine it is very stressful."

Jon snorted. "Terrifying is more like it. But I'm relieved." He chuckled. "I'm not going crazy after all. How about that?"

"I will help you, Jon. I have been trained, and I can train you."

He examined her earnest expression and wondered why he trusted this alien woman who had helped kidnap him. There should have been all kinds of internal alarms sounding.

But when he looked at her, at her lovely, open face, what he felt was…kinship. It surprised him and also reassured him. He wasn't the only one with crazy dreams. "Thank you," he told her. "It will help immensely."

She nodded. "Are you ready to speak with the others? I can have

233

them bring you food and water."

He took a deep breath. "That would be good. Nourishment and answers."

Jon watched Perin rise and cross over to a small panel on the wall, marveling at how easily she moved without normal sight. She touched the panel. It made a small *ping* and was answered. She spoke into it. It *pinged* once more and she turned away.

"Eloch and Wren will be here soon," Perin said, returning to her seat at his side.

"You move like you can see," Jon said.

"I know this ship," she replied. "And I am not totally blind. I see people's energy patterns and can tell where they are and who they are. And I wasn't always blind. It was when I began to Dream True that I lost my normal sight."

"Then I will go blind as well?" he asked.

She shook her head. "If you were going to go blind, it would have happened already. Perhaps it is the way of my people and not your own."

The door panel slid open, bringing the scent of food, along with two people Jon immediately recognized. They were the petite woman with the auburn coils and the giant man who kidnapped him. He stiffened.

"You look better. Rested," the woman with the coils said, a tray in her hands. She moved like a fighter, Jon noticed, graceful and smooth despite the slick black prosthetic replacing one leg.

"Hungry?" she asked. "I sure was."

Suddenly, Jon was ravenous. "Very," he replied.

"My name is Wren," she said as she placed a tray on his lap. "Enjoy your meal."

234

The man handed a second tray to Perin, who smiled delightedly and immediately began to eat.

Jon swallowed and looked at his food warily. It smelled delicious. But hadn't he just been abducted?

Wren laughed, watching him. "We didn't bring you here to poison you," she said. "Look," she plucked a bit of fruit off his plate and popped it into her mouth. "Go ahead and enjoy. We'll wait."

"I'll trade my meal with you, Jon, if it will make you more comfortable," Perin offered.

Jon looked at the plate in his hands and shook his head. "Not necessary. Thank you, though." He looked at the woman named Wren. "I…well, it's all damn strange, and I'm on guard."

Wren nodded sagely. "*Caution First* is this crew's motto. But go ahead now. Eat."

Deciding to trust them, he took a bite. The meal was delicious, and he focused on that while the three sat quietly and waited. When he was finished, Jon handed Wren the empty tray and sat back with a sigh. "Thank you," he said.

"Not at all. I was ravenous after that crossover, and I assumed you and Perin would be as well."

"Crossover?"

Wren nodded toward large man sitting beside her, who was studying Jon. "This is my mate, Eloch," she said by way of introduction. "He's the one who brought you to our ship, and I think he's the one who should explain things. We have a lot of questions, and we've traveled hundreds of light-years to get them answered."

She rose. "Why don't we all go to another room and have a conversation? Perin, just leave your tray there and come. We can collect them later."

CHAPTER 19 – COMPARING NOTES

Jon considered Eloch. He was a big man, several inches over six feet tall, Jon guessed, and well made, fit, strong, with dark good looks. His face conveyed a keen intelligence.

But his clothing. Jon had no idea what the man Eloch was wearing. His tunic was a sturdy dark green cloth belted around the middle. His legs were encased in what Jon thought could be animal skins, but he wasn't sure. But regardless of his strange clothing, the man made Jon wary. Even standing quietly, he radiated a dangerous power and the kind of authority that proclaimed him a leader.

Eloch smiled. It wasn't a friendly smile, to Jon's mind. "Would you like to take a tour of our home?" he asked. He turned to Wren and Perin. "Why don't we take Jon up to our Bridge and introduce him to the rest of our crew?"

"I shot you," Jon said.

"Yes, you did."

"With a fission generator wand."

He lifted one brow. "Is that what it's called? Genji and Spider will be overjoyed to finally know its name."

Jon shook his head. "It's just not possible for a man to survive being shot with a fission generator wand. So how are you still living?"

"Eloch is more than he seems, Jon," Wren said quietly. "I think if you tour the ship with us, you'll begin to understand."

He barked out a laugh. "I'm glad you have faith in my mental capacity. I feel more confused than ever."

"Jon is a Seer," Perin said. "He Dreams True."

"Ah," Eloch said. He glanced at Wren.

"More puzzle pieces fitting together?" she asked him.

"It makes sense, don't you think? Their connection."

Jon looked at the two, resenting their private conversation.

Perin covered Jon's hand with her own. "They do that a lot. You'll get used to it. Sometimes they don't even use words."

He felt his eyes widening. "You two telecommunicate? Mind to mind?"

Wren nodded and grinned. "I think it's best, Jon, if you suspend your disbelief and just hear us out."

Perin squeezed his hand. "You will come to understand us, and you will help us. I have Seen it." She gently tugged at his hand. "Come tour our home. Trust me."

"I do," Jon told Perin. "I don't know why, but I do. You, Perin, I trust. These two? I'm not sure."

Perin's smile dazzled. All she needed was wings. And if she unfurled a pair he wouldn't be surprised. "Come," she said.

"The *Valiant* is a modular ship," Wren said as they walked down a wide, well-lit corridor. "Are you familiar with modular starships, Jon?"

"No, I'm not," he replied.

She nodded. "A modular ship is comprised of different modules configured together to meet a particular expedition's requirements."

"Okaaaay," said Jon. "Still not understanding."

Wren smiled. "I didn't understand it either at first. Let me explain it the way Aiko, one of our pilots, explained it to me." Wren paused. "Imagine a flying box, Jon, made up of several different boxes fitted together inside the larger box. The larger box is the ship's hull, its outer skin. Each of the smaller boxes is a room that provides a specific function. The med lab we just left is an example. Our galley would be another box, individual sleeping quarters are other boxes, and so on. With me so far?"

At Jon's nod, she continued. "For the *Valiant,* all the individual boxes were fitted around a middle box. The middle box was originally a three-story rectangle housing our Solar Farm and large enough for flying."

"Flying?"

"We'll get to that. Before the *Valiant* became ours, it was a colonizer vessel, equipped to house nearly ten thousand people, who would use the modules as their homes when they reached their destination planet. It was huge, much larger than what we needed, so we sold off many of those modules to pay for what we needed for this journey." Wren waved her hand, "Probably more information than you needed. Anyway, when we left our solar system, that's what the *Valiant* looked like, a bunch of boxes surrounding a larger box, all contained within an even larger box— the hull."

The group came to a stop at a wide door panel.

"And now?" Jon prompted.

"Over the years, Eloch here has been making some modifications." Wren tapped the door panel and it whooshed open. She walked in.

Jon froze in the doorway. Beyond the doorway was a world, a paradise of trees, fields of flowers, blue sky above, a river flowing freely from a large lake. The warm breeze on his face smelled slightly of salt, as if there was an ocean not far away. "How can this be?" he gasped.

"Like I said," Wren responded, "Eloch is more than he seems."

Jon glanced at Eloch as he strode into the world and joined Wren. They turned and waited for him, but he was still frozen in the doorway.

Perin took Jon's hand and gently led him through. The door panel behind him slid shut, and Jon could swear he was standing dirtside.

"Sit," Perin said and drew him down on a bench beside her. She started to slip her hand out of his grasp, but he clung to it like a lifeline.

The other two sat in the grass in front of him, Eloch cross-legged, Wren leaning against him, her legs outstretched.

"Long ago I was the Champion of Entean," Eloch said, leaning over to pluck a long blade of grass.

"What does that mean? Who is Entean?" Jon asked.

"Entean is my home planet," Eloch said, twirling the grass as he spoke. "As Her Champion, I would travel around Her surface, solving issues and resolving disputes. It was my responsibility to maintain Her balance. So when a ship from Spur arrived, Entean sent me to investigate."

"Spur is my home planet," Wren said, picking up the narration. "The ship was on a scouting mission. The people of Spur were too numerous and had targeted Entean as a candidate for colonization."

Eloch continued the narrative. "Entean asked me, as her Champion, to travel to Spur to find out why Spur's people were leaving. Spur had fallen silent. In order for me to communicate with Spur, Entean gave me a part of Herself...a seed...which grew into a plant that coexists with me within my body."

"When Eloch woke Spur," Wren said, "Spur needed a Champion to put things right on Her surface. Eloch was Her Champion until she found one from Spur."

"As a reward, Spur gifted me some of her Power and sent Wren and me on a mission," Eloch said.

"To Longwei," Wren said. "To make amends to the planet Longwei and to re-gather Her people—those colonizers now living on Longwei—and bring them back to Spur where they belonged."

"But while we were on Longwei," Eloch continued. "Entean notified me that Something Was Coming. The Something That Was Coming was attacking planets and sucking away their life force. As the life force was drained from the planet, the life on that planet could not be sustained, and eventually all that remained was a lifeless planet. Entean tasked me with finding the Something That Was Coming and stopping it before it reached our galaxy."

"Because Eloch was now Champion not just of Entean, but also of Spur and Longwei," Wren said, "Longwei remade Eloch so his body could contain the power of a planet so he could defend all the Sisters against the Something That Was Coming."

Wren paused. "The power of a planet is its creative life force. And so," Wren swept her arm in an arc, "Eloch is creating, the same way a planet creates. This ship, the *Valiant*, is now a part of Eloch and Eloch is a part of the ship. This ship is our ship...and it's our planet."

"Like a planet, I am aware of everything within and outside my self," Eloch said. "Like a planet, I could sense the Something That Was Coming. So we have been on a course to intercept and stop the Something That Was Coming."

Eloch focused all his attention on Jon. "That Something is you, Jon. You and your ship."

Jon swallowed, his mouth suddenly dry.

"Which brings us to the reason you are here on this ship," Eloch said. "To explain to us why you and your ship would destroy planets."

"Come," Wren said, getting to her feet. "Let's meet the others."

CHAPTER 20 - ANSWERS

Jon didn't know if his knees buckled voluntarily or not, but he found himself back on the bench. Perin, who had been holding his hand, landed beside him with an "oof."

"I'm so sorry," he exclaimed and helped her straighten, then looked across at Wren and Eloch, who were squatting in front of him.

Jon shook his head, thinking that might clear it. "I got lost in the narration," he said. "Forgive me, but it sounds like fiction. I need to get something straight." He squinted at the pair. "I know there is life on other planets, but are you telling me planets themselves are actually alive? As in conscious and aware?"

The pair nodded and waited.

"They're alive. And they talk to you." He smirked.

"In their different ways, yes, they do," Perin said quietly.

He turned to look at her. "You talk to your planet. Which one? Entean?"

She shook her head. "No, I am from Talamh, and I speak with The Lady Talamh, yes."

"Are you that planet's Champion?"

"No, I'm the people's Seer. The Lady also has a Champion, the High Priest."

He looked at all three of them. "Either I am a raving lunatic," he said slowly, "or the three of you are."

243

Wren laughed. "I warned you you'd need to suspend your disbelief. I didn't believe it either until I met Spur, the spirit of my home planet. She had gone dormant because Her people stopped believing they could actually have a relationship with Her. Eloch brought Her back. Perhaps your planet is dormant, too." She stood gracefully and offered her hand. "Let's meet the others."

Jon let Wren haul him to his feet, surprised at how strong she was. Then he helped Perin, taking comfort in her warm grasp. In silence, the four crossed to the other side of the meadow, down a shady path by the little creek, and over to another panel. He paused and turned, looking at where they had come. The land stretched for miles. "Shouldn't this have taken us longer to get across?" he asked.

"Eloch has done something to time and space in here," Wren said. "Genji says it has to do with quantum physics."

"And I say if it works, why do you need to know how?" Eloch said.

Wren snorted. "You say that about everything you don't want to take the time to explain."

After they exited, Wren continued with her narrative. "This corridor leads to the Bridge, where the others are monitoring your ship," she told him. "If you go the other way, you come to the sleeping area and galley."

"How many on board?"

"There are ten of us."

Jon halted. "Ten," he repeated. "All this space, and only ten people."

"Yep," Wren nodded. "Like I said, Eloch has been expanding over the years, but we like the space. We each have a lot of privacy this way."

"What about maintenance? A ship this size would need constant monitoring. Even if it's automated, people need to check the

244

readouts."

"Not if Eloch is aware of everything inside and outside of this ship. He takes care of it. You're going to have to—"

"I know. I know," Jon said, interrupting her. "Suspend my disbelief. I got it. I'm just trying to understand. It's as if I'm in some sort of weird alternate reality."

"Well, in some ways you are. But I'm going to let Genji and Spider explain that to you. Come, let's go."

Jon followed, shaking his head. What kind of a name was Spider? Come to think of it, what kind of name was Wren? "Who *are* you people?" he muttered to himself.

Perin touched his hand. "You're not crazy," she whispered.

~ ~ ~

They entered a flight deck different from every other flight deck he had ever seen. And the group who studied him as he made his way over? The word *motley* came to mind.

A man and woman slowly rose, their movement drawing his attention. Their clothes were even more different than the three accompanying him, Eloch in his skins, Wren and Perin in their tunics and flowing pants.

This pair wore bright, colorful garments which left their arms, legs, and feet bare. Both were tall, with lean, well-defined muscles which rippled underneath golden skin. Their hair was thick and dark, nearly black, and the woman's was tied and hung down her back.

He didn't want to stare, but he couldn't help studying the strange, intricate drawings etched into their skin running down half of their bodies, mirror images. They were quite stunning, Jon decided, yet somehow dangerous. It was the way they watched him, as if they were trying to catch his scent, just like a large predator. It was rather disconcerting.

The other two women present were small and fine-boned like Wren, although one was round and feminine, with short wavy hair and a beguiling smile, while the other was more serious and sharp-featured, with a thick plait of straight, dark hair.

There were also two men sitting near the smaller women. They were closer to his age and height, but leaner than he. One of the two had thick, dark unruly hair, thick brows, and dark eyes. The other had more open features and lighter hair and eyes. The women and men were dressed extremely casually. Jon decided it was safe to assume the crew had no regulation uniforms. He wondered about it because, as casual as they appeared, they still seemed a very disciplined and well-organized group. He turned his attention to the last man.

The final man was nearly as tall as the golden couple and was the motliest of them all. His hair was shaggy, he needed a shave, and Jon noticed a small tear on one of his shirtsleeves. He stood, sleeves pushed up, arms crossed with arrogant confidence. Jon was sure when he walked it would be with a swagger. This man, he noted, also bore a drawing, a handprint, on his right forearm.

The man caught Jon studying him and smirked. "This the Sleeping Beauty we've been waiting for?" he asked. "Looks to me he could have used another forty winks."

"That's Grale," Wren said. "He's our comic relief and one of the pilots." She nodded at the serious, sharp-featured woman sitting in the chair just to the right of where Grale stood. "And that is Aiko, our other pilot. Over there," Wren continued, gesturing toward the golden couple, "are Genji and Kalea. They're one of the reasons our ship's center module is so enormous. In their Nuri forms, they're much larger."

"Nuri forms?"

"Yeah," drawled Grale. He glanced down at Aiko and winked. "They change into big lizard things that fly and spit fire. They're also rather protective of Eloch, so watch your step."

Jon gaped at Genji and Kalea.

Genji and Kalea stared back.

Jon swallowed.

"Genji," Wren said, frowning. "Ease up."

Genji almost hissed when he said, "He does have some explaining to do, Wren."

"And he will, Genj," Wren said mildly. "But I don't really think he's the enemy." She sent a smile to Jon. "At least not an intentional one."

Genji shrugged and pinned Jon with a glare until Kalea touched his arm.

"The guy with dark curly hair over there is Spider," Wren continued. "He and Genji are our lead problem-solvers, although we all get to dabble in the problem-solving arena, but Spider and Genji are the scientists.

"And these last two are Mink and Wade," she said nodding at the feminine woman who dimpled at him and the man with the light eyes. "Wade and Mink keep us well and alive. They're our Cryo-stasis and med lab specialists." Wren clasped her hands together. "So now you've met everybody." She turned to the group, "Everybody, this is Jon."

Jon saluted. "Jon Gaylord, navigator of the *Defiance*." He glared at Genji. "And I have some questions for you all as well, one being how did I get here and how were we unaware of this ship's presence?"

Then he caught a glimpse of what was on the table in front of Spider and gasped. "And how did you get your hands on my Fission Generator Wand?"

Spider glanced at Genji. "So that's what it's called."

"Makes more sense now, too," Genji said to Spider. He returned his gaze to Jon.

247

Spider raised his brows, "You're right, Genj. Much more sense. Good name for it."

Genji glared at Jon. "We got it because you shot Eloch with it," he hissed. "You nearly destroyed him, and our ship along with it." Something rippled under Genji's skin, something wanting to get out.

Jon sucked in his breath and took a step back.

Kalea touched his arm. "Genji," she cautioned.

"I warned you to watch your step," Grale said. He grinned as he leaned back and refolded his arms.

"Ease up, people," Wren said and then glared at Jon. "You, too."

Eloch cleared his throat. "Let's keep in mind why we're here," he said serenely.

Genji touched Kalea's hand, which still rested on his forearm. He took a breath before speaking to Jon. "Sorry," he told him. "Grale's right. I'm a little protective of Eloch."

"His Nuri has a temper," Kalea said apologetically. "And they are both very loyal."

"I think we should explain to Jon exactly where he is," Spider said. "That way we can all be on the same page."

"Good idea," Wren said. "Jon, why don't you take a seat in the copilot's chair, over there by Aiko?"

Jon glanced at Perin, uncomfortably aware that he was still clutching her hand.

"I will take you," Perin said with a gentle tug.

Wren and Eloch exchanged a smile Jon suspected he wasn't supposed to see.

Jon sat, and the others arranged themselves around him so they could all see the viewing screen easily. Aiko glanced at Jon with a slight smile and nodded at the viewing screen. "Empty space, right?"

Jon nodded.

"But look at the readouts," she said, pointing at a flat panel of screens easily accessible to both the pilot and copilot chairs.

Jon looked and then looked back at Aiko, "I see numbers, but I don't know what they mean. I can't read your language."

Aiko flashed him a grin. "Of course you can't. I'm sorry." She pointed at one screen specifically. "These are the coordinates of something that should be right in front of us."

Jon looked out the viewing screen. "Still empty space."

"Exactly," said Aiko. "Now I'm going to split the viewing panel in two. The left side is what we are seeing out front and the right side." She paused as her hands flew over the flat panel of screens. "This is what we can see using sensors Genji and Spider threw together."

"We're still perfecting it," Spider said humbly.

"The images could be sharper," Genji agreed.

Jon shot them a glance before turning back to the viewing screen. There, on the right hand side of the screen, was his ship. "The *Defiance*! That's my ship, but I know she's not cloaked. You should be able to see her on both sides of the screen."

Aiko nodded. "That would make sense. Look." She gestured again at the panel of screens. "Here are the coordinates for the left side of the screen, and here are the coordinates of the right side of the screen. They are the same coordinates."

Jon rubbed the back of his neck. "I don't get it. Why can't I see her on the left-hand screen?"

249

Aiko peered up at Genji. "Want to explain to Jon what he's seeing, Genj?"

Genji glanced down at Jon and gestured at the screen. "On the left screen is where we are, our reality. We can't see your ship because we're functioning on a completely different wave frequency than where your ship is. Since your ship exists in a different frequency of reality, the only way we can see her is to target that range of frequency. Do you follow?"

Jon shrugged. "Maybe. Keep going."

Genji nodded. "Spider and I made a device that can take the frequency range where your ship exists and translate it into the frequency range where we are. That translation is what you're seeing on the right-hand side of the viewing screen."

Jon let go of Perin's hand and scooted closer to study the screens. "So what you're saying is there are parallel worlds, and I live in one world while you live in another."

"Exactly," Genji said.

"Fascinating," Jon said.

"I think so," Genji said.

Jon looked at Genji.

The two shared a grin.

"So my hallucination wasn't a hallucination," Jon said to himself. "I can somehow see between dimensions."

"You can see between dimensions?" Genji asked.

"Not all the time. Well, once, really. And then the dreams."

"Jon is a Seer," Perin said, "like me."

"Is he blind in that other world?" asked Spider.

Jon scoffed. "No, I'm not blind. I'm a navigator. I need to see to be a navigator."

"Not just like Perin, then," Spider said. "Interesting."

"How did I get here?" Jon asked, already knowing the answer. He craned his neck to look at Eloch, who towered behind him.

Eloch smiled. "I raised my frequency to match the frequency of your world and brought you back. The same way I brought back the stake you shot me with."

"I did not shoot you with the wand," Jon said. "I locked onto a power source and discharged the wand into that source in order for us to utilize the power. How could I shoot you if you were living in a completely different frequency? And why would I even want to shoot a person with a fission generator wand? It would kill them."

"Nearly did," Grale said.

"To answer your question," Spider said, "we believe that a part of Eloch resides at that frequency level. We think these parallel worlds overlay each other, since we could still pick up a reading on your ship even though it was invisible to us."

Jon nodded. "I buy that. It validates my hallucination-that-was-not-a-hallucination."

He snapped his fingers. "Okay. I think I know what's going on here." He looked over at Eloch. "In my parallel universe, my home world is expanding its trade routes. To do so, we create these jump portals we call star gates." He nodded toward the split-viewing screen. "The *Defiance* is a military ship. Our military is also expanding its reach to protect the new trade routes. Our mission is to create different star gates—military star gates—that will eventually surround our galaxy so we can quickly be anywhere we're needed to keep peace. As navigator, I scout for strong energy signals, the stronger the better."

He paused. "You told me a Champion maintains the balance of the planet he serves, correct?"

Eloch nodded.

"Our military serves a similar purpose, and since a galaxy is bigger than a planet, we needed to find a way to get to the hotspots fast in order to keep the peace. So we developed the star gate technology." He looked around. "Everyone with me so far?"

He was greeted with silent nods. "Okay then. There's a certain power level we need to maintain in order to keep our star gates open and functioning. Throughout our galaxy, we have found natural pockets of raw energy. As navigator, my job is to locate those natural energy pockets with high enough output levels to maintain a star gate. When I find one, we launch a fission generator wand and begin drawing energy to activate a gate. In my universe, we're drawing energy from these natural pockets."

He jolted around to look wide-eyed at Eloch. "But in your universe, we're draining planets—sentient planets—of their life force, aren't we?"

Eloch nodded.

The room was silent.

"That's horrifying," Jon whispered.

Chapter 21 - Next

"Typical," Spider spat with a scowl. "They think they are tapped into the Universal Core Essential Thermals and are using fission technology to extract and amplify it for their bloody star gate. But, as often happens when we combine physics with big business, they didn't do the research required to understand the full ramifications."

"Exactly. They aren't amplifying the UCETs at all," Genji stated. "Instead, they created a parallel draw of a planet's life force that is inextricably connected to the geothermal energy, thus weakening the planet so it's unable to sustain life." He paused and looked at Eloch. "If it goes on long enough, not only will the planet cease to sustain life, it will die. We know this already."

"It must stop," Eloch said through clenched teeth. "Before any others die."

Jon shook his head. "I don't see how that's going to happen," he said mournfully. "The costs involved, the time to find an alternative energy source, all of that...they aren't going to stop what they've got going."

Genji hissed.

"Don't let him go all Nuri on us, Kalea," Grale warned.

Kalea pinched Genji.

His head snaked around with a hiss. He looked at her expression and then slowly nodded, smiling sheepishly.

"We will explain to your leaders exactly what's happening, Jon, and if they do not see reason, then I will stop them myself," Eloch said.

"He can do it," Aiko said. "I've seen him do it before."

Jon frowned. "I hate to disappoint, but that ship there," he pointed to the *Defiance*, "could totally disintegrate this ship and everyone on it."

"Not from where we're sitting," Aiko said quietly. "From where we're sitting? Your ship doesn't even know we exist, Jon."

"It's true," Wren said. "You really can't touch us."

Jon sighed. "Look, I'm not your enemy. I had no idea the damage we've been causing to your dimension with our star gates. Had I known, I would have protested. I'm sorry I had anything to do with this project." He paused. "So, I'm not your enemy. However, I do think like the enemy. I understand the enemy."

"What are you saying?" Wren asked.

Jon craned his neck so he could see her expression. It was alert, impassive, yet approachable. "I would like to help," he said. "This may sound crazy, but I think I might be destined to help." He held up his hand. "But I'm also not thinking too clearly at the moment. As you can imagine, this has been quite an unusual day for me. And you all threw a lot of information at me."

"Understatement. I like him," Grale whispered to Aiko, who grinned back.

"I need to..." Jon paused, searching for words, "...settle. I need to settle in a bit."

"We can arrange that," Wren said as she moved around to face him where he sat. "But there's something you need to think about, and think hard." She squatted beside him so they were face-to-face. "If you decide to help us, Jon, we will be sharing our technologies, our plans, and our secrets with you. More than we have already. If you help us, then we can never allow you to return to your world.

Really think about this, Jon. If you help us, you will never see your friends or loved ones again. Not just for our safety, but for your own."

"I...I hadn't considered that," Jon said numbly.

"Well, consider it. Then let us know." She glanced at Perin. "Perin, will you show him the room next to yours? He can stay there while he's here."

"I will," Perin said.

"Okay, Jon," Wren said and rose. "Off you go. Just ping us if you have any questions or when you're rested and have made your choice. If you decide it's too much of a sacrifice, then Eloch will put you back where he found you and that will be that."

She grinned. "One of us will be bringing you a food tray. I'm sure you're still hungry."

~~~

Jon glanced at Perin as she serenely led him down the corridor to his assigned quarters. What was it about this woman that made him feel so comfortable, so at peace?

"It's because we are both Seers. We are the same." she replied when he asked her. "I have Seen you in True Dreams. More than once. I know you, Jon."

He shook his head as he tried to calm his churning thoughts. "It doesn't make sense. None of this makes any sense."

She laughed, the clear bell-like sound he enjoyed so much. "I gave up trying to make sense of it a long time ago. It has made my experience so much easier. I recommend it." She paused in front of a door. "Here is your room." She waved her hand in front of the door panel and the door slid open. "Rest. Gather yourself. Food should be arriving soon." She touched his hand. "Trust your True Dreams, Jon. It will be all right. You'll see."

255

He watched her move down the corridor, her fingers gently trailing along the wall until she disappeared into the room next to his.

Inside his room, he found all the amenities of a well-appointed hotel suite. The lighting could be raised or lowered at his voice command. So, too, the drape covering a viewing port. The bed was expansive, with a light, downy duvet. The carpeting was deep and plush. There was a WC off the room with a full bathing area, not the cramped WC he was used to. The dark blue upholstered sofa and twin chairs seemed even nicer than his father's. The restful grey wall covering, definitely nicer.

Before he had a chance to sit, the door chimed and Eloch entered at his invitation, carrying a covered tray.

"I have food," Eloch said as he placed the tray on the table in front of the sofa. "An assortment of things," he said, lifting the cover.

Jon felt his eyes widen when he saw the bountiful variety of meats, cheeses, breads, and strange spheres in a bowl he assumed to be a fruit of some sort. He eyed Eloch. "There seems to be more here than one man could eat," he said noticing the two plates, a large pitcher of water, and two glasses accompanying the food.

Eloch smiled. "I decided to join you. We can talk while we eat." He took a seat in one of the chairs and began filling his plate.

Jon sat on the sofa and followed suit.

The food was quite good and he said so.

"Thank you," Eloch said. "We grow the food in the Solar Farm, and the automated galley does the rest."

"No cook?"

Eloch shook his head. "Unless someone wants to, but it's not necessary. This ship is fully automated." He raised his hand, "Not my doing, though. It was designed to be."

"Really? Quite the sophisticated technology. I'd love to have a look at it. New technologies fascinate me."

Eloch grinned. "You sound like Genji and Spider. They are perpetually hungry for information." Eloch took a bite of his sandwich and chewed thoughtfully. "Please tell me about your people, Jon. What are they like?"

Here it comes, thought Jon, and he took his time before answering. "We are a very old society made up of many planets and peoples. We're peaceful but are prepared to defend ourselves against aggression. That's what these star gates are all about. We're forming a ring around our galaxy and establishing a perimeter of outposts. As you are well aware, a galaxy is billions and billions of light-years across. As I mentioned earlier, without the star gates, it would be impossible to keep peace."

He looked up to meet Eloch's gaze. "And so, if you were to destroy our star gates, we would consider it an act of aggression and would do all we could to stop you."

Eloch nodded thoughtfully. "I can liberate the planets from this frequency without setting foot in yours. You can't stop me from here."

"True, but we can track you by your energy signature. After all, I found you twice. Even if you kept me here, in this reality, another navigator would find you again," Jon said. "And we would simply replace any fission generator wands you destroyed as soon as you destroyed them."

"I will be teaching the Sisters—the planets—how to guard Themselves so you will not be able to access their energy any longer."

Jon shook his head. "And then we would create something else. We're a tenacious lot. Don't you see? It will go on and on and on."

He took a breath. "As I said earlier, I'm on your side. I meant it, Eloch, and still do. I don't like the thought of draining the life force of a planet until it cannot sustain life and can barely sustain itself. If there were another way to travel across our galaxy, I'd be behind it one hundred percent."

Eloch rubbed his chin. "What if I told you there is another way?" he asked after a moment.

"There is?" Jon set down his food. "There truly is?"

Eloch nodded. "We travel using the space-time connections that are found throughout all space, and I am told, in all dimensions."

"Wormholes," Jon whispered.

Eloch nodded. "Wormholes."

"But how?"

"Your technology sniffs out energy sources that happen to be planets, and our technology sniffs out wormholes."

"It's impossible to travel through one," Jon said. "It would kill you, destroy your ship."

Eloch shrugged. "Yet our pilots do it all the time."

"And how do you know where you will end up if you go through one?"

"It's our technology." Eloch sat back, steepled his fingers, and studied Jon for several moments. Finally he continued. "I have a proposal for you to consider. I know you don't speak for your people, but," he chuckled, "you're the only one I can ask."

He sobered. "Jon, if we were to share our wormhole navigation technology and teach your pilots how to safely travel through them, do you think your people would be open to shutting down their star gates?"

Jon was quiet for several minutes before he answered. "I honestly don't know," he said. "But, underneath it all, we are truly peace-loving and life-affirming. We are thriving throughout a galaxy comprised of many peoples and cultures, and without war.

Skirmishes, yes, but those are usually solved through negotiation and kept on-planet." He smiled. "And there are a good many of us who are as curious as your Genji and Spider. I know many of our kind would embrace this new technology and be eager for the challenge."

Eloch smiled. "There is hope, then."

"There is hope," Jon agreed.

"Whom would I need to speak with?"

John grimaced. "I'm not sure. Let me think about who would be best."

Eloch nodded, then rose, towering over Jon. "Thank you for our conversation. It was very enlightening. I feel hopeful." He smiled. "I will leave you now to think. And allow you to finish your meal in peace and to rest."

"It was enlightening," Jon said, rising. "Thank you for the delicious food."

Eloch paused at the door, "When you wish to contact us, just ping." He pointed to a small panel underneath the door chime. "You'll find several of these placed around your room."

After he left, Jon went back to his food. As he chewed, he let his eyes wander around the space and wondered what else was placed around the room. Although Eloch was gone, it felt as if a part of him was still present.

~~~

Later, after a shower, Jon lay on his bed, arms folded behind his head, and considered his choices.

Although he was abducted only a few hours ago, it seemed much longer. If he agreed to help, it would be much, much longer before he saw home. Most likely never.

But if negotiations were involved, he was sure he would end up in a mediator position, and he could still see his loved ones.

He stilled. But suppose he couldn't? What if he never saw his loved ones again? Most of the people in his life he rarely saw anyway, he reflected. Friends had come and gone, but his reputation as *the* prime navigator in the empire brought him more jealousy than friendship. Because of his fame, his life really wasn't his own. If he were to stay, become part of this motley group of people, maybe it wouldn't be too bad. His thoughts drifted to Perin. Maybe not bad at all.

He was so drawn to her. Yes, she was beautiful and exactly the type of woman he was normally attracted to, but it was more than that. It was as if he'd known her for a long time. Had he experienced what she called True Dreams about her before? Was that why he felt so at home with her? He really wasn't sure. Maybe? Long ago?

He wasn't even sure what a True Dream was, and he had certainly never been trained to decipher such a dream's meaning. But he had had recurring, extremely vivid dreams, although when those dreams became reality, he had labeled those episodes more of a déjà vu-type experience.

Jon blew out a breath. He would need to discuss this with Perin so he could better understand what Dreaming True was about.

One thing he did know. If he stayed and allied himself with this small, fascinating group of characters, Perin would be one of the deciding factors. He also already knew that if he chose to go home, he would always wonder what could have happened between them.

His thoughts shifted to his conversation with Eloch and the new technology he described. To travel through a wormhole! He would love to experience it. And to learn a whole new technology! With that technology, his navy could still fulfill its mission of surrounding their galaxy with protective outposts—without sucking planets dry.

But the cost! They had spent billions on these star gates. Who could convince the government's accountants this new technology would be a good long-term investment?

Jon shot up straight and reached for the small panel located conveniently at his bedside.

Who, indeed?

CHAPTER 22 - SOLUTIONS

They sat around the familiar galley table, various beverages in various stages of consumption in front of them.

Jon smiled and shook his head.

"What's so funny?" Mink asked, her eyes flashing, dimples disappearing.

Jon held up his hand, "No offense, Mink. I was just thinking about recent events. I was taken from a naval ship only a few hours ago, all orderly, uniformed, and clean. And I arrived here, on this motley ship where you dress as you please, and you drink what you please, when you please. It strikes me as funny is all."

"I get it," Aiko said. "I worked for the Ring Colonizers, a branch of our military. Life on board this ship, it's different, true. Much more relaxed. But underneath we do have structure. Just like in the military, we…what did you call us?

"Motley?"

Aiko smirked. "Yeah, motley. Where was I? Right, just like in the military, we motley folk are either on or off duty at any given moment." She held up her wine glass. "I happen to be off duty."

"As am I," Mink said, leaning forward to clink glasses with Aiko.

"Sadly, I am not," Grale said, holding up a mug of tea. He clinked with both Aiko and Mink.

Jon grinned. "It goes deeper than that. Your behavior. It's beyond on or off duty. You are a cohesive unit, comfortable and relaxed together," Jon said. "It's refreshing. In fact, I'm envious."

"We've been traveling together a long time," Spider said. He smiled at Wren. "And many of us knew each other for years before this current adventure. We've worked out the bugs."

"So, what's the common denominator?" Jon asked.

All eyes turned toward the broad-shouldered man sitting by his mate. "Eloch," they said in unison.

"Have you made a choice?" the Common Denominator asked.

Jon felt his heart rate increase as he nodded. "I've always wanted to support a cause. Have a purpose." He shot a glance at Perin. "I'm choosing to back the motley folks with the common denominator. I want to help this current situation come to a peaceful resolution. We just need to figure out what to bring to the negotiating table that will create the result we want."

Eloch nodded with a quiet, peaceful smile. "I'm glad, Jon."

Jon glanced around at the closed and impartial expressions. It was impossible for him to get a read on any of them, save Perin. She seemed pleased. "Remind me to never play a betting game with any of you," he said, trying to lighten the mood.

"I know I'm going to need to convince you all." He glanced at Spider. "Work out a lot of bugs, but if you want to know what made me decide to join you? Honestly, I believe it's my destiny, whether I want to or not. It's a feeling that has nothing to do with True Dreams or any other mumbo-jumbo. It's my gut, which I trust.

"And I can't have the peace my people strive for be destroyed fighting against someone or something like you, Eloch. We are trained from childhood to negotiate. Yes, as I've told you, tempers flare, skirmishes erupt, but then our mediators are called in to evaluate and guide those in disagreement into an agreement. Everyone is willing to compromise because everyone wants the same thing: peace."

Jon focused on Eloch. "I wish to offer myself as your mediator, Eloch. I think this new technology we spoke about is a marvelous bargaining chip."

"Wait," said Genji. "What new technology, Eloch? Not the ability to see within the different frequencies."

Eloch shook his head. "Of course not, Genji. Jon and I had a private conversation earlier, and I proposed that we teach his people how to travel through wormholes and make the star gates obsolete."

"They will need trained pilots," Grale said.

"And we've got two excellent pilots who can train them," Wren said.

"We can only train those with the right amount of knack," Aiko said. "How are we going to find them?"

Wren winked at Spider. "Spider and I know how. Way back when I was a KinLord in SubCity, Spider and I came up with a way to pre-cull our Kin. That way we could hide those we knew the Martials wouldn't want. Spared many lives. Kept the most gifted for ourselves of course."

A slow grin spread across Aiko's face. "I never knew that."

"That's because we never talked about it," Wren said. "Only Spider, Mouse, Flick, and I knew what we were doing."

"Crafty," Aiko said. "SubCity crafty. I always wondered why we got along so well."

Wren laughed.

"So we'll offer the FNs the wormhole technology and the training. In exchange, they will shut down their star gate system," Eloch said. "Is that agreeable to everyone?"

"Wait," said Jon, "FN? Let me guess, I'm an FN, but what does that mean, exactly?"

"Frequency Neighbor," said Spider. "You are our neighbors, but living in a different frequency."

"We shortened it," Grale said wryly. "Some of us objected to all the syllables."

Spider looked at Grale. "You had to bring that up now? Really?"

Grale widened his eyes. "Just giving Jon here all the details."

"Is this agreeable to everyone?" Eloch asked again.

"Not only is it agreeable, it's doable," Genji said. He looked at Kalea's worried expression. "They won't need us, Kalea. We'll still be going home."

"What if these FN aliens don't agree? They already have their space travel system up and running. Why would they want to bother with the expense and training of developing a new system?" Grale said. "Do we have a Plan B?"

Eloch sighed and looked at Jon, then Grale. "We do. One neither Jon nor I like. If the FNs don't agree, then we will destroy the stakes as Spider and Grale taught us how to do. And I will teach the Sisters how to defend themselves against them." He looked at Jon again. "Jon said his people would come up with something different, and we, in turn, would have to destroy that. Sadly, it would go on and on."

"Grale makes a good point about expense," Jon said. "I think we can use it in our negotiations. It will be just as costly to continually replace the wands and to develop new technology. Plus, with Eloch destroying star gates, they will develop a reputation for unreliability. We will eventually need to develop a new technology anyway. I believe we can convince the bean counters that in the long run they will save money by agreeing to our proposal."

"And how do you know, Jon, that the agreement will be honored?" asked Wren.

Jon smiled. "That is one thing I do know. Negotiations take a long time in our world because once a resolution has been agreed upon, it will be honored. That is the core infrastructure of our government. We solve our problems with peaceful resolution because then we all can thrive. The mediators we will work with all know this." He sobered. "Unfortunately, this is going to take a long time, and I worry about the planets."

"As do I," Eloch said. "I may need to rescue those in greatest need."

"And it will be my job to help my people to understand why."

"Then the sooner we begin all this, the better," Wren said. "Do you know someone we can approach to begin the negotiations?"

Jon nodded. "I do. I think I know the perfect person. In fact, he's the admiral overseeing the star gate implementation, and he happens to be presiding over the *Defiance.*" Elbows on his knees, Jon clasped his hands. "If we can convince him to enter into negotiations with us, then he will convince the others of its importance. He is planning on retirement, and he wants to leave a great legacy.

"I think we can use his desire to leave a legacy to our advantage. He wants to be remembered for the star gates. But wouldn't it be far more satisfying, and confer more greatness, to be remembered as the man who created peace with an alien intelligence and introduced a new and safer technology to circumnavigate the galaxy?"

Wren squinted at him. "You seem to know a lot about this admiral," she said.

"Known him all my life. He's my father. And he does like safety. If he knew what we were doing to the life over in this dimension, he would be as mortified as I am. Introducing a safer and less detrimental technology is something he could get behind."

"I wouldn't know about safer, unless your pilots are well trained," Aiko said "But there's far more freedom using wormholes. For the most part, they're readily available." She looked at the others. "Granted, between galaxies there are fewer. We needed the Cryo beds to get here. But within a galaxy?" She grinned at Mink and then Grale. "Cryo beds are used more for keeping you young and combat-ready."

"And it's going to be way cheaper," said Wade, who had been quietly nursing a beer. "Wormholes are already there. Star gates need to be manufactured."

Jon's brows drew together. "Cryo beds?"

"Cryogenesis. A deep-freeze sleep state for when you're traveling great distances to a destination," supplied Mink.

"We could offer that technology as well," said Wren.

"Maybe," Jon said. "We have something similar."

"Really?" Spider asked excitedly, darting a look at Mink. "We'd love to compare technologies."

Eloch raised his hand. "Let's not get too ahead of ourselves," he said. "We first need to speak with Jon's father. Now, do we go to him or do I bring him to us?"

Jon sucked in a breath. "He's much older than I am. I don't know if his system could take the transition. There was a lot of pain involved."

"I understand," Eloch said, "It will be fine. I've learned how to make the transition nearly painless."

"I have one question to throw into the mix," Genji said.

Aiko laughed. "Of course you do."

Genji offered her a slight smile, then looked at Eloch, "How can we be sure wormholes are even traversable in the FNs' dimension? Our planets show up as energy sources. Jon tells us they have wormholes, but will our piloting technology work?"

"There's only one way to find out," Grale said. "I'll volunteer."

Aiko put a hand on his arm. "No, I should."

"I can send an unmanned ship through," Eloch said. "After all, it's the technology we're testing, and you two are a resource I can't afford to be without."

Both Aiko and Grale sat back with their arms folded and glowered. "Unmanned," they said in unison.

"That's how it's going to be," Eloch said quietly. "I will be able to monitor it."

He looked at Jon, "This technology requires a pilot," he explained. "The only reason we can send an unmanned ship through is because of my unique relationship with this ship."

Jon raised an eyebrow and glanced around the table. He noticed they accepted what Eloch told him as truth. He mentally shrugged, deciding if one man has the ability to bring another across dimensions, why not?

"But you haven't tested your unique relationship by going through a wormhole before," Aiko protested.

Grale coughed and looked sheepishly at Aiko.

She glowered and punched him in the arm. "You didn't tell me?"

Grale rubbed his arm. "You and Wren were in Cryo. We were bored. You came out of Cryo. It just never got mentioned before it was my turn to sleep. Then things got crazy and I forgot. What can I say? I'm sorry, Kitten."

"But you didn't even bring it up with me when Genji, Kalea, and Wade made their plans to leave us," she groused.

"That's because I was thinking you were wanting off this rust bucket. I wasn't thinking clearly, you know that." He looked at her pleadingly. "I said I was sorry. I'll make it up to you." He winked and lowered his voice to a growl. "Kitten."

Aiko glanced up at the ceiling and sighed, nearly managing to keep her face straight when Wren chuckled.

"When do we do the test?" Wren asked.

"What about now?" Eloch said. "I don't want to lose this opportunity to meet with the admiral."

Grale stood and offered his hand to Aiko. "Would you like to find the nearest wormhole with me?" he asked in the same throaty growl.

"Oh, Cowboy, the things you say," Aiko said, batting her eyelashes at him.

Wren laughed out loud, and the others joined in.

Jon shook his head and caught Eloch's eye. Eloch grinned and shrugged.

Chapter 23 – Admiral Gaylord

Admiral Xerxes Gaylord needed to make a decision, and he needed to make it sooner rather than later.

He couldn't sit, dead in space, for much longer. Not only was the crew beginning to grumble, but he was receiving more and more inquiries as to the status of the mission—his Mission, his magnum opus. The final jewel crowning his long, glorious career.

The final jewel, he thought with a glower, he would never claim if he couldn't relocate his navigator.

But none of it mattered at the moment because the lost navigator was his son. His only son, Jonathan.

The shock of it. He was still reeling from the impossibility. No matter how many times he reviewed the ship's computer recording of the event, he still couldn't wrap his mind around it. *How could this be? How could a man open up some sort of vortex, reach out, and pull his son through?*

And his son—his expression, as if he knew what was coming. What secrets had Jon been keeping from him?

What secrets was he now keeping?

The admiral had ordered his Bridge crew to maintain strict secrecy until they could uncover the cause of Jon's disappearance. It was an easy order to obey, he knew. Nobody on the Bridge that day wanted to describe to anybody else what they had seen. It was impossible. It was madness.

And so Admiral Xerxes Gaylord did something he had never done before in his entire career. He lied.

He covered up.

He came up with as many reasons and excuses as he could in order to keep the *Defiance* exactly where she was, dead in space, until he could locate his son and bring him home.

But time and excuses were running out. Although there were no higher ranks he reported to, he did have committees who had been nudging him for explanations. And colleagues, many of whom were friends, and those friends had begun to contact him privately to express their concern.

Yes, time was running out. Perhaps he could finagle one more week, but then he would have to abandon his search, abandon his mission, and go home, the conquered conqueror.

His ego would mend, he knew. He would recover. *But to abandon Jon!* From that he would never recover.

"Sir? Sir!"

Xerxes blinked and looked around. He had been so lost in gloomy thoughts, he had forgotten he was sitting on the ship's Bridge. "I'm sorry, Captain. You were saying?"

"I was asking for your orders, sir."

The admiral sighed. "We will continue to stay put for one more week. I would like all available scientists, engineers, and whoever else we can think of, trying to locate and bring home our navigator."

The captain nodded, concern wrinkling his brow. "I'm sorry, sir. I believe you misunderstood my question. The energy signal has returned, and I was asking what your orders are regarding the signal, sir."

Xerxes straightened. "It's returned? Good lord, man, have

someone lock onto those coordinates ASAP and prepare to launch the fission generator wand. Navigator or no navigator, we need to at least establish a star gate so we can get home."

"Yes, sir!" the captain said, relieved to be issuing orders after so much inactivity. Once the generator began to operate and the power source was contained, they could all go home.

He was ready for his nice, long leave. He saluted smartly and had turned to do his admiral's bidding when he felt something shift, and the hairs on the back of his neck rose. He whipped around and gasped, unable to believe what he saw.

It was happening again!

Before the captain had a chance to call out a warning, the very fabric of time and space seemed to ripple and open with a bright flash of light that left him seeing stars. The same large man reached out through the opening, snatched the admiral, and pulled him through. There was another bright flash, and the opening was gone, along with the admiral.

Too stunned to do anything else, the captain sank to the deck and stared at the admiral's empty chair.

~~~

For a brief moment, Admiral Gaylord felt intense pain, but before he could even react, the pain vanished and in its place was a warm suffusion of energy. His arm was released, and he sensed movement and a hand being placed on his shoulder.

"Are you okay, Father?"

His eyes flew open. Joy flooded through him. "Jon!" He reached out and pulled his son into his arms. "You're alive! I thought I had lost you."

He felt Jon patting his back. "Easy, Father. It's okay. I'm fine. You? Do you hurt?"

The admiral shook his head. "No, not in the least. In fact, I feel much better physically than I have in a long time."

"That's good, Father, that's good." Jon smiled and gently extricated himself from his father's embrace. "I'd like you to meet some people, Father," he said, helping the admiral to his feet. "This is the crew of the *Valiant*, upon whose Bridge we are standing."

Admiral Gaylord straightened as he tugged down his jacket. He scanned the faces, his eyes resting on a tall, broad man dressed in what appeared to be a tunic and leggings made from animal skin. "*You!*" he hissed, and reached for the sidearm he kept on him at all times.

Jon stayed his hand. "Wait, Father. They mean us no harm."

"Mean no harm? How can you say that when both of us are here against our will? Get behind me, Jon," he commanded as he wrested himself from his son's grip.

He drew his weapon, the barrel weaving among all his potential targets. "Stay where I can see you or I promise you I will shoot." One of them, a woman, hissed and stepped forward.

"Wait!" said another woman, this one small, with a mass of auburn coils snaking down her back. "Everyone just calm down. Can't you see the man's terrified?"

"I am not terrified," the admiral exclaimed. "I am livid. I consider this abduction an act of aggression, and I am acting accordingly. Jon, get behind me like I told you," he stated, aiming his weapon at the small woman who appeared to be the leader. "I demand you return us to the *Defiance*. Immediately. Or I will be forced to shoot you."

"Of course you're terrified," the woman said calmly, ignoring the sidearm pointed at her chest. "Any brave and intelligent individual would be terrified under the same circumstances. But we're not here to hurt you. Look at your son. He's moving around freely. We simply want to have a conversation with you. And then you may leave."

The admiral took a deep breath. "And Jon? Is he to be held as hostage?"

The woman smiled, her grey eyes kind. "Not at all. Jon can do what he wishes. Please, don't be frightened. Just hear us out."

The admiral took another deep breath and glanced at Eloch. "I am not frightened," he huffed and lowered his weapon.

"I was frightened when I first laid eyes on him," a woman said.

The admiral looked at her where she sat in a chair facing a viewing screen and assumed she must be the ship's pilot.

"So was I," another man said.

The admiral noticed how close the second man stood to the woman who had aggressively hissed at him. He was broad in the chest, although not as tall as the other, and had some sort of strange markings running down his arm. "Nearly soiled myself, in fact."

Someone laughed.

"The Knack Man's so full of knack, only a fool wouldn't be afraid of him," the pilot said matter-of-factly.

The man in question turned his head to look at the pilot, one brow quirked. "Knack Man?" he asked in a deep baritone.

The woman smirked. "My little nickname for you."

The man snorted and returned his gaze to the admiral. "Will you put your weapon away, sir?" he asked calmly. "We have a proposal which requires your expertise and advice."

Then Xerxes looked at his son, who nodded encouragement. He sighed and re-holstered his sidearm. "I suppose it wouldn't hurt to listen."

"Thank you, sir," the woman with the masses of coils said. She grinned suddenly, and the admiral felt himself relax.

Jon touched his arm. "Do you trust me, Father?"

Xerxes looked at his son and rubbed his chin. "You know," he said after a brief pause, "until this very moment, I'm not sure if I've ever thought about whether I trust you or not. But yes, I believe I do trust you, Jonathan. Indeed I do."

"Good," Jon said with a smile. "Then believe me when I tell you you're going to need to suspend your disbelief and sit down because I doubt you'll be able to stand after you hear what you're about to hear. Come with me."

He led his father to the copilot's chair by Aiko, and, standing in front of him, said, "It was only a week ago, but seems like an eternity since I was sitting in this very same chair, Father, about to listen to the very same remarkable story you're going to hear."

He gestured toward the tall man who had pulled the admiral up and out of his ship. "The man standing over there, Eloch by name, is not at all what he appears to be. And…"

With input from Genji and Spider, Jon proceeded to tell his father everything he had learned during his week's stay aboard the *Valiant*. "And so," Jon said as he finished his narration, "I have taken it upon myself to be the mediator representing Eloch and his crew on the *Defiance*. I would like you, Father, to help us. They are as peace-loving as we are, and I think with what they are offering—the new technologies and assistance with testing and training pilots.—we have a solid case to present."

Admiral Gaylord looked at his son through eyes he was sure appeared glazed over. "I am impressed with you, Son. Extremely." He ran his hand over his short military haircut. "But you must know this is an immense amount of information for me to grasp all at once. I require some time to assimilate what I have just heard. And be assured, I will no doubt have many questions."

"Understood," Jon said and grinned. "You're handling this so much better than I did, Father. I was so overwhelmed, my mind

276

shut down, refused to think, and I surprised myself by taking a nap."

The admiral nodded. "A nap sounds like a splendid idea," he said.

Jon looked questioningly at Wren and Eloch. "May I take my father to my quarters?"

"Of course," Wren said. "We'll bring him some tea."

The admiral cleared his throat. "Perhaps something a little stronger than tea?" he asked.

Jon laughed. "I already have some of that in my room. Come, let me take you there."

With a last look at the split-view screen, the one where he could clearly see the outline of his ship and also clearly see it was not there at all, Admiral Gaylord followed his son off the Bridge.

"What do you think?" Wren asked Eloch when the pair was out of hearing range.

He nodded. "I think it went well. Better than expected."

"He did seem intrigued," Wren agreed. "Jon made a great case."

"And he really perked up at the thought that his final act as admiral would be to bring harmony to their galaxy as well as new, potentially cost-effective technology," Spider said.

Wren slid him a glance. "You caught that, too, eh?"

Spider smirked. "Hard not to. Our Jon sure knows what motivates his father."

Eloch tapped his lip. "It will take longer than I had hoped. The Sisters of Vela Kentaurus...I worry about them."

Wren slid an arm around his waist. "Is there something you can do to make them more comfortable?"

"I don't know, Wren, but now we have the time to explore it."

He turned toward Genji, Kalea, and Wade. "Now then, when would you three like to go home?"

Chapter 24 – Endings and Beginnings

Mink hugged Wade fiercely. "You have been my Cryo partner for so many years," she said and straightened to look up at him. "I don't know what I'll do without you."

He rubbed the tear-stained spot on the front of his tunic. "It will be strange, Mink, but," he continued with a glance at Spider, "I'm sure you'll manage." He grinned suddenly. "One more long sleep and I'll be back on Longwei. First thing I'm going to do is grab some ferment and find a nice, sandy patch by the ocean to enjoy."

"First thing I'm going to do is to shift into my Nuri form and fly," Kalea said, her eyes shining.

"Now, you know what to do going through the wormholes, right, Genj?" Aiko asked, gripping his tunic front. "There are only three you need to traverse."

Genji patted her hands. "I do. I've been practicing like you wanted me to." He looked over her head at Eloch. "Besides, I'm just the copilot. This bird can fly herself. Eloch's proven that to you."

Aiko nodded. "Still…" Her voice trailed off.

Genji smiled at her, his throat tightening. He nodded and squeezed her hands. "I love you, too."

"My turn," Wren said and waited for Aiko to release Genji.

When she took Aiko's spot, she hugged Genji hard. "Where do I begin?" she asked, blinking up at him, "Thank you for being

Eloch's first real friend. Thank you for saving my life and trying to save my sausage leg. Thank you for your loyalty and your steadfastness. Thank you for that curious brain of yours."

She sniffed and released him with a watery smile and took a step back. "Take that fission generator thing far away. Learn it inside and out, and then destroy it. Keep the Sisters safe, Genji." She brushed a tear off her cheek, "And have lots of little Nuris and live happily ever after. That's my final order." She pushed him toward the small walkway connecting the *Valiant* with the new ship Eloch created, which they had christened the *Vigilant*.

Genji reached for Kalea's hand and nodded to Wade. "Ready?"

"You bet," Wade said, already in motion. "Got a Cryo bed with my name on it," he said over his shoulder.

Genji looked at his friends one last time, memorizing each face, burning the image of them into his mind exactly as they were in that very moment. Grale's hands were on Aiko's shoulders, and she leaned back against him. Spider and Mink stood side by side, fingers brushing. Eloch had his arms wrapped solidly around Wren.

Perin stood a little to the side, raising her hand when she felt his gaze upon her. He still didn't quite understand how she could see energy yet still be blind.

Perin would be leaving soon as well. She was going with Jon to the *Defiance,* acting as an ambassador of sorts.

"We're waiting until we know you made it through that first wormhole," Aiko said. Her voice trembled. "Safe travels, Genj."

He saluted her. "Safe travels, Captain, and thanks. For everything."

He looked at the others, a part of him wishing he could go with them to that other frequency. So many adventures he would be missing.

And then he looked at Kalea, his mate, the mother of his unborn children, his home. "Let's go," he told her with a laugh that sounded a great deal like a roar, and pulled Kalea across the small walkway, muscling past Wade so he would be the first one to step aboard the *Vigilant*.

As Eloch locked and sealed the opening, Genji heard Spider laughing.

"I just love it when you go all Nuri, Genj!" he shouted.

EPILOGUE

"Your Champion was successful, Entean."

"Yes. I take great joy speaking once more with our neighboring Sisters, Longwei."

(A Pause.)

"When We lost Our connection to him there was...concern he had failed."

"There is still concern, Longwei. Not that he failed, but that there was...sacrifice."

"There is enough of Us within Our Brother, Entean. Before the disconnect, I felt His power. It has grown."

(A Pause.)

"He thrives, Entean."

(A Pause.)

"Agreed."

THUS ENDS THE ENTEAN SAGA

GLOSSARY

A Hide – going into hiding (i.e. take a hide)

A Solo – similar to Australian walkabout, personal journey

Animates – prosthetic device/artificial limb

Coilmats – dreadlocks

Entean – uncolonized planet in The Ring

Ferment – rum-like beverage

Knack – term used by residents of Spur to identify inherent skills and abilities

Longwei – colonized planet in The Ring

Metacrystal Instruments – device used by mining companies to locate crystal deposits

Nuri – symbiotic shape-shifting dragon persona, native to the planet Longwei

Rock Pounders – slang for miners planet Spur as the hub

The Narrows – Wren's code for speaking privately

Sniffer – a predator native to the planet of Spur, bred with canine and feline traits used as guard animals

Span – a measure of time

Spur – hub planet in The Ring

SubCity – underground portion of the city on plant Spur where the poor, criminal and dregs of society were forced to reside; divided into KinLands ruled by KinLords

Talamh – first planet in The Ring to be colonized

Timekeepers – timekeeping device, similar to a watch

Trummer – a wasp-like assassin's weapon with a hypodermic needle like a stinger, programmed to targets via their DNA

Stardust – Aiko's transport ship.

Uni - uniform

UpperUppers – slang word used by residents of Subcity on planet Spur to refer to the wealthy and powerful residents occupying the upper levels of the city

Valiant – a colonizer's scout ship recovered on planet Longwei

Vela Kentaurus – neighboring galaxy

ABOUT THE AUTHOR

C.B. Williams is the author of several fantasy books that span the subgenres of Young Adult, Space Opera, Science Fiction and Romance. While each story is a grand adventure into time and dimension, her stories are also reflections of contemporary issues such as social norms, relationships, spirituality and environmentalism. She writes with keen emotional depth, insightful observations on human nature, and a fabulously quirky sense of humor. Visit her online at www.cbwilliams.us